The LIGHTKEEPER

THE
Kinkades

The LIGHTKEEPER

BESTSELLING AUTHOR
DR. REBECCA SHARP

Love N. Books Press
An Imprint of Wolfpack Publishing
1707 E. Diana Street
Tampa, FL 33610

www.lovenbookspress.com

Cover design by Okay Creations LLC
Internal graphics design by Rachel Chaya Design
Edited by My Brother's Editor

The Lightkeeper was originally self-published in 2024 by Dr. Rebecca Sharp.

Paperback ISBN 979-8-89567-159-7
Ebook ISBN 979-8-89567-158-0
LCCN 2025942773

The LIGHTKEEPER

CHAPTER 1
KIT

The sunrise steeped the horizon in deep crimson, the color bleeding onto the distant ocean surface. A caution to those familiar with the sea: *Red sky at night is a sailor's delight. Red sky in the morning is a sailor's warning.*

I wiped clean the last corner of glass in the lantern room and shoved my rag into my back pocket, my morning ritual complete. Every day for the last nine years, I'd woken before dawn and made my way up the spiraling staircase to the very top of the Friendship Lighthouse to clean the windows encircling the tower; one of my many tasks as its lightkeeper. Dirt and dust were easier to see before the sun was fully up.

I'd existed at the edge of the ocean for nine years' worth of sunrises to heed nature's forewarning. It wasn't going to be a good day.

My footfalls were heavy back down the stairs. Normally, I'd prepare for a stormy day by moving my easel to the small office that sat at the base of the tower, moving the desk so the space could transform into a makeshift studio as the picture window afforded a wide panorama of the storm over the sea and a new scene to paint. However, inspiration had run dry lately, and worse than that, today I had to go into town.

A tremor ran through me. Unwelcome but unsurprising. I didn't like cramped spaces or crowds. Or people in general. I liked my corner of the earth, tucked on the bare, jagged edge of the continent, secluded in my lighthouse. It was on the very edge of civilization, my only neighbors being feathered nomads and crusted sea creatures, and it suited me. *It had to;* I'd never have a normal life again.

It had taken time, but I'd whittled my errands down to a single day out of the month. One day to get groceries. To pick up any necessary tools or supplies for repairs to the lighthouse. And to see my family. Only one day where I had to prepare myself to deal with the world.

But some days, one day felt like one too many. *Some days like today.*

I wished I could put it off for longer, but as I entered the kitchen from the little office at the base of the tower, the empty shelves, empty bread basket, and empty fridge echoed that I couldn't. *I was supposed to go three days ago, and I had kept pushing it off.* If the fact that I'd run out of food wasn't enough, the increasingly insistent texts from my younger sister, Frankie, warned that if I didn't see her and my siblings and Mom soon, I'd be getting a house call—*a lighthouse call.* And that was worse.

I didn't want them here. I loved them—I loved them too damn much to want them to see how I lived because

I didn't live. I existed. And the state of the lighthouse made that painfully clear.

The inside of the small house was wrapped in either wood panels or wallpaper—the kind that was washed of all color and design by the tumble of time, leaving only a thin, gray barrier that had started to peel in spots. After the desk in the little office space, the living room was inhabited by the second of my three pieces of furniture: a single, solitary recliner that faced the fireplace.

A hint of smoke clung to the air, the ashes of last night's fire piled in the small hearth. Only in the depths of winter did I have a fire burning since consistent electricity and heat were...questionable...out here during a storm, but now, as winter cracked open into spring, I usually only lit one at night to keep the chill away.

I walked into the bedroom to pull on a thick sweater, the fabric at the elbows wearing dangerously close to holes. There, the third piece of furniture sat just off the floor: a mattress with a flat pillow and a haphazard collection of blankets. I'd slept on far worse in Afghanistan, but my family wouldn't see it that way. They'd look at the sparse furniture in the cold, dreary house on the edge of the world and they'd worry. They'd worry so damn much, and it would kill me.

I reached up and dragged my hand roughly through my hair, my fingers snagging on the heavily scarred skin at the back of my skull hidden underneath my thick waves.

"Shit." I pulled my hand away instantly and balled it in a fist. It didn't hurt, but the memory did. Worse than the original injury.

Next week was the anniversary. The first one. After

a decade, I thought it'd get easier. After isolation, I thought it'd get easier. Nothing got easier. I went over to the cases of water bottles I had stockpiled next to the fridge—the only thing left in the kitchen—and took one, chugging several big gulps and swallowing down the demons that clawed inside my chest.

Time to go.

Time to get this over with.

I strode to the living room and grabbed my brown jacket and hat from the nails I'd driven into the wall next to the door.

Even on my broad shoulders, the worn, weather-proof brown jacket hung stiff and loose. My cap was black with the words *Candle Cabin* stitched into the rim—the name of my sister Frankie's handmade candle shop.

I plucked my truck keys off the third nail in the wall, pulled the collar of my coat high, and headed outside.

It took three cranks to start Dad's old truck. I should've had the starter looked at a year ago when it started taking two cranks for the engine to wake, but it wasn't a priority. If the truck didn't start, that was one more reason to not leave the lighthouse.

The streets of Friendship still slept as I drove into town. In a few months, summer vacationers would swell the coastal towns of Maine, but at this time of year, it was only locals who traversed the streets. And this early in the morning, the locals knew that nothing was open yet save the town's only coffeeshop, the Maine Squeeze.

My first stop.

I parked right out front and left my keys in the

cupholder. No point in locking things around here. The town was too small to need anything like that. And again, if someone stole the truck...*one more reason not to leave the lighthouse.*

The bell chimed above the door, a twinkling welcome into the retro café with its checkered vinyl floor and bright orange walls.

"Good morning! Welcome—Kit!" Lou squeaked and bolted around the counter straight for me.

I grunted as my sister barreled into me. "Morning, Lou." I held her close for a good hug.

Elouise was the youngest Kinkade—but only by seven minutes. She and her sister, Frankie, were twins and, technically, my half sisters since we only shared Mom. But there was nothing half about my or my brother's relationship with them. Their dad hadn't been a good man, so Jamie had stepped in as the eldest, a pseudo-father figure to them...and me.

One more reason I kept to myself. Having to see the look on Jamie's face, wanting to help me and knowing there was nothing he could do, was one of the worst things.

"How are you? How's the lighthouse?" She drew back, a serene smile on her face. Her warm brown hair was braided back on both sides, every strand collected and contained—which was one hundred percent Lou.

"Still shining." I ignored her first question. "How's work?"

"Good. Busy." She moved back behind the counter. "Your usual?"

Plain black coffee.

"Yeah. And a bag of fresh grounds, please." I pulled my hat off and took a seat at one of the counter stools, watching as she poured the piping hot brew from the fresh carafe.

"Are you stopping to see Mom and Frankie and Gigi?"

Both my sisters lived with Mom and our grandmother, Gigi, on a farm just outside of town.

"Planning on it."

"Good, because Frankie's been worried."

I sighed and took the travel cup from her. She knew better than to pour it in a regular mug; I wouldn't stay for long.

"Frankie should worry about herself a little more," I muttered and took a sip of the fresh, hot coffee, savoring the treat.

Once a month, I was reminded that the coffee I made myself every morning was a poor substitute for the real thing.

"Never." Lou laughed. "She has a bag of candles and jam for you, and Jamie had to talk her out of bringing it to you on Friday."

I took another drink, swallowing down my groan.

Lou and Frankie were paired together like day and night, essential to each other but opposites. They both had the same warm brown hair we all got from Mom, their eyes the same chocolate as their father's, but that was where the similarities ended. Lou was reserved while Frankie was bold. Lou was thoughtful while Frankie was daring. Lou was temperance while Frankie...Frankie was trouble.

"One day, those plans of hers are going to come back and bite her in the ass," I grumbled.

"Hopefully that day comes before they bite me in the butt, too," Lou said with a sigh. "She tried to set me up with one of the Fulmer boys last week—*'Elouise, he's perfect'*—it was horrible."

The only person who ever called her 'Elouise' was Frankie, and usually when Frankie was concocting one of her hair-brained plans and roping Lou into it.

"Sorry." I grimaced.

Lou pursed her lips. "You're just happy she's not trying to set you up."

"She's too smart for that." There was no setting up a man who lived in a lighthouse.

"She does like a challenge..." Lou grumbled and then changed topics. "Did you drop off any new stuff at the gallery?"

"No." I cleared my throat. "Still working on something new."

I never intended for my paintings to become a business, but art took up space—space I didn't have in the lighthouse keep, so I started selling them. Well, I paid Lou to sell them for me. Half of every commission. First, at a booth at some small local fairs and festivals. Pretty soon, the fairs weren't frequent enough, so I rented a small gallery space in town.

It was two blocks from the Maine Squeeze, and I only went inside when I dropped off paintings, which was once a month, if that. I'd set them inside the door, and then Lou would arrange them in the space when she worked there on the weekends. If it weren't for her —if it weren't for the money it was making her (I was still paying her half of the commissions), I probably would've just tossed the paintings when I was done with them.

Art was my escape. Most of the time. Lately, though, that well of creativity felt bone dry. It was the time of the year, I told myself. Once the anniversaries were over, it would get better. It had to.

"I told you the painting of the lighthouse all wrapped up in lights for Christmas sold in minutes, right?"

"Oh, yeah?" I grunted. I didn't pay much attention to what sold and what didn't; that was Lou's job.

"Yeah. Everyone loved that one."

A low noise rumbled from my chest. The Christmas painting wasn't my usual subject; most of my works were shorelines and seascapes. But a year ago at Christmas, I'd watched my brother fall in love.

Jamie, who always took care of everyone to the point where he never thought of himself, had fallen in love with Violet, and it changed everything. Seeing their whirlwind romance sparked something in my chest—something I'd be tempted to describe as hope the way it drove me to paint the lighthouse all wrapped in twinkle lights for the holiday.

Whatever it was, hope or not, it was gone now.

"What's new with you?"

Lou sighed, arranging the pastries in the display. "Mom's trying out a new flavor for spring—"

"I don't want to hear about Stonebar," I broke in. "I want to hear about you."

Stonebar Farms was Mom's company. Homemade jams, preserves, and jellies from only the finest, locally sourced ingredients. At first, her concoctions were only a local delicacy, but it didn't take long for their goodness to spread. Now, she had a storefront, a commercial kitchen, and shipped nationwide.

The only thing more famous around here than Mom's jams was my grandmother's fortune telling.

Yeah. Fortune telling. And not via crystal ball or Tarot, no. Gigi's prophecies came via handwritten labels on specialty batches of preserves.

We'd laughed about it when we were younger. Until we were old enough to see how each and every one she'd written had come true in one way or another.

Her latest victim was Jamie. *Purple Princess,* she'd written on a label for blueberry jam, and a few weeks later, Jamie had fallen in love with Violet Royale.

Lou bit her lip and then came over to me and lowered her voice like this was some big secret. "Rumor has it, the real owner of the inn is planning to sell."

"Oh?" I lifted my brow.

Everyone in my family had their thing—their passion. Mom and Gigi had Stonebar Farms. Jamie had his woodworking and furniture business. Frankie had her candles. I had my art and my lighthouse. And Lou... Lou's thing was getting the old Lamplight Inn back.

Yeah...back.

God knew I was the poster child for unbelievable life circumstances, but what happened earlier this year with my family and the inn certainly made them a respectable contender for the title.

Up until the middle of January, Mom and my uncle George were the owners of the Lamplight Inn. *Or so they thought.* Years ago, when the original owner passed away, Mom and Uncle George bought the inn from his son, planning on one day restoring it to its former glory.

But life and Stonebar got busy, so it continued to sit and decay until Violet came into Jamie's life and took an interest in renovating it. For the last six months of last year, Violet and Lou had been working on plans and proposals and ideas, the new year signaling the start of the new business venture.

Until they went to apply for permits and were denied.

Apparently, Mom and George didn't own the inn. In a fucked-up twist of fate—or a random ancestry test —the original owner had another son—an older son— with a woman who wasn't his wife. The will specified the inn was to go to his oldest son...which was now this prodigal son and not the man who'd sold it to Mom.

It was fucked up. It took a whole month of legal back and forth before Mom and George got their money back after all these years. Violet...as excited as she was for the venture, the months she'd spent working with Jamie in his business gave her a different passion to focus on. Really, the only one to feel the magnitude of the loss was Lou—the one who'd just found her passion in the prospect of restoring the inn only to lose it.

Honestly, I didn't really care who owned the inn, the only reason it was important to me was because it was important to Lou. She'd been adrift in what she wanted to do in life until working on plans for the inn had brought a spark to her I hadn't seen before.

"Ginny told Marla who told Tess that the new owner sent someone up to take a look at the inn last week. She saw them going in when she was opening up her store." Ginny owned a chocolate shop on Maine Street.

"You really think he's going to sell?" I didn't want her to get her hopes up. He hadn't been interested in letting Mom and George keep the inn they thought they'd bought.

Her lips firmed. "Of course," she declared. "Frankie and I looked him up. Matthew Collins. He's a real estate mogul from New York. There's no way he has an interest in restoring a small-town inn. He probably just knew he could get more for it with his commercial contacts than Mom and Uncle George paid."

I made a low sound. I already didn't like this guy, and hearing Lou's objective assessment only made me dislike him more—especially because it meant she'd need even more money to offer a competitive bid on the building.

"Don't worry," she assured me. "I won't let it go without a fight."

A shadow of a smile crossed my face.

When Lou first told me her dream of owning her own business—whatever it ended up being, I promised to invest in it the second the opportunity was available. But she wanted to do it on her own, so that was when I decided to have her sell my art. Based on my own profits, I knew she had a sizable nest egg by now, but compared to what a big-city development corporation could offer...

"Well, whatever happens, we'll figure it out." Everyone saw the change in Lou when she'd started helping with plans for the inn. It was like she'd finally found her missing piece, and I'd do anything I could to help her keep it; the rest of our family would, too.

The bell at the door sounded, and two policemen walked in, bringing with them the chill of reality. The uniforms. Their guns.

My chest tightened.

Even though Lauren was at the register to take their order, I stood and said, "I should get going."

Sadness crept into the corners of Lou's eyes, but she didn't protest, only nodded and smiled.

"Thanks for stopping by." She walked me to the door, and when she put her hand on my arm, I tensed.

Instantly, self-loathing washed over me, and I saw hurt cloud her face as she pulled her hand back. This was why I stayed away.

"I miss you, Kit. We all do."

"I know." I missed the man—the brother I was, too. But he was gone, and I didn't know how to tell them that. "Love you, Lou."

"Love you, too."

I dragged my cap back onto my head and when I went outside, the first thing I did was look up.

Shit. I didn't like the shape of those clouds. I didn't like their shape at all.

I WAS IN AND OUT OF MIKE'S HARDWARE STORE IN fifteen minutes. My list of maintenance on the lighthouse was never-ending, but at the very top was patching some of the shingles on the roof of the house where they'd dislodged, allowing water to drip into the bedroom every time there was a good rain. Next, the windows needed to be replaced. Minimally, the two that were cracked. They were so old, they couldn't be repaired because the glass had lead in it. And last, I needed to figure out why there was no hot water in the shower. Plumbing wasn't my strong suit, and my showers were too quick to care about heat, but it should really be fixed.

It was my job, after all.

"Hey, Kit!"

I stopped short in the canned goods aisle, almost making it through the grocery store without being stopped by someone who recognized me. With my cap on and my beard grown out a bit, I hoped it was enough to obscure my identity. "Hey, Brian," I greeted the older man and braced for conversation.

Brian Fuller's farm abutted Mom's property.

"Good to see you. I haven't seen you around much, even at your mom's," he said, and when I realized he was going in for a hug, I quickly extended my hand, forcing a handshake instead.

I didn't like contact. Not from someone who wasn't one of my siblings.

"Just keeping busy," I replied. "How's the farm?"

"Oh, your mom is keeping me busy needing all those blueberries, but we should have a good harvest this year." Bryan's family farm supplied the bulk of the blueberries used in Mom's most popular jam.

"Good to hear." I started to turn away, about to say goodbye, but he wasn't having it.

"How's the lighthouse?" he probed. "I'm glad they kept a keeper for that old thing."

Me, too. My hands tightened on my cart. It was no secret that with modern-day technology and charting, lighthouses were no longer necessary in the way they once were. The Coast Guard, who was in charge of all the lighthouses in the country, had even started selling some of them off—the ones that couldn't be saved as tourist attractions. Thankfully, the Friendship Light-house had been spared so far.

And I had Jason to thank for that.

Jason Salter was the officer in charge of the light-houses along Maine's coast. I'd known Jason since I was a kid; his family was from Friendship. He was the reason I got a job as the lighthouse keeper—a volunteer position with the Coast Guard to take care of the light-house and keep it in working condition. The pay was halfway decent, but I wasn't here for the money. I was here because I couldn't bear to be anywhere else.

And Jason knew that.

"Needs some work. Some repairs. But otherwise has good bones." I eyed the end of the aisle, tempted to just walk away.

"Good to hear." He nodded and lifted a finger. "You know, Ginny told me the other day she heard they're going to start doing some research out that way. You know anything about that?"

I winced. "No, she must've heard wrong," I answered a little too sharply. *Damn Ginny and her rumors.* My chest tightened, wondering how far off she was about Lou's inn if this was the kind of news she was spreading. "They talked about doing that a year ago, and it never amounted to anything. Anything that happens at the lighthouse gets run by me, and I haven't heard anything."

I didn't actually know if I would have a say in something like that, but minimally, Jason would've given me a heads-up; I was the keeper. Even if he didn't exactly know I was living at the lighthouse, he still would've warned me if someone was going to be poking around.

"Oh, interesting. I wonder where she got that idea then..." Brian trailed off, looking flustered. *Shit.*

A month avoiding town and my ability to "people" was sorely lacking.

"Good seeing you, Brian." I took the opportunity to interject a goodbye with the friendliest pat on the shoulder I could muster. "Don't work too hard."

I walked away to the tune of his *"hope to see you around more"* and wondered why, considering how I'd just been so curt and dismissive. I chalked it up to politeness as I started adding random cans of food to my cart. Beans. Ravioli. SpaghettiOs. I wasn't picky; as long as it wouldn't perish in the next four weeks, I'd take it.

MY FROWN DEEPENED BY THE TIME I REACHED THE lighthouse. A storm was definitely brewing, angry and threatening on the horizon. I pulled up close to the door and parked. If I could unload and get over to Mom's before the skies opened up, then I'd have a good excuse to leave as soon as they did.

With that goal in mind, I rounded the front of the truck, hefted the two massive paper bags, one in each arm, and carried them to the house.

One step. That was as far as I made it inside before I realized something was wrong. Very wrong. *Someone was here.* I stared at the backpack and two massive duffel bags on the floor in my living room, one of them opened, clothes piled inside.

I didn't move a muscle, listening carefully, but only

hearing the creak of the windows as the wind blew against them.

"Hello?" I called, but no one answered. I set the grocery bags on the counter with a loud thud and did a quick sweep of the space. Office. Kitchen. Living room. Bedroom. *Nothing.* "What the hell..."

I stalked outside, dirt flying up like smoke from my stride as I scanned for another car—or any sign of the person who'd left their shit in my lighthouse. When I came up empty, I turned and looked at the tower. *Could someone be...*

A low sound broke from my chest. If this was some fucking prank or dare from some dumb kid to climb to the lantern room—

A squeal—*a distinctly feminine squeal*—sounded from the side of the lighthouse.

"Shit." I bolted across the gravel pad and over the boulders that framed the base of the tower, rounding the white brick edifice and preparing to take a dive into the frigid sea when I saw her.

And the sight stopped me cold.

Petite. Plump. Glossy obsidian curls pulled high on her head, cheeks tinted a dusty rose, and round wire-framed glasses—the definition of "spectacles"—perched on her pert nose. She straightened, examining whatever was in her palm so intently that she didn't even notice me. But it was impossible not to notice her.

She had on...waders. It took me a second to remember what the fuck they were called because they were so ridiculous. *Waders.* Giant, puke-yellow rubber overalls with built-in boots. *What the hell was she doing?*

"Excuse me!" I shouted.

My sharp tone startled her, and she jumped; her glasses bounced, and her bright blue eyes snagged mine for a moment before they snapped back to whatever was in her hand, so determined to protect it that she didn't catch her foot sliding on the wet rock. In an instant, her sound of surprise turned into a cry of dismay as she started to topple.

Instinct. I hadn't used it in so long that I almost didn't recognize the sensation as it took over and sent me charging to save her.

Nine years of living in the lighthouse and weathering all kinds of tasks were the only reasons I made it across the uneven boulders to her in the span of a second, my feet finding steady purchase as I hauled her into my arms to keep her from tumbling into the churning sea.

And as soon as I did, that *instinct* was replaced with something else. Something that couldn't ignore the soft, generous curves that, while hidden by waders, couldn't be obscured when they were pressed against me. Something hotter. Sharper. Hungrier—*something I couldn't afford.*

"Oh my," she said breathily, her head slowly tipping up as mine lowered. This close, I could tell how petite she was. The top of her head hardly reached my chin. Her vibrant blue eyes were wide—the color of the sea on a sunny day—and curious but held no trace of fear. And for some reason, that irritated the hell out of me.

"Who are you?" I demanded.

And what the hell was she doing invading my world?

CHAPTER 2
AURORA

W ell, this was decidedly *not* the specimen
I'd come out here searching for.

No, the man who crushed me to his
chest was hard and large and oh, so warm. Even
through the thick rubber of my waders, I swore I could
feel the heat radiating off him like the pulse of an open
flame. And he was tall. So very tall. My head tipped
back farther and farther...and farther until I could
finally look at him. A giant. A gorgeous giant. And from
underneath the ridge of his brow, charred brown eyes
glared back at me, glittering like two burning coals. *A
gorgeous, glowering giant.*

"Who are you?" A deep rumble carried his question
out.

No, he was definitely not one of the cold-blooded
invertebrates I'd come here to study.

I gasped loudly, suddenly recalling what I'd been
doing in the moments before. "Oh my god. The
dendronotus!" I scrambled to pull myself out of the

giant's arms, praying it hadn't been crushed in my grasp.

"The what?"

I ignored him and carefully peeled open my fingers. The peach-colored mollusk curled in my palm, its tendrils a little squished but otherwise no worse for the wear. Slowly, I watched its condensed form unfurl, awed as the speckled maroon edge transitioned to the soft pink.

"You're okay, little guy," I breathed, my fear allayed.

"Are you fuc—are you kidding me?" The low demand claimed my attention as it finished with a noise that sounded suspiciously like a growl.

My head tilted, and I blinked. I'd never heard a man growl before. The sound was deep. Rough. *Powerful*. Like saltwater rushing over large, craggy rocks. I wouldn't have thought the idea of it appealing, but the goose bumps that ran over my skin and the heat that charged low in my stomach told a different story. All because of a growl. *Interesting*.

"You almost died for a damned sea slug?" the giant grunted.

"I didn't almost die." I waved off his concern. "I just lost my balance a little, that's all."

"A little?" he gaped. "I just had to save you from falling into the damned ocean."

Goodness, he was grumpy. I huffed and pushed my glasses higher on my nose, though his displeasure was already crystal clear. "Well, I wouldn't have needed saving if you hadn't startled me."

"Me?" His head cranked to the side, the muscles in his jaw tensing and releasing in a way that reminded me of how the waves crashed and retreated on the shore. An endless cycle of power. "You shouldn't be out here alone—*you shouldn't be out here*."

I waved my free hand in front of me. "I absolutely should be out here. I can't do my job anywhere else but out here—"

"Your job?" he croaked. "Who are you?"

I tipped my head and did a more thorough assessment of the grumpy piece of granite interrogating me. Worn, dark jeans rose from his weathered work boots and molded to his thighs with the same precise adaptation as green algae on the surface of ocean rocks. His sweater, I would venture to say fit the same, but it was hard to tell with the large brown jacket he had on. All I knew for certain was that his chest was as broad as the jacket hinted, and that was only because I had firsthand experience pressed against it. Very broad. And warm.

I shivered. Why was I shivering? Why was I hot?

Why was I shivering and hot?

"Who are you?" I returned, noting the tendrils of dark-brown hair that peeked out from the brim of his cap and pressed to his neck.

There were muscles there, too. Ones that pulsed every time his jaw flexed—which was quite frequently. *Fascinating.* I'd never seen such an active muscle on a man before. Then again, I couldn't recall ever meeting a man who seemed to have as many muscles as this one did.

To be fair, I spent the majority of my time either in a textbook or in the lab. Though some might argue men were spineless, they weren't technically in any of the taxonomic phyla of invertebrates and therefore distinctly outside my educational purview.

"I'm the lighthouse keeper."

My mouth formed a small "o," seeing him in a whole new light. I was told about a keeper—a Mr. Kinkade, but I'd never imagined he'd be...*this*. He wasn't what I envisioned, yet...my head tipped in the other direction. He fit perfectly into the persona. He stood just as mighty and weathered and...solitary as the tower that rose next to us. It made me wonder what storms he'd faced to make him so.

Not your business, Aurora.

"I'm Aurora Cross." I extended my free hand and offered him my biggest smile.

He looked down at my outstretched fingers and then back up, his expression blank as he rumbled, "What are you doing traipsing around my lighthouse, Miss Cross?"

My brow creased. *Did he really not know?* Maybe they just hadn't given him my name; that had to be it. "I'm not traipsing. I'm researching."

Still no sign of recognition.

"I'm here to study coastal invertebrates for the semester to complete my master's in marine biology."

I was used to being stared at. It was a common occurrence for the majority of my twenty-three years of life. I was short and happily plump—I got that from Mom—and I spoke my mind without worrying what other people thought—and that was from Dad. On top of that, from the time I was young, I wore big, round glasses because contacts irritated my eyes, and I was the only girl in my class who loved snails and slugs and all things slimy.

I used to wonder sometimes if my parents encouraged my love of science too much. They were both scientists and nature enthusiasts themselves, so we were always studying one creature or another. Sometimes, I thought maybe they'd nurtured a part of me that was *too much*, but then they reminded me of the alternative, and that seemed far more horrifying. So, I'd grown accustomed to the stares—like any of my hundreds of specimens under the microscope; people looked because they didn't understand me, and that was okay. *What was the purpose of life if not to learn more about the things we didn't understand?*

But the way Mr. Kinkade stared was unlike any other stare I'd gotten before. It made my skin prickle and my heart quiver. It made me feel different, not because he looked to understand who I was but because he saw me and already knew.

Impossible. I blinked rapidly.

"You're...studying...here?"

"For the semester." My head bobbed. "I did speak with Jason already, and he mentioned you. He said he was going to tell you about me—about my project."

"Researching?" There was that rumbly growl again. "That's what you call risking your life for some sea worm?"

"Okay, first off, we've already determined I wasn't risking my life. I was entirely stable until you showed up. And second, *Dendronotus frondosus* isn't just some sea worm," I declared, affronted for my little squishy friend.

"Is that supposed to mean something to me? Because it sounds like some made-up Harry Potter spell."

"Made up—" I shook my head, but admittedly, had to bite the inside of my cheek to stop a small laugh from escaping; the Latin classification did make it sound a little fantastical. "It's not made up at all. Maybe you've heard of Frond eolis?" I asked, rattling off another more common name for the snail.

"No—"

"Bushy-backed nudibranch?"

"No—" He choked. "Bushy-what now?" The stoicism of his expression broke so completely that my smile couldn't help but coil higher.

And I couldn't help but repeat myself.

"Bushy-backed nudibranch." I took another step closer to him, watching the way his arms lifted just a little like he expected me to fall again. Grumpy but chivalrous. "See?" I extended my palm so he could look at the colorful creature. "Bushy-backed because of all its tree-like arms. This little guy has six. Sometimes they can have up to nine." I tipped and tilted my hand so that the little tendrils moved and swayed. "It's because of their little branches that it's easy to mistake them for algae or seaweed."

I loved biology. Ecology. I loved all the ologies that gave us a better understanding of the world around us. How everything was connected. How the tiniest sea snail affected the environment as expansive as the ocean.

How all of us, even down to a frilly colorful sea snail, tried to fit in.

"Miss Cross—"

"Nudibranch is the suborder of its taxonomy," I went on, wanting him to understand, too. Maybe then he'd understand why this little guy was so important. *And maybe then he wouldn't be scowling at me the way he was.*

From a distance, the scruff of his short beard hid the details of his face, but up close, I could follow the sharp edge of his jawline and the firm bow of his lips. The bob of his Adam's apple drew my attention down the thick column of his throat. A nice throat that led to an even nicer chest that I couldn't help but observe because that was what I did all day, every day. I observed specimens in their natural habitats. And now, I observed him.

A lightkeeper in his lighthouse. Broad and strong but weather-worn. Steady and protective. Cautious and warning. I wondered what the pulse on his neck would feel like under my fingers. What the ridges of his chest looked like underneath his shirt. I inhaled sharply, heat oozing through my veins. *Had the temperature risen out here? A heat wave in the beginning of March?*

"It sounds like nude because he's naked—I mean, without a shell like most sea snails. Or any male—*snail* really."

Oh my. My eyes went wide—probably even wider to him through my glasses. What was I thinking? *Mr. Kinkade wasn't a specimen. I couldn't be wondering what he looked like without his shell.* But how could any woman not wonder about the big, burly man with shadows in his eyes? I sank my attention back to the *snail* in my palm, my eyelids fluttering like they could dust off the pink embarrassment in my cheeks.

"They're also called the shaggy tree snail."

"You couldn't lead with that?" He folded his broad arms over his chest.

I shrugged. "A nudibranch by any other name would still be—"

"Unbelievable." He shook his head and wiped his hand over his mouth in frustration. "How long are you here for, Miss Cross?" Even though I'd already told him, he asked as though hoping this time I'd give a different answer.

"The rest of the semester—ten weeks or so," I repeated. "Did they not tell you?"

He let out a sound of displeasure and then spun on his heel.

"Wait, Mr. Kinkade—" I huffed when he didn't stop. *Rude.* Turning, I quickly replaced the tree snail back into one of the tide pools and trudged after him, waddling over the rocks as quickly as I could.

I wanted to let him know that I didn't need a lot of space—I'd set up my stuff on a desk inside the cottage, but I could easily move it if it was in his way. Laptop. Camera. Notepad. Specimen containers. Textbooks. It was a fair amount of stuff, but I could move it to the kitchen if he needed the desk; judging by the sparse shelves and empty fridge, it didn't seem like the kitchen got much use anyway, so maybe that would be better.

"Mr. Kinkade!" I called, watching him disappear inside the house.

We'd clearly gotten off on the wrong foot, and I wanted to remedy that. I didn't know how much time he spent at the lighthouse each day, but the last thing I needed was to be on bad terms with the man I would be sharing a working environment with for the next ten weeks.

My rubber boots tripped me up when I reached the flat gravel path; they were made for wading, not chasing. I unhooked the clips of my waders at the entrance to the cottage and began to finagle myself out of the cumbersome attire. They were such a pain to get out of—especially in a hurry. One socked foot landed on the entryway as I grabbed the door handle, swinging it open as I hopped and swung my other leg free.

"Mr. Kinkade, I'm sorry—" I called, stumbling forward through the door and straight into him. *Again.* "Oomph!"

I felt the rumble of his chest more than I heard it this time. And the heat...the heat of him soaked through me as though I'd been doused by that wave. A giant masculine wave that oozed amber and sea salt into my nostrils, and I inhaled deeper, the scent fueling the rolling bang of my heart against the front of my chest.

"I'm *so* sorry." I gulped, blinking up at him, his expression even more stern than the first time he'd saved me from falling.

Big, strong hands gripped my upper arms and slowly pushed me back.

This time, in addition to the hardness of his chest muscles, I also observed the slight bump of his shirt where it rested over a necklace, the chain peeking out ever so slightly from the collar. But before I could determine anything more, his voice demanded my attention.

"Have you considered pursuing a master's in balance instead of biology?"

My jaw dropped a little, and then I smiled. "That was my first choice, but I decided on something I'd have a chance of succeeding at."

His lip twitched as though it wanted to crack a smile but was held back. He released me and took another full step back, his gaze raking down me once more. Now, it was my turn to feel...nude. I wasn't. *Obviously.* I had on black leggings underneath my waders; they were comfortable and convenient, but the subtle flare of his nostrils reminded me that they also revealed every one of my curves.

I wasn't ashamed of my body—or anything about myself, really. Plump and peculiar were just fine with me. But his stare made me hot; it made me feel like I was under the microscope. Not for my body to be picked apart, but for him to assess how best to devour me.

"Is there something else you needed from me, Miss Cross?" he rumbled, and I watched the dark centers of his eyes widen.

A kiss.

My breath caught. No. That was wrong. So wrong. Impossibly wrong.

"I just wanted to tell you that I can move my things to a different room if you want," I said, backpedaling toward the kitchen and pointing through it to the desk where my stack of folders, books, and my laptop sat on the desk. "I put everything there when I got here because you weren't here, and I didn't know where to go with it," I babbled on, wanting to distract his focus from me. The intensity of it was making my mind go haywire. *Wanting to kiss him. How ridiculous.* I'd only just met him. And he was as congenial as a crab. "I'm not sure where you work from in here, but I can set up anywhere—even in the bedroom—"

"No."

Okay then.

"If you're sure—"

"I...store things in the bedroom. It's off-limits. You can use the desk."

"Thank you." I swallowed and nodded. "I promise I won't be in your way. I'll be outside and around the lighthouse most of the time. I mean, I do have to collect some specimens and analyze them, which I'll do inside. Also my notes...and importing photos and things—"

"I don't care what you do, Miss Cross, just don't disturb me."

"Oh, of course, I would never—"

"And don't fall in the ocean," he growled. "I'm the lighthouse keeper...not yours."

My jaw dropped for an instant. The words stung. More than I really wanted to admit. So, I scooped up my indignation with a defiant tilt of my chin. "You're very unpleasant, you know that?"

His eyes crackled with something electric, and my skin sparked.

"I hate to break it to you, but social butterflies aren't native to lighthouses," he said lowly. "There's a reason only certain animals live at the edge of the world."

My breath hitched. Why did he live at the edge of the world? Was there a reason he was so...prickly all the time?

"And what is that?" I asked, wanting to hear his answer.

"You're the expert." He zipped up his jacket with a flick of his wrist, and the room felt like it lost several degrees of heat. "What time will you get here in the morning?"

"Early. Around seven or seven-thirty, if that's okay—"

"I'm here for the dawn, Miss Cross."

Right. "I'll finish up outside by sundown, and then I just do my notes for the day if you want me to lock up—"

"Don't bother," he said and headed for the door. "No one comes out here."

Except me.

He stopped, his body completely filling the frame as he looked back over his shoulder, pinning me with his stern stare. "It's going to storm tonight," he warned in a low voice. "I wouldn't be traipsing around the water much longer."

"Okay..." The word hung in the room longer than he did.

I walked to the door and watched him get back in his truck, wondering what it was about him that turned my heartbeat into an unsteady tumble and made my skin sizzle with heat.

No sooner did his truck disappear down the winding gravel drive than a fat raindrop landed on my nose. I looked up, the second one landing square in the middle of my glasses. *Crap.* I ducked back inside and within seconds, there was a steady shower coming down outside, the patter of the rain mingling with the riotous churn of the ocean against the rocks. *Crap, crap.* My shoulders slumped, and I stared longingly in the direction of the tide pool where I'd returned the *dendronotus*.

Tomorrow. I'd find him again tomorrow.

Crouching, I reached out and hauled my rubber waders inside, hanging them on one of the nails driven into the wall by the door. I had a feeling Mr. Kinkade had been the one to drive them into the wall; it seemed like his style. Rugged. Rough. Sturdy.

"Oh," I muttered and reached for the small chest pocket on the waders, remembering the shell I'd tucked in there before I'd noticed the dendronotus.

A northern moon snail. Well, what was left of one.

The large shell had taken on an almost purple-pink hue which stuck out immediately among the brown and gray rocks, stranded there from one of the recent storms. It was too beautiful not to save before the tide washed it away.

I carried it to the kitchen and set it on the counter, the dulled opalescent hues of the shell practically the only color in the dreary room. And then the thought struck me. With a grin, I went to the desk and grabbed a pen and a sheet of paper from my notebook.

Mr. Kinkade, I think we got off on the wrong "foot."
I hope you have a spe-shell day!

I pushed a loose strand of hair back from my face and smiled as I tucked the note underneath the edge of the shell. *Perfect.* Dad always said there was nothing that couldn't be cured with kindness. Maybe this would soften Mr. Kinkade's prickly demeanor a little.

Satisfied with my little olive branch, I walked over to the window and watched the rain drench the shore. Hopefully, by tomorrow the storm would pass and I could be back outside—back to my research on the coast's aquatic biology.

My phone buzzed and I fished it from my bag, smiling as I answered, "Hey, Dad."

"Hey, honey. I just finished class but I wanted to check and see how you're settling in—"

"Oh, I'm at the lighthouse already."

"I'm not surprised." Dad chuckled. "Find anything good yet?"

"A northern moon snail shell and a dendronotus." *And a grumpy lighthouse keeper.*

"Oh, how wonderful!" he exclaimed. "Can you send photos? I'd love to show my class."

Dad was a biology professor at Tufts, so there was no shortage of things for us to share our excitement on. We were like two peas in a pod for almost my whole life after Mom died. Always exploring. Learning. It was because of Dad that I wasn't afraid to ask questions. That I wasn't afraid to search for answers—for understanding. And it was because of him that I'd decided to finish up my master's here in Maine rather than in the halls of Boston University.

I didn't like leaving him for such a long period of time, but he wouldn't hear of anything else. *"There is no education without experience."*

"I'll send one of the shell," I said. "It started to storm, so I'll have to try for the dendronotus tomorrow."

"Oh, of course. Of course." He chortled. "All right, I'll let you go. I can't wait to hear about all the species you find."

As I murmured my goodbye, I had to remind myself that the inhabitant *inside* the lighthouse wasn't part of my studies. *I wasn't here to understand him...or the effect he had on my very rational brain.*

CHAPTER 3
KIT

Bushy-backed nudibranch.

I didn't know what was more ridiculous—
that a living creature had such a name or that I
couldn't stop thinking about the woman who'd told it to
me. I checked my phone and laid back on the stiff
mattress with a huff; my alarm wasn't set to go off for
another twenty minutes. *But what was another twenty
minutes when I'd hardly slept all night?*

I rarely slept well—nightmares were my frequent
bedfellows. But last night was different. Last night, it
was dreams of a different kind that kept me restless.
Aching. Dreams of a woman I never should've met.

Aurora Cross. The woman invading my lighthouse.
My closed-off corner of the earth.

I didn't want her there—I didn't want anyone there. It
had taken me years to whittle my life down to the bare
essentials and the very barest of interactions, and in one
fell swoop—or one quick slip—she'd crashed right through
those barriers and brought with her a whole host of chaos.

I couldn't believe what I was seeing when I found her on the side of the tower. It was as unbelievable as a damn mermaid washed up on the rocks, too preoccupied with the aquatic equivalent of a dinglehopper to pay attention to her surroundings. *And just as damned enticing...even in those ridiculous waders.*

Even more so when I saw what was hidden underneath.

Those big, curious eyes and wild black curls were nothing compared to her curves. I hadn't looked at a woman in so long—not like that. But Christ, the way she crashed into me left me no choice. She was all softness and warmth packed into a lush frame—a shot of temptation straight into my veins. There was no stopping it. No stopping the fantasy of those curves overflowing my big palms, her almond eyes hooded with pleasure, and her full lips leaking unencumbered moans as I fit myself to her hips and buried myself—buried all my broken edges in her softness.

"Fuck," I muttered and pounded my fist into the mattress, but the second I squeezed my eyes shut to try and wipe her from my thoughts, it was only her face I saw.

"You're very rude, you know that?" It was the look on her face more than her brash words that struck me. The recollection of her pink cheeks, wide eyes, and full fucking lips...she had no idea what rude was. Rude was what I wanted to do to her mouth. The way I wanted to stuff it full with my—

"Enough," I warned and sat myself upright with a harsh exhale. I hadn't been with a woman in so long—which was no fucking excuse. I had enough demons to deal with—ones far bigger, far more vicious than desire. "*Enough.*"

It was only ten weeks, I'd reminded myself countless times in the hours since I'd left her standing in my doorway. Ten weeks where she should be working outside and I, inside. Ten weeks where I'd figure out every possible way of avoiding her just like I avoided everything else that provoked my damned demons.

"Hello?" Jamie's voice rang through the barn.

Shit.

I should've expected this—did expect this, but at the same time, I hoped I'd be able to avoid it.

"Yeah," I croaked and threw off the thin blanket I'd slept with last night, dragging my hand through my hair and along my beard. I pushed myself off the cot in the loft with a grunt, adjusting myself in my jeans, the stiff fabric no match for the stiffness of my cock.

"Kit?" Jamie's heavy footsteps clunked closer.

"No, your other brother," I quipped and exhaled slowly. He appeared at the bottom of the ladder a second later, his gaze meeting mine.

So much of us was similar. Our brown eyes. Our smiles. The way our protectiveness strengthened and sharpened after Dad died. We both looked after Mom, though Jamie thought it was his sole responsibility as the oldest. And then, after Mom got caught up with Frankie and Lou's father...I shuddered. Thank God that gold-digging piece of shit was out of our lives. *Thank God, the only father figure the twins had ever known was Jamie.*

"You all right?"

I tensed, his concern like hot water on burned flesh. To be fair, I was sleeping in the loft of the barn on Mom's property that he'd long ago converted into his woodworking shop. The loft was relegated to unsold or unfinished pieces of furniture, historic furniture that Jamie sometimes put on display, and excess wood.

After my dreams last night, a little more excess wood than usual.

"Fine." I grabbed my sweater and pulled it over my head, stuffing my dog tags underneath the fabric. "On my way out."

Dawn was fast approaching, and I had work to do. My list of tasks—my routine—was what kept me sane. Gave me purpose. And I wasn't going to let anyone interfere with that.

"Surprised you came here in the first place," Jamie said, holding his place at the bottom of the stairs. "Everything okay at the lighthouse?"

I gritted my teeth. Last night, I almost didn't bother texting him to let him know I was going to crash in the loft. I knew there was an extra bed up here from the days when Jamie would work into the early morning hours on his custom furniture or when the weather was too bad to risk leaving. That was before Violet—before he had every reason to go home.

Still, I'd given him a heads-up, and now I regretted it.

"Yeah."

"Then why are you here?"

"Change of scenery?"

His scowl rivaled my own as he folded his arms. "Bullshit."

"There's a student doing research at the lighthouse," I revealed carefully, tugging on my boots. "It's just better—easier if I'm not one more curiosity for her to study."

"Her?"

"Yeah." I cleared my throat. "Jason didn't exactly give me a heads-up, so I'm adjusting."

I'd dialed Jason's number as soon as I got in my truck yesterday, smoke practically blowing out my ears. I didn't even make it to the first ring before I'd ended the call. I had no place to be angry. The lighthouse wasn't mine—not to control who was allowed there. *Not even to live there.*

Technically, I'd never been given permission to live at the keep, but neither had I been forbidden; I'd just never asked. Yeah, there were times I was sure Jason knew. That the old *don't ask, don't tell* policy extended to my living situation. But I didn't want to risk it, so I swallowed down my irritation about Miss Cross, afraid it would invite more questions I didn't want to answer.

"So, this is more than one night?"

"A few weeks." I climbed down the ladder.

"Weeks?" His brows lifted. "Why don't you stay with Mom?"

I answered him with a look. I'd stayed with Mom... after everything. I thought being there with her and Gigi, Lou, and Frankie would be easiest. So many reminders that I was home. *Safe.* Instead, they'd been a litmus test for my trauma, showing me just how crippled my life was—would always be.

"It's only a few weeks." I tugged my hat securely over my head and offered him a tight smile.

His hand anchored onto my shoulder as I tried to walk around him. "Kit..."

I stopped but didn't look back. It killed me that he

couldn't help me just as much as it killed him wanting to.

"You can't hide forever."

Slowly, I met my brother's gaze. "You can't protect me from everything."

I knew it was his nature, just like it was mine. And when he'd stepped in to take care of the family, leaving no room for me to do the same, I enlisted instead. If he was going to protect our family, then I was going to protect our country. But fate had other plans.

"Not trying to protect you from everything, Kit. Just from yourself."

I felt myself tense, but before I lashed out when he was only trying to help, I said instead, "Tell Violet I said hi," and shrugged off his hold.

"You coming to Mom's for the twins' birthday?" he called as I approached the door.

I breathed out slowly. *April first.* Frankie and Lou's day. After all these years, I didn't know if it was better or worse that their birthday fell on the day I was released from Walter Reed. A day that should've been a celebration from every angle, but it was always a celebration shadowed by what happened two weeks later.

"I don't think so." I hated myself for the answer, but only a fool would agree to something that was beyond my limits. Their party would be full of friends and family. Full of smiles and laughter and loud noises. Full of all the things that crippled me. So, I would do the smart thing and stay away. Just like I always did.

The last thing their celebration needed was the presence of a dead man walking.

Dawn stretched its fingers over Friendship's main street, catching on the details of the buildings and bringing them to light. Postcards of Maine—of New England were less picturesque than the main drag in my hometown. The small shops and wrought-iron lampposts romanticized the coastal town image that was cozy and quaint even on a dreary day in that muddy season in March where it was too cold to be spring but too wet to still be winter.

Water sloshed under the tires and rain tapped on the windshield, remnants of yesterday's storm still dragging their feet. Part of me was tempted to stop at the Maine Squeeze and pick up a coffee on my way to the lighthouse, but I couldn't risk Lou's sympathetic look two days in a row. Especially if Jamie had mentioned to anyone that I'd stayed at the barn last night.

The sympathy killed me. The pity. The pain. I wanted to get better—to be better. But I just fucking couldn't. After what happened...coming home...I couldn't adapt. I couldn't find a way to be around anyone, even my family, for long periods of time. I couldn't stop the nightmares. The panic. I couldn't change what had become of me...and so I did the only thing I could: I tried to protect my family from having to see it.

My blood began to pump as I turned onto the road to the lighthouse, the wooden sign faded and weather-worn to the point where the *Friendship Lighthouse* engraving was hardly visible.

Two miles of gravel path led to the secluded keep, lined the whole way by evergreen sentries on the left and boulders barricading the sea on the right. In the winter, snow could make the drive so treacherous that the only safe way to access the lighthouse was via snowmobile.

I scanned the perimeter, waves still chopping at the rocky base as the drizzle of rain ushered out last night's storm. The off-white house and tower appeared a dreary gray, coated with rain and clouds, but the red roof was still bright. Undimmable. Kind of like the determination in Aurora—*Miss Cross's* gaze.

Goddamn, I needed to stop thinking about her.

I pulled all the way down the narrow lane, exhaling in rough relief when there was no sign of a soul, and parked in front of the house.

Salt air hit my nose like a dose of disinfectant. The kind of scent that went right to the very core of a person and purged anything that wasn't meant to be there. Except memories. Those, I'd learned, weren't strong enough to erase.

I hustled inside, stopping short at how starkly the interior of the cottage changed in less than a day. *Because of her.* Miss Cross's things littered through the rooms like algae on the seafloor, pervasive yet as though it all belonged.

I went to hang my jacket, but her waders had claimed the hook. Empty jars lined the edge of the kitchen counter just waiting to be filled with some hocus-pocus-named creature or another. And my office...I strode to my desk chair, but the seat was stacked with textbooks and notebooks, all tabbed with colored Post-it Notes along the edges. I reached out, my fingers splaying over the one on top, tempted to open it just to see what her handwriting was like.

In the hospital—the second time—writing was how everyone communicated with me until my hearing came back. I hated being back in that bed with nothing to focus on except all the tiniest details of being stuck there—and one of those details was handwriting. From my nurse Nikki's loopy, bubbly cursive to Jamie's strong but sloppy scrawl. And the twins...Frankie's bold print and Lou's thoughtful strokes; sometimes it was hard to believe that two people who were so genetically similar could be so different. And now, I wondered how Aurora wrote. I lifted the edge of the notebook, imagining stocky, block letters. Efficient and emboldened, but with softened, rounded corners.

Gritting my teeth, I let the cover—and the thought —go and instead reached in the drawer for my logbook, closing the drawer hard enough to make the desk rock, and then made my way to the spiral stairs.

The staircase wound up the center of the tower like an artery straight to the heart of the lighthouse. Some towers were big enough to house entire rooms at different points along the ascent; the Friendship Lighthouse wasn't that big, but at eighty feet tall, it was big enough. Just before the top, there was a small landing with the mechanical and electrical components that operated the light, so I stopped there first to check all the indicators, noting all the levels in my leather notebook.

Logbooks were a thing of the past when lighthouse keepers needed to track the conditions of the sea and sky on a daily basis—something that modern navigation and meteorology made obsolete. I kept a log though. Not so much for the lighthouse, but for me.

The therapist I'd seen for a year after being released from the hospital had suggested a daily journal. Something about connecting with routines to find a way back to normal. She'd also wanted me to track every time I had a nightmare. Every time I had a panic attack. When they occurred. Where. If something triggered them. *She'd wanted me to track every time I was reminded of my reality.*

And I couldn't do that.

Instead, I'd compromised with this. A daily log as the lightkeeper. The top corner of the page noted with the date. Below it, I recorded all the information from the mechanical room each day, including the battery levels. I noted the weather each morning and the forecast for the day. And then I went back to the previous page and marked if I'd done any repairs or if anything of note happened.

There was rarely anything put in that spot because rarely did anything happen. Until yesterday.

I flipped back to the nearly empty page, staring at the faint lines for a long moment before I scribbled in the space: *Aurora arrived.*

My pen hesitated. *Why hadn't I written Miss Cross?* I should cross it out and fix it, but for some reason, I couldn't. The notebook slapped shut, and I took the stairs two at a time to the lantern room, the automated light beaming out in steady, measured bursts.

"Mr. Kinkade?"

I spun with a low curse, the burst of adrenaline in

my veins making me see stars. I barely wiped the pained shock off my face before Aurora's head poked into the lantern room, her curls loose and wild around her face. My fingers tightened around my pen, itching to know if her hair was as soft as it looked. I didn't deal with soft things. The scars and calluses on my hands were a testament to the roughness of my work: manual labor and repairs, most days outside and in inclement weather. But Aurora—*Miss Cross*—was made of layers of soft temptation, the kind of thing a hard, broken man like me could only ever dream of feeling.

Warm eyes found mine as she stepped fully into the tiny room, wearing another pair of black leggings and a similar long-sleeve black shirt. This time, I was close enough to see that her clothes were a kind of cold gear to help keep her warm in the waders; unfortunately, all that meant to me was that they clung to her lush body like a second skin, making my dick so hard, so fast, I had to shift my weight to stop my jeans from pinching.

"Miss Cross," I growled, prepared to order her out of the tower in another second when her attention was stolen by the sea.

"Wow." She faced the panoramic views, her jaw dropping, those full lips of hers rounding around the "o" in a way that was dangerously erotic.

Miles of sea stretched like a banquet of beauty all the way to the horizon. It was breathtaking. Every morning, rain or shine, snow or storm, the sight steadied me. Comforted me.

Until now. Now, the only thing I felt was uncomfortable. She was in my space—my haven. And with her back to me, the view I had was of her wide hips and full ass. I could just imagine sinking my fingers into her warm flesh, holding her steady while I marked her with all my hard, sharp edges.

"You shouldn't be up here," I said low, tearing my gaze away as lust blared like a warning siren through my veins. This was one more reason I shouldn't be around people. Years without sex—without intimacy—turned me into a snarling caveman around a woman who looked like a raven-haired Venus rising from Botticelli's sea.

"I saw your things but couldn't find you..."

"You don't need to find me to do your research," I said, and then added even more harshly, "I'm not one of your specimens."

Her shoulders slumped, but I knew better than to hope she'd give up and leave me alone. "What do you do up here?" she asked, reaching behind her and holding onto the railing that circled the room. "As the lighthouse keeper, I mean?"

I forced myself to look away from her. This room was far too damn small for the two of us when my body reacted to her the way it did.

"I make sure the light is working properly. That the battery and generator are functioning optimally. Make sure the windows and lens are cleaned. And then take care of the whole keep. Patches. Repairs. Anything it needs..."

"You write that all down?" She pointed to my notebook and instinctively, I clutched it tighter.

"Most of it. I note the weather each day. Precipitation levels. Quality of the ocean." I didn't know why I was even answering her. I wasn't the one being studied here, but for some reason, it felt like not answering her would only make her curiosity even worse. The last thing I needed was her snooping around the damn house and finding all my art supplies or—worse— evidence that I actually lived here.

"It's comforting, isn't it?" Her smile came out of nowhere, so bright I thought for a second that I'd stared directly into the beam of the light.

I started. "Excuse me?"

"Cataloging—tracking the environment each day," she clarified with a contented sigh. "I do the same thing. Not for the lighthouse, obviously. But for my research, I keep track of a lot of similar things about the environment so I can see any trends and if they affect the animals I'm studying."

I grunted.

"I think it's fascinating to see how much things stay the same...and to be able to pinpoint the exact moment something changed. Fascinating and comforting."

I didn't know how to agree because I'd never thought of it like that before. I kept a log because it anchored me to reality—to each day. It reminded me that even though I was broken, I had a purpose. But maybe there had always been something more...something I hadn't given a name to until she'd translated it.

"Also, lonely," she went on, shifting just enough that I could see her reflection in the glass, her eyes blankly pinned to the horizon. "So focused on keeping track of the world around you, you don't have to think about your place in it. Or wonder if you have one."

Who was this woman? Who went from sea slugs to existentialism in a matter of minutes without missing a beat? And more importantly, how did she know? I didn't want to think about my place in the world because I didn't have one. Not out there. Only here, on the very edge of existence, was there a place for me. Here, where the weather and the sea were as harsh and unforgiving and solitary as I was.

"My place is right here." *Unlike hers.*

I refused to let myself consider why she sounded like she didn't have a place. I refused to let myself wonder how someone who was clearly smart, breathtakingly beautiful, and too damn kind for my own good could think she didn't have a place. Literally anywhere would be lucky to have her. Anywhere but here.

"Is there something you needed?" My jaw clenched, and my gaze traitorously returned to the slope of her back down to her perfect ass. *Goddamn, she was crafted for pure temptation.*

I went to move behind her at the same moment she turned, her upturned face within inches of mine. Her small gasp immediately drew my attention to her mouth. Full, pink lips that were so close. So damn close all I had to do was bend down to taste them.

"How did you know about the storm?" she asked, the huskiness in her voice unmistakable.

For a second, I let in the insane thought that if I kissed her, it would stop her questions.

Fuck.

"Everything dangerous in nature comes with a warning, Miss Cross, if you're smart enough to recognize the signs," I rasped.

"What's your warning?"

A low sound erupted from the depths of my chest. *She should've recognized the signs for that instantly.* I moved back, needing space from her.

"For the storm, I mean."

"Blood red sky in the morning," I said roughly.

"Oh."

"You should go. I'm sure you have plenty of work to do." *Like I did.* "They're not calling for a lot of great weather in the coming weeks."

The forecast predicted a halfway decent day once the drizzle stopped, and that meant I wanted to get up on the roof and replace the dozen or so shingles that had been damaged in the last big storm. After today—after the end of this week, really—that was when things took a turn for the worse.

I opened the door to the stairwell, holding it ajar for her. Single file, we made it back downstairs without incident.

Almost.

"Oh," she exclaimed and spun. Somehow, I managed to not crash into her, but it was a small victory considering that stopping in time meant stopping within too-short inches from her. "Did you like the shell?"

"What shell?"

Color fused to her cheeks. "Here." She went to the kitchen, and I took the opportunity to take a deep breath, preparing myself for several more minutes in her presence.

"Your shell and note." She pushed both along the counter until they were in front of me.

Somehow in the midst of...*her*...I'd missed the cotton-candy-colored shell and paper in the center of the counter.

I picked up the paper. Block letters. Slightly curved. On a slant. *Everything I thought her handwriting would be.*

Mr. Kinkade, I think we got off on the wrong "foot."
I hope you have a spe-shell day!

Foot. Shell. I gritted my teeth, forcing myself not to react to her snail puns as she watched me with a smile. I set the note down without a word and picked up the shell, the whole thing swallowed up in my grasp.

"What is this?" I was almost afraid to ask.

She beamed. "A northern moon snail. Well, the shell of one. I found it in the rocks yesterday," she said as I turned it in my hand, examining the intricate whorls and vibrant coloration. "They're not as commonly found in the intertidal areas, but I think with all the storms, it washed this one ashore."

"Moon snail..." I ran my finger along the edge and then snapped my gaze to hers. "And it's for me?"

"A peace offering." Her smile widened, bringing out the dimples in her pink cheeks.

No. Absolutely not.

"A carcass," I declared roughly.

"What?" Her jaw dropped.

"This is a carcass." I rotated the shell in my fingers, pretending like my classification wasn't exceptionally harsh. "You're giving me a snail carcass as an apology."

Her mouth opened and shut. I'd made her speechless, and I liked it. Almost as much as I liked the rich, almost-red blush on her cheeks...and being the reason for it. God, this woman was just as colorful as the world she was here to study.

"Well, I guess...technically...it's a shell." Her tongue swiped over her lips, wetting the pink flesh, and my dick started to leak in my jeans. *Fucking hell.* I should've worked one out last night, but it felt fucked up to do that in my brother's barn.

"A carcass," I grunted and set it down, moving back to my desk and replacing my logbook in the drawer. "I have work to do." Anything to make the torture stop. Anything to put a damn bit of space back between us.

When I looked back, I found Aurora staring at me with an expression that drew a sensation up my spine that I didn't care for. *Not one bit.*

"Mr. Kinkade, have I done something to upset you or to make you dislike me?" she asked softly.

I tensed.

Yes. You made me aware of your existence. Aware that my body was still capable of feeling, wanting, and aching for things the rest of me can't have. And because you're not leaving, I have no choice but to figure out how to handle...temptation.

"As you said, we both have worlds to watch, and you're not a part of mine, Miss Cross, just as much as I'm not a part of yours." I grabbed my cap from my back pocket, tugged it on my head, and then strode back outside. Drizzle be damned.

We could cohabitate the lighthouse the same way the fish and the fisherman cohabitated the sea, but that didn't mean she was part of my world.

CHAPTER 4
AURORA

"Black coffee, please. Biggest one you have. And one of the cider donuts." I pushed the hood of my yellow windbreaker back but made sure my cap stayed securely on my head. No one needed to see my hair after the morning I'd had. Missed alarm. Late shower. Rushed out into the rain.

Just another manic Monday.

"Absolutely." The woman behind the counter smiled wide. She'd been working here every morning I'd been in for the last two weeks, usually with one or two other girls who normally took my order, but today she was alone.

Of course, I'd observed her all those mornings in action. Noted little details and facts. It was my habit—the way I engaged with my environment. I noted that her name was Lou. Her chestnut brown hair was always braided back either in a single braid or two braids down either side of her head. She knew almost everyone who came in by name. And her smile was the warmest, most welcoming thing about this place—like hot tea on a cold day.

"Thanks." I wiped the wetness from my face.

For two weeks, I'd had nothing but sunny, brisk spring days to work with. The conditions were perfect to examine the numerous saltwater species living in the tide pools and rocky shoreline around the lighthouse. Mollusks. Echinoderms. And arthropods. *Oh my!* Their habitat—their existence—consumed me. I'd spent every minute of the growing daylight hours observing, recording notes, taking photographs, and collecting specimens, and then far too many minutes of my nights cataloging and collating, slowly building the framework for what would become my thesis.

How they existed, how they existed together, how they evolved...it fascinated me. But for some reason, it didn't consume me like it normally would. Instead, if given just a moment for distraction, my mind went to a different speci-*man*—one who I swore had almost kissed me that morning.

Heat hummed along my spine, and my eyelids fluttered. If I let them shut, I knew I'd see his face just inches in front of mine. His gaze anchored to my mouth like it was the only thing keeping his mind from losing its moorings.

I was a smart woman. Not just in my field of study, but in general. I was observant. Patient. And quick to pick up on the slightest nuance of behavior. *At least when it came to invertebrates.* But it had to be the same for humans—for men, right? Unfortunately, my experience with *that* species was the equivalent of abysmal.

"For here or to go?" She lifted both cup options.

"For—" I glanced over my shoulder and heaved an

exhale, changing my mind. "For here." Normally, I took my coffee to go, wanting to get to the lighthouse and to work as quickly as possible, but the rain made me hesitate.

It wasn't a thunderstorm, but it was raining hard enough to make outdoor exploration a little too risky, which meant I'd be relegated to the indoors. Normally, that wouldn't be a problem. I had plenty to do inside— plenty of live and dead specimens I'd found and preserved in jars that now covered the counter in the kitchen, including my prized pet, Stuart. A sea star who'd lost two arms and was in the process of regenerating them. However, *inside* was Mr. Kinkade's domain, and the rain would certainly trap us both there.

For the last two weeks, we were like ships passing in the night—except we passed in broad daylight. *Each watching our own worlds.*

If I was outside, he was inside. The days when I was collecting my specimens and bringing them inside, he was outside. First, on the roof, and later, around the side of the house repairing one of the windows. For two weeks, wherever I was, he wasn't. *Except for in my thoughts.* But today...today might break that cycle, and I wasn't sure I was ready.

"It's Aurora, right?" Lou asked, grabbing my donut while she waited for the fresh pot of coffee to finish brewing.

She had a good memory for names; another detail I'd picked up on. She knew most every customer by name, and in my case, even though she'd only taken my order once, she still recalled my name.

"Yeah." I smiled.

"I'm Lou," she introduced herself before I could

ask. "I keep telling our manager that we need name tags, but he doesn't listen. Says the only names that matter are the customers."

I chuckled. "It's nice to meet you, Lou. Is that short for Louise? Or Louisa?" I wondered and began to scarf down the donut.

I liked names. *Genus. Species.* Learning Latin nomenclature felt like being able to see the root system of the tree rather than just the leaves on the branches. It shaped everything. Put it all in place. For the invertebrates I studied, it gave clues to their existence. Explanations of their composition. Human names were less indicative of those kinds of things, but they still fascinated me.

"For Elouise." She poured my coffee into a giant mug and set it on the counter in front of me.

"Oh." My eyes rounded. "I like that." I'd have to look up its origins later. I sighed when the warmth from the cup seeped into my fingers.

"Only my sister calls me Elouise, and usually when she wants to get us in trouble," she went on as I brought my mug to my lips and took a sip of my coffee.

It was still hot enough to burn the tip of my tongue, but I didn't care, it tasted so good. I'd passed the little coffee shop on my taxi through town to the lighthouse that first day, but when I saw Mr. Kinkade wearing a hat with the name on it, I knew I had to try it. Anything that passed that man's muster was something worth trying.

"You seem more like a Lou," I agreed. Elouise was beautiful, and the woman was definitely that. But Lou was something more relaxed. Approachable. "What's your sister's name?"

"Frankie. Francesca," she revealed with a grin and added, "We're twins."

"Identical or fraternal?" I took another big gulp of the strong brew.

"Identical, but if you ask anyone who knows us, we're only clones on the outside." Her tone was rueful.

"Did you know sea stars are one of the few animals capable of producing complete clones of themselves? Some species can regenerate their entire body from a single severed arm." I shouldn't sound so enthusiastic about a sentence that had the word "severed" in it.

Lou wrinkled her nose. "I don't know if I should be impressed or grossed out..."

Way to go, Aurora. "Sorry, I should explain." I ducked my head and laughed. "I'm a biology nerd. I'm here finishing my master's degree for the rest of the semester."

She nodded. "Well, that makes sense. Usually anyone I see for more than a week has moved here, but usually, when someone moves to Friendship, I know well before the week is up."

"Nothing evolves quite as quickly as news in a small town."

"Very true." Lou chuckled. "So, what are you studying here? Ocean life?"

I laughed. "Coastal biology—things that live in intertidal and coastal ocean waters."

"Oh, that's really cool," she said and began restocking the stacks of to-go cups and lids near the register. "So, are you out on the beaches then, or like snorkeling in the water?"

"Oh, no." I shivered at the thought, quickly downing another gulp of coffee. "My focus is on the species that live on the rocky terrain closest to human habitats, so my workspace is confined mostly to the perimeter of the Friendship Lighthouse. It's just outside —" I stopped short when the stack of paper cups in her hands tumbled to the floor.

"You're working at the lighthouse?" She approached me, staring like I'd just sprouted a third eyeball.

"Yeah..." I paused with my mug halfway to my lips, her tone making me feel like I was missing something. "Have you been there?"

"Have you met the lighthouse keeper?"

My jaw dropped slightly and then snapped shut. Was everyone as intrigued by him as I was? Did that make me normal? Or jealous?

"Yeah." I quickly chugged the remainder of my coffee.

"He's a little rough around the edges, right?" she asked with a knowing smile.

"I'd say he's the male equivalent of a sea urchin— sounds approachable until you meet him and realize he's covered in venomous spines," I countered wryly.

Lou let out a full laugh. "Don't let my sister hear you say that, she'll never let him live it down."

"Does she—do you know him well?" I adjusted my glasses, hoping my eagerness to learn more about the reclusive keeper wasn't as obvious as it felt.

Her head bobbed in slow motion. "You could say that."

My brow furrowed.

"Kit is our brother."

KIT. HIS NAME WAS KIT. *WAS IT JUST KIT? OR WAS it short for Christopher?* I swallowed the questions before they bumbled off the tip of my tongue.

"Oh. I didn't realize..."

"I'm Lou Kinkade," she re-introduced herself as she picked up the cups she'd dropped. "Kit's my older brother. Well, one of them. Jamie's the oldest."

"I see." I gulped. "Well, I'm sorry for saying he's not friendly...and calling him venomous." *This was why I stuck to science, not social sciences.*

"Don't be sorry." She sighed. "He's not so bad once you get to know him."

"Oh. I don't think that's going to happen." I shook my head. "He doesn't like me very much."

"It's not you," she offered kindly, and I wished there was a way to *kindly* tell her she was wrong. It was definitely me he had a problem with. "Kit's not used to having anyone at the lighthouse with him."

"I'm mostly working outside for my research, so I try to stay out of his way. I know he has a lot of work to do."

"He does, but he could use someone to get in his way once and a while."

"I did that the first day and barely lived to tell the tale," I joked.

"What? What happened?" Her eyes were wide.

"We just got off on the wrong foot. I left him a

moon snail shell as an apology. He called it a carcass." I shrugged and sighed.

"Oh, Kit." Lou shook her head.

"To be fair, I'd just surprised him in the tower, and I think I probably crossed some invisible boundary by doing that, but sometimes I get curious and I don't think—"

"He let you in the tower?" She balked.

"Well, I wouldn't say he let me..." I trailed off. "Anyway, I think we're kind of out of feet to get along on." I stared into my empty cup for a moment and then looked up when Lou didn't respond right away. As soon as I saw her dismay, warm guilt flooded my cheeks. "It's fine though. Nothing to worry about."

What was I thinking? I shouldn't be complaining to her about her brother. This wasn't her problem. It wasn't even really a problem. Sure, my heart raced and my body temperature elevated every time he got close, but that physical...attraction clearly didn't change anything.

I stood. "I should get going—"

"You should ask him about his art," Lou blurted out.

"Art?" I froze.

"Yeah." She nodded. "Paintings mostly. He has a gallery in town. But you should ask him about it. Maybe that will get him to open up a little bit."

I hummed and then muttered without thinking, "I'm not sure even a jackhammer and vise grips would be enough to pry him open, but I'll give it a shot."

Lou threw back her head and laughed. "Well, if it doesn't, you'll still have one Kinkade that you can call a friend," she declared with a wink.

"Thank you." I smiled, wishing it was always this easy to make friends.

I could've stayed longer. It probably would've been smarter since it was still raining outside. But I found myself bundling back up and calling a cab. I couldn't help myself. I wanted to know more about Mr. Kinkade.

Kit.

I wanted to know more about Kit.

And the only way to do that was by going back to the lighthouse.

GOODNESS, IT WAS REALLY COMING DOWN. I'D SPENT that extra time at the Maine Squeeze thinking it would give the storm longer to pass through. Instead, it only gave it time to worsen.

"You sure you want to be here, miss?" my taxi driver asked.

"Yes." I gripped the door handle and then flung it open, rushing out into the rain before I had another chance to think better of it.

Head down, I sprinted until I reached the house and barreled inside, the door rattling as I pressed my back to it and heaved an exhale of relief.

I opened my eyes, and the first thing they focused on was him.

Mr. Kinkade. *Kit.*

He stood in the kitchen, elbows propped on the counter as he examined one of my glass jars that held the purple sea star. His eyes snapped up, their warm brown instantly growing darker. *He wasn't expecting me.* Slowly, he straightened, the edge of his jaw hardening underneath the coat of his beard.

"I figured the rain would keep you away."

I knew it.

"Oh, no. I'm not afraid of the rain, and I still have plenty to do." I unzipped my trench coat and slid my arms from the sleeves. Carefully, I hung it on the nail next to the one that held his massive brown jacket, shivering when I felt his gaze lock on my back.

When I turned, his head dropped back to the jar in his hand, and he quickly replaced it on the counter as though he'd forgotten for a second that he was holding it.

"*Solaster endeca.*" I walked over, keeping the counter between us as I picked up the same jar, the glass still warm from his hold. "Purple sun star."

He grunted.

"There aren't very many sea star species that survive in colder waters, but this guy is one of them." I turned the glass as I spoke. "Everyone is always attracted to the color on the top of sea stars. The scales. The exoskeleton and spine. But I find the underside the most fascinating." Spinning the container, I held it out for him to take a closer look.

He didn't. So, I held it for him.

"Sea stars have hundreds of tube feet on their bottom surface. It's how they move. How they hold their prey." I pointed all along the bottom of the arms. "But here is their mouth in the center," I said. "The way sea stars eat is by holding onto their prey—some kind of mussel usually—and pushing their stomach through their mouth. They digest their food outside of their body and then slide their stomach back in." Without thinking, I made a slurping noise with my mouth. *Crap.* My cheeks flamed, and I quickly barreled on. "It's one of the most fascinating characteristics they have because it allows them to eat prey larger than would actually fit in their mouth."

My eyelids fluttered, and I hazarded his gaze for a single second and prepared myself for another one of his *rough edges.* But when I looked up, he was closer than before. We were both hunched over the counter, staring at the sea star floating in the glass.

"So, I guess they never bite off more than they can chew." His deep voice rumbled.

My head snapped up, eyes wide. *Was that...had he... just joked?* For a split second, I swore he was going to smile. The movement of his lips was less of a twitch and more of a tug, and my breath caught in anticipation. *As though I were about to watch him push out something vulnerable through the hard, immovable layers of his shell.*

But just as quickly as I noticed it, the tug was gone.

"Don't move."

Before I could ask why, his fingers pinched the arms of my glasses and carefully pulled them off my face. Instantly, the world was a blur, and he moved like a giant blob over to the sink.

"What..." I trailed off when I heard the rip of a paper towel.

Seconds later, he returned and aligned my glasses to my face, sliding them onto my nose. Slowly, the blob of him came back into focus. The frown lines on the weathered skin of his forehead. The dark hairs of his beard where they tried to hide the curves of his lips.

This close, I could see he had nice lips. Full, but still able to be obscured by his beard. And soft. Surprisingly, for all the hard words that came out of his mouth, his lips looked so soft.

I inhaled deeply, the scent of him, leather and sea salt, sinking into my nostrils. Gritty and masculine.

"They were covered with water," he grunted in explanation.

From the rain.

"Oh, I didn't realize...thank you." I blinked several times, feeling my face redden again. "You know, if I were a sea star, I could just grow a new pair of eyes." My throat bobbed, afraid he was going to move back at any moment, so I kept talking, hoping I could distract him to stay a little longer. "That's their other fascinating characteristic; they can regenerate themselves. Like Stuart."

"Stuart?"

I went to the desk, grabbing the saltwater container that held the mangled, three-legged sea star inside. "Stuart." I pushed the container in his direction, forcing him to take it.

"You named a sea star?"

"Of course." My smile faltered when his eyes dropped to my mouth, and I realized how close we were. Warm tingles began to shoot over my skin. Was it a warning? *Or something else?* I wasn't thinking when I'd walked up to him; I'd just wanted to show him the jar. But now...now, there was no counter between us, only a few perilous inches. "I found him last week. You see how he's missing two arms," I said, hoping he couldn't hear the quiver in my voice as I pointed to the nodes where the limbs had been torn off. "He'll regrow those arms over time."

"That's convenient," he said hoarsely, his eyes stuck on my mouth.

So, I kept talking.

"Actually, depending on which arm is severed, the organism could regenerate the rest of its entire body just from a single piece." I reached out and took one of his hands in mine, lifting it up between us. "Can you imagine? Growing a whole new body—all your organs and systems and parts—from just your hand?"

I caught his eyes, and my heart swan-dived into my stomach. *Oh no.* Why didn't I think around him? Why did I just go and do and say and *touch* without a moment of hesitation? Where exactly did my brain go when he was around?

Because it certainly wasn't here to do its job—to warn me away from his boundaries. *To stop me from touching him.*

Everything registered at once. The heat of his skin. The size of his hand—it was massive compared to mine; I had to use both my hands to hold his fingers wide. And to think about holding his hand...his palm would swallow mine up. But it was the roughness in his gaze that made my breath hitch. It traveled down my cheek, along my neck, my arms, and finally to where we touched.

I swallowed hard, my fingers inching toward the breaks in his as though we were two puzzle pieces I needed to try and fit.

"It wouldn't have to be a hand," I murmured, unable to stop my gaze from roaming every inch of his face. I didn't know if I was moving or if he was, but we were getting closer. We were definitely getting closer. "It could be a foot. Or a nose. Or a mouth."

He jolted. His focus burned the skin of my lips with its intensity. He wanted to kiss me. The way he looked at me. The flare of his nostrils. The rough nature of his warm breaths. He wanted to kiss me, and I felt it all the way in the marrow of my bones because I wanted to kiss him, too.

And I'd never wanted to kiss someone before, not like this.

I had, of course, kissed men before for experimental purposes. Ten times, to be exact, because I didn't want my research to falter on a poor sample size. Initially, I was curious what happened. When I was in high school —middle school, even—girls in my class were always giggling over kissing boys. *Making out. Seven minutes in heaven.* I never felt the same, so I buried my head in books and figured one day I'd feel that same urge. When I got to college without having the inclination, I decided to take matters into my own hands and did what any good scientist would do: I experimented.

After the first five kisses proved lackluster, I tried five more because I thought I had to be missing something. In the end, I determined I was. *Missing something, that is.* I was missing whatever part that made most women enjoy it—or want more.

Or I thought I was, until this moment.

I hadn't even kissed him, but I already knew Kit would be different. It wouldn't be an experiment, it would be an explosion. Unstoppable. Consuming. Life-altering.

"Kit..." I breathed out, realizing my mistake too late.

The haze in his eyes cleared, their black pits darkening furiously as he tugged his hand away and straightened, Stuart's container hitting the counter with a thud.

"Shit," he muttered, the word so low under his breath I was surprised I could hear it with the rain beating against the windows.

What was I doing? Taking his hand? Thinking he wanted to kiss me?

Calling him by his name?

"I'm sorry," I blurted out, binding my arms over my chest, which only made him back up even farther until he collided with the counter behind him. "I was at the Maine Squeeze this morning, and I met your sister, Lou..." I trailed off, hoping it was obvious how I'd come by the personal information.

"Oh yeah?" he grunted and turned to face the sink, whipping on the faucet and washing his hands like he was desperate to scrub my touch from his skin.

Rude.

I tried to swallow, but it felt like I had a sea urchin lodged in my throat, round and prickly and painful. While he was able to wash me off, my body was still recovering from the way his made it go haywire.

My heart continued to pound in my chest. My lips tingled like they were just starting to get normal circulation back. But the ache that started lower, that didn't seem to be dissipating at all.

"I went there because I saw your hat that first day and the mug you always use, so I figured the coffee had to be good."

"Or maybe it's just the only coffee shop in town."

I pushed my glasses higher on the bridge of my nose. "And while that might prompt you to get coffee from there, I doubt it would entice you to wear their branded paraphernalia."

He turned, tucked his arms to his chest, and narrowed his gaze on me. "And how do you know what would entice me, Miss Cross?"

My mouth parted as it felt like all the air was suddenly suctioned from the room. *Entice*. What a poor choice of word I'd picked. My eyes dropped to the floor for an instant. "You're right. I don't," I said, and then because I couldn't stop myself, I added, "But I don't think there are very many things that would."

When I looked back at him, he tumbled with heat like storm clouds churning with lightning. "Well, you're right about that," he said, his voice growing rougher as his eyes did a quick, cold flick over me.

In an instant, that ache that gnawed inside me shriveled up so hard and so fast that I swore I felt it shatter. I'd never been attracted enough to feel a man's rejection before, but I swore that was what this was. Which was odd because I didn't realize there was anything between us to reject until it happened.

"Lou said I should ask about your art." I forged on past the lump in my throat. *What else was I going to do?* I'd already gone off the deep end, so either I was going to let his surliness drown me or I was going to try to make it back to shore.

"Did she?" he said tightly and faced me, his eyes narrowing. "What else did she tell you?"

"That she has a twin. Frankie. And another older brother, Jamie." I licked my lips. "Your name. Well, she called you Kit. Is it just Kit? Or is it short for Christopher?"

His jaw pulsed. "Short for Christopher."

That fit. He'd turn every part of himself into something short and sharp if no one stopped him.

"Do you have any of your paintings here?" My eyes flicked to the locked bedroom; if he did, that was the only place they'd be.

"No." His lip twitched. "I see my sister conveniently forgot to tell you that all my work is at my gallery in town...that she manages," he said with a low rumble. "You're welcome to call a taxi and go there if you want to see them."

And leave him in peace went unsaid.

"Maybe I'll stop by another day." I brushed off the dismissal. "What do you paint? Sea creatures by any chance?" I let out a weak laugh. "I started to sketch some of these guys for my paper, but my art skills are sorely lacking."

"Seascapes. Storms."

I hummed and pulled my bottom lip between my teeth, imagining what kind of style he had. Were his paintings dark and foreboding? Or were they storms on the verge of breaking?

"You're going to be in here then for the day? Staring at your starfish?" His hard tone broke through my thoughts.

"Technically, the name starfish is a misnomer since they aren't fish at all. They don't have scales or gills or fins; they're from a completely different order altogether, which is why we prefer to call them sea stars—"

"You know what I prefer, Miss Cross?"

I blinked at him, guessing sheepishly, "Sea snails?"

His frown deepened. Clearly, he still wasn't entertained by our prior *nudibranch* conversation.

"Solitude," he clipped. "Are you going to be inside all day, Miss Cross?"

I blinked at him and then nodded. "There's not much I can do outside with the rain, but I'll leave you in peace, I promise—"

He barreled around me, his shoulder and chest brushing along my arm no matter how hard he tried to avoid it.

I spun just as he yanked his coat off the hook and threw it on.

"You're going out there? In the rain?" *All to avoid me?*

Kit pinned me with a sharp stare. "You don't become a lightkeeper if you're afraid of a storm."

"No, I guess you don't," I said quietly once he'd barreled through the door.

Then again, if I were the storm, I think I'd be more afraid of him.

CHAPTER 5
KIT

I had to stop watching her.

I gripped the sandpaper block in my hand and scrubbed the bottom of the window frame for the millionth time. At this point, the area where I'd patched the wood couldn't get any smoother, the only thing I was sanding now was the skin from my fingers.

But if I moved, I'd lose sight of her.

The sun was out, which meant so was she. Traipsing around the building in those ridiculous waders of hers. They were so big and clunky, it should literally be impossible for me to be attracted to her, but goddamn if my dick wasn't as polished as the damn window frame from the number of times I'd jacked off in the shower thinking of her.

It was the pink in her cheeks. The wisps of hair that always escaped around her face. It was knowing what was under those waders. Curves on curves on curves.

It was impossible not to watch her. At first, it was self-preservation. I refused to let her sneak up on me again like she had last week when she'd barged into the house from the rain.

It was a miracle I hadn't dropped her damn jar with the bolt of adrenaline that injected straight into my veins. My pulse had spun like a top out of control, spots dotted my vision, and my fight or flight was so intense, it took me far too long to realize she'd caught me looking at her things.

But she hadn't cared.

It would've been better if she had. Better if she'd scolded me and told me to stay away from her damn starfish—*sea star*.

Fuck.

This woman was getting under my skin in the way an anchor gets under the surface of the sea—*by sinking suddenly and completely to the deepest goddamn parts of me.*

Parts that were so dark they rivaled the bottom of the ocean. At least in the way they tormented me.

Instead, she'd shared with me about her work. The things she thought. The things that interested her. She was just a goddamn open book, and that was what infuriated me the most—how easy it would be to let myself in.

But I couldn't.

I wasn't like her damn sea star. *Stuart.* I was broken beyond repair—beyond regeneration. There weren't enough pieces of me left to make a whole.

Her little squeal drew my attention. I knew the sound well enough by now not to be worried. It wasn't a cry of distress but excitement.

"Dammit," I muttered, yanked my hand off the sill, and dropped the sander into my tool bucket.

After three weeks, I knew her routine by now. She'd already stopped in for lunch—a ham and cheese sandwich, which meant she'd be out there until the sunset. Everything about her was predictable except when she was with me. When she talked to me. *Touched me.* I shuddered and clenched and released my fist, my fingers still able to feel the press of hers.

Hands were okay, I reminded myself, trying to recall the countless handshakes I'd exchanged in the years since I'd come home. Handshakes I could stomach. It was everything else that made my mind go haywire. My body, according to my doctor, was fine. The skin. The muscles. Everything had healed and responded normally to nerve testing. It was only my brain that continued to register touch like I was still on fire.

Aurora let out another sound, light and high-pitched with success as she couched in front of another tide pool, her hand furiously moving across her notebook.

I felt like a creep watching her from the window. Her expressions. The scrunch of her nose when she was focused. The smile she had when she found something new—she smiled and bit her lip at the same time, like it took pain to hold back her excitement. *Fuck.* I grunted and widened my stance, the thought always made my dick swell. I couldn't remember the last time I'd fantasized about a woman this way. I wanted to say high school, but I never imagined a woman like this in high school.

Those dark curls tangled around my fist. My other hand full of the flesh at her waist. And my cock ramming into her so hard it made those damn adorable glasses of hers bounce on the bridge of her nose. I wanted to fuck her like an animal. Like living in this damn keep hadn't just turned me into a man on the edge of reality but a savage on the brink of sanity.

I wondered if she made those same gasps and whimpers of excitement when she was fucked. I wondered if any of the men she'd been with before had made her scream. If they hadn't, they didn't deserve to live. If they had...*they didn't deserve to live.*

"Christ," I muttered and ran a hand through my hair.

I was really losing it. Close proximity was like a daily dose of poison. The way my need for her felt like it was slowly killing me. I couldn't get close to her. I knew that. But neither could I get her off my mind. So, I'd found a compromise—just like I did with everything else that haunted me; I captured the emotion in the confines of my art.

Leaving my perch by the window, I went and unlocked the bedroom, pulling out my sketchpad and pencils from the closet. It wasn't my usual medium, but neither was it my usual subject.

I returned to the kitchen, pausing for one more glance out the window to confirm Aurora was busy, and then flipped to the most recent partially finished sketch: the damn sea snail.

The sketches were supposed to be fast and crude. An outlet for my frustration and what I'd hoped would be a stepping stone to my next painting that should've been finished long before now. Case in point: Lou left me a message yesterday that the painting displayed in the front window of the gallery had sold, and she didn't have a good-sized one to put in its place. *Basically, it was a reminder that I needed to get my act together and create new content before my gallery was filled with empty frames.*

But as soon as I started the sea star, my plans went out the window. *Just like everything else about Aurora did.* The drawings had taken on a life of their own, capturing all the details of the sea star while Aurora's voice described them in my head. Before I knew it, the sketch was a full-fledged drawing that I inked over in black, and for a split second, I considered putting it in my gallery.

And then I'd quickly flipped to a new blank sheet and started on the sea snail. *The nudibranch.* That was two days ago. Now, I had the body finished and was working on all the tiny extremities that stretched out like crystallized fingers. One after another, I added the creature's little branches as though it were counting all the reasons I needed to stay far away from its captor.

I wasn't sure how long I'd been working, but the sound of her approaching voice broke my bubble of concentration.

"It's going really well. I'll send you some photos of what I collected today; you'll love them." I tensed, hearing the smile in her voice. *Who was she talking to?* "I miss you, too, Dad."

Dad.

I caught the rim of her yellow hat as it passed by the front window I'd been sanding earlier. *Shit.* I flipped my sketchbook shut and beelined for the bedroom, tossing everything on the bed and quickly shutting the door. My hand was on the key in my pocket when the front door opened.

"Love you, too," she said just as our eyes met across the living room.

She was on the phone—*wasn't talking to me*—and yet something cracked open inside my chest, and it was damn uncomfortable.

I saw the moment she started to look too long—to wonder what I was doing standing by the bedroom door. So, I quickly spun and strode back to the kitchen for some water.

"Hey, can you do me a favor?" she asked, standing in her waders in the doorway.

I stared at her.

"Can you grab me another jar?" She pointed to the box of empty jars underneath the desk. "Otherwise, I have to get out of these waders just to get back in them."

I gritted my teeth and headed for the box. Anything to spare myself the sight of her in the tight leggings she always wore underneath.

"I found a *Buccinum undatum* that I want to bring inside," she went on blithely, her excitement making her words bounce. "More commonly known as a waved whelk, they're like bottom-feeding conch snails. Not particularly special, although their numbers have been declining in certain areas where they are common, but my dad loves them. So, I had to call and tell him."

My throat felt tight. *What would it be like to be the person she called when she was excited?* It wasn't just her face that lit up when she found something new, it was the whole of her. Every inch fucking glowed. *What would it be like to be the first person to bask in that?*

I extended my hand with the jar, and before I could stop myself, I asked, "Any other dinglehoppers or snarfblatts I can get for you?"

Her eyelids fluttered, taking a second to process the reference. If she was going to speak Latin, I was going to speak *Little Mermaid*; with two younger sisters, I was fluent in mermaid.

"No." Aurora smiled and blushed, the sight like a punch to the gut. She took the jar, brushing my fingers in the process. I felt the heat—the fire—but not the pain I usually anticipated. "Thanks, Kit."

Air hissed from my lips. How much longer would the husky way she said my name continue to drive a bolt of lust through my veins? I stood there for only a second longer, watching her quickly waddle back to capture the waved whatchamacallit, and then decided I needed to get out—away from the lighthouse for a little bit.

And that was when I knew it was bad—whatever this was, whatever I felt—when I was willing to leave my own sanctuary rather than torment myself with her presence any longer.

TEN. I'D COUNTED TEN DEEP BREATHS AS I SAT IN my truck in front of Mom's house, Frankie's old Volkswagen Beetle parked on one side of me.

I was pretty sure Lou was working because she was always working—always saving for her inn—but I couldn't be positive because she didn't have a car. *Part of that whole "always saving" mantra.*

I injected one more breath into my lungs, preparing myself for my family. It wasn't that they were a lot, it was that I wasn't enough—that I wasn't better. And if I couldn't make them happy by getting better, then I could at least spare them the pain of seeing me broken.

Gravel crunched under my boots as I walked up to Mom's farmhouse, the path leading to the wide, wrap-around porch that we used to sit on as kids and watch the rain. I pulled my cap off as I climbed the front steps, not bothering to knock before I let myself in.

"Mom?" I called and wiped my feet on the mat.

"Kit." Frankie stopped in the hallway, her hands filled with candles as she blinked at me. "Hi." She looked down and then to me again. "Can you smell these?"

She didn't give me a choice, walking over and shoving one and then the other in my nose, the scent of the sea bursting in my nostrils.

That was Frankie.

Once she set her mind to something, she didn't give anyone—even herself—a choice in the matter. In my case, she was determined to be normal around me. Determined to not show a single tremor or crack no matter how different I was now or how bad things got. Come hell or high water, she was going to treat me like the brother I'd always been.

Meanwhile, Lou was the complete opposite. Sensitive. Affected. She guarded her words and her emotions, trying to look out for me at every turn as much as I tried to take care of her.

"Do they smell different to you? I thought they did, but now I can't tell. And Mom and Gigi are jamming, so they're useless..." She continued to alternate one and then the other.

"I don't..." I sniffed again, wishing I could help, but all I smelled was sugar and lemon and *her*. "What am I smelling for?"

She huffed. "Well, they're both sea scents, but one I did with a little hint of citrus."

I shook my head and tried again. "The right one."

She squealed. "I knew you'd figure it out. I was about to drive them over to the lighthouse to get an answer."

"How'd you know I'd figure it out?" I folded my arms.

"You have a good nose." She shrugged.

"Are you saying I have a big nose?"

It was almost imperceptible—the hesitation and widening of her eyes—but I caught it. *Surprise.* I was joking with her. I couldn't remember the last time I'd joked with her—with any of them. But here I was, emitting the smallest piece of light from somewhere I swore was only filled with darkness.

Where had it come from?

And was it because of her?

My teeth locked. "You said they're in the basement?"

She hummed, her head bobbing as she continued down the hall. I followed a step behind into the kitchen; I heard Mom and Gigi going at it before we even reached the basement steps.

"Crisis averted!" Frankie exclaimed. "Kit found the one with the citrus."

"Oh, Kit." Mom sighed as my feet landed on the basement floor.

"There he is." Gigi's cloud of cotton-candy-purple

hair floated over to me as she wrapped me in a hug. "Hello, Christopher."

Is it just Kit? Or is it short for Christopher?

"Hi, Gigi." I gently hugged my grandmother back. She was the only one who called me by my full name.

"I didn't know you were coming today." Mom was next in line for a hug and kiss, quickly wiping her hands on her apron that was smeared with all colors of jam.

"Neither did I," I muttered under my breath as I approached their work table and stared at the jars of jam strewn over the top. "What are you making today?" I picked one up, the contents a bright red.

"Seaside Strawberry," Mom answered.

Gigi gasped, drawing all of our eyes as she pointed at me with her pink Sharpie. "For you."

"No." I lifted a finger and warned. "Not for me, Gigi. I don't want—" I broke off, tensing when Frankie put her hand on my arm.

Why was it that my body rejected my own family but when Aurora took my hand, it felt like a balm on an open wound rather than a brand on bare skin?

"You don't get a say," my sister quipped, a smile teasing her lips. "That's how it works."

I let out a long exhale, watching Gigi scribble on one of the labels.

A majority of Stonebar Farms jam production was done in bulk in a facility that was just outside of town. Making the jam. Canning it. Labeling it. Start to finish, everything happened there. But here, in Mom's basement, she and Gigi made special batches just like they'd done at the start.

And some of those batches...I shook my head. Some

of those batches, my dear, purple-haired grandmother claimed were *Premonition Preserves*.

In all the years I'd been home—more or less—I'd be spared one of those jars. Sometimes, I thought it was a kind of ridiculous proof that there wasn't anything else left for me. *No fortune to tell for a man who had no future.* But apparently, I was wrong.

"Here you go, young man." She stuck the label to the jar, the angle noticeably skewed, and plopped it in my open hand.

I looked at the label, my eyes tracing the delicate, trembling swirls of my grandmother's handwriting. It was frilly but full of fortitude.

"Well? Spill the beans," Frankie urged.

"It doesn't matter." I lowered my arm, but not fast enough before Frankie grabbed the jar from my hand.

"Of course, it matters. C'mon, it can't be as bad as mine." Frankie was notoriously unimpressed that her fortune label only said *Chandler*. A chandler was a candlemaker, which was what she was. There was no mystery. No excitement. None of the crazy things that Frankie thrived on.

"Okay." I waved at her. "Then read it."

Her brow scrunched. "*Chasing Dawn*."

I swallowed. "Happy?" I plucked it from her fingers. "You got a *Friends* character and I got the title to a *Twilight* movie."

"First off, that's *Breaking Dawn*," my sister corrected. "Second, what could it mean? Chasing light? Because you're the lighthouse keeper?"

"Yeah, that's probably it," I grunted.

"I don't think that's it," Gigi said with a smile I

didn't like, and then started humming a tune while she went back to work.

That was definitely it.

"I'm glad you're here. Lou was just telling us the other day that there's a lovely student doing research at the lighthouse. I didn't know about that." Mom adeptly changed subjects, but there was a reason we all called her *CI-Ailene*. If there was information to be found out, she was going to get to the bottom of it.

"Yeah. She's collecting stuff outside, so we don't really interact." Except for when she touches me and I almost lose my mind and kiss her.

"Oh, that's a shame. Lou said she's so nice."

"We should invite her over for dinner," Frankie said, munching on a piece of cheese.

"That would be—"

"No." I practically growled at them. Aurora wasn't coming here. She wasn't meeting my family. She wasn't...going to sink any deeper into my life if I could help it.

"Why not?" Mom probed, her brow arching.

And there it was. *CI-Ailene*. Looking for what was buried underneath my denial.

"You're right," I conceded with a flash of a smile. "Invite her over. Whatever you want." *I was hardly here for dinner anyway, what did it matter?*

"Oh! We could invite her to our party. Then she can meet everyone," Frankie declared, popping another piece of cheese in her mouth and darting around me for the stairs. "I'll text Lou!"

"Looks like you're going to have to fill in as our label placer," Gigi said, handing me a label stuck to the tip of her finger.

I sighed and picked up a blank jar, rolling the label around it.

"I don't have to invite her over, Kit. I just thought it would be nice. Lou said she's here all alone for a few months—"

"It's fine, Mom, really. Whatever you want to do, it doesn't matter to me. I've got a lot going on anyway." *So, I won't be coming to that dinner.*

"How are your paintings coming, Christopher? I haven't seen any new ones in the window recently. Have you thought about doing something other than the sea?"

Like a sketchbook filled with sea creatures?

"Still keeping it in mind," I said, plucking a cracker from the tray of snacks. "Lou mentioned that the inn might be for sale soon?"

"Oh, we're hoping." Mom clapped her hands together and then passed me another jar to go with the label Gigi wrote out.

"Who's the owner again?"

For the next hour, I let the two of them go around on the topic of the old inn. The man who first owned it. What happened to him. What happened to the inn. The mysterious real estate mogul who owns it now. At some point, Frankie returned and added in the rumors that it was haunted.

I didn't say much, but that was okay. I hadn't come here to talk. I'd come here to escape. I'd go back to the lighthouse later once it was dark to check on the light. In the off-chance that *Chasing Dawn* had anything to do with Aurora, it was better I steer clear of finding her.

"Shit," I swore when the wind caught my truck door and slammed it shut harder than I'd intended, the rain hitting me like a wet sheet.

These storms were common for March, but damn, if I'd been stuck outside in them too many times for my liking. *Her fault.* Because I kept having to avoid my own lighthouse.

I jogged toward the house, the windows glowing with light from inside. *Dammit, she'd left the lights on.* She'd never left the lights on before. If anything—aside from her specimens taking over the kitchen—Aurora was very careful about making sure she didn't disturb anything else. But now that she'd been here for three weeks, she was probably getting too comfortable. Either that, or she'd left in a hurry to try and beat the rain.

I kept my head down as I threw open the door with a low curse and quickly shut it behind me as the wind howled. I shook off the water from my jacket, shoved my hood back, and stopped short.

Aurora hadn't left the lights on by accident; she'd left them on on purpose because she was still here.

And she was looking at my drawings.

While that was the first thing I noticed, it was quickly superseded by everything else about her.

What the...

Her hair was soaked. Her face was bright red. Judging by the puddle of water at her feet...and the trail

I could see through the house...her clothes were soaked. But it was the way her teeth chattered that brought the whole picture together—their vibration making her entire body shake.

"Jesus Christ," I swore and closed the space between us, gripping her shoulders. She blinked up at me, her skin pale and clammy and wet. "What happened, Aurora?"

CHAPTER 6
AURORA

What happened, Aurora?

I trembled at the angry vibration in his words.

What happened was what always happens...I got too caught up in what I was doing that I didn't see the danger—the warning signs. The beating rain. The agitated sea. I felt a chill, but even when the wave hit, I wasn't that cold.

"Tell me what happened," he repeated, and then I felt his hands cup my face.

Strong fingers. Big palms. I let out a soft whimper; they were so warm. I shivered and placed my hands on top of his. I wanted him to hold the whole of me in his palms, then the cold wouldn't get to me because it wouldn't get through him. *Nothing got through Kit Kinkade's shell unless he wanted it to.*

He pressed the back of his hand to my forehead. "Jesus, you're burning up."

I tried to shake my head, but instead my whole

body shook. He was wrong. I wasn't burning up, I was freezing. "No, I'm cold. S-s-so cold."

"Because you have a fever," he growled, and then the world started to tip.

Wait. No. It was just me that tipped—sideways as Kit lifted me in his arms. *God, he was like a furnace.* I pressed my face harder to his chest, wishing the heat of him would seep all the way to my bones and pool warmth and safety into my marrow.

Were all men like this? Hot? Strong? Protective? Or was he a different species of male? Maybe I should've paid more attention—studied them a little more before writing off their entire sex in favor of science.

"We have to get you out of these clothes."

My eyes felt too heavy to open, but my brow creased. Had I heard him right? *Maybe I was hallucinating.*

"What?" My voice was a distant mumble.

"Your clothes are soaking wet and freezing, Aurora. They need to come off. Now."

"I like when you say my name." I sighed and then immediately wondered if I'd actually said the words or only thought them. It was just that he was saying my name so much right now, whereas before it was always *Miss Cross.*

I pushed my eyes open, the width of his chest almost completely blocking my view. I turned my head and saw he'd brought me into the bathroom, the white subway tile swimming in my vision for a second as he leaned around me and turned on the shower.

"Arms up."

I shivered again, and my arms felt like logs as I tried to obey him.

Steam started to spill out around us. He'd shut the bathroom door and closed us in the cramped room, so it wouldn't take long for the steam to heat it. But it wouldn't be enough. Not for the way I shook.

"Kit..." Was that my voice? It sounded thick. Husky. Maybe it was because I was so cold.

"Let me." A second later, my arms lifted as though by marionette strings.

My shirt started to peel up my stomach. Inch by inch, the cold air hit my wet skin and then was immediately chased away by the heat of his hands. I shivered uncontrollably, my breaths punching in and out of my lungs. I'd never been naked in front of a man before. When kissing felt like a flop, it seemed like a waste of effort to continue to something more.

I kept my gaze locked on his face. It seemed like it helped the shaking if I really focused on something steady—and Kit Kinkade was the most immovable thing I'd ever met.

"I like your beard," I blurted out, staring at the pulse of his jaw underneath it.

Only his nostrils flared in response as my shirt reached my chest. He was so focused. So...angry. His eyes dark, their centers stormy as he bunched the fabric in his grip. And then his jaw muscles squeezed harder for an instant as he carefully lifted my shirt over my breasts.

There was a noise. A rumbled sound of pain. I bit into my bottom lip, thinking it came from me—from the cold rush of air against my sensitive skin—but when I looked at Kit, I wasn't so sure...he looked like a man who'd been stabbed. Wounded. *Tortured*. But unable to remove the knife—the source of the pain without risking further harm.

"Sorry, they're big." Why was I apologizing for my boobs? I had no idea what I was thinking—what this fever was doing to me. He just looked so angry, it seemed like I should apologize for something, and I was willing to let my boobs take the fall.

Air hissed from his lips, his eyes snapping to mine as he said, "They're perfect."

Oh my...I inhaled tremulously, trying to hold onto the low words that shook me—warmed me to my very core. And just as quickly as he'd said it, his gaze lowered again and my nipples furled so tight against my bra, their outline pressed through the padded, wet fabric.

Perfect.

Had he really said that?

I focused on his mouth, wishing the words had stained the curve of his lips so I knew for certain he'd spoken them.

"Kit..."

He pulled my shirt the rest of the way over my head, taking whatever I'd been about to say with it as he let it land with a slap on the floor. Another burst of cold made me quake, but instead of lowering my arms around me, my hands reached for his shoulders.

"You're so warm," I murmured when his sharp stare pierced mine. "And I'm so cold."

Even in the steam, the air felt like a thousand nettles prickling my skin.

If he said something, I forgot what it was as the warm hooks of his fingers curled under the waist of my leggings. *Right. Those were wet, too.*

"I didn't see the wave," I murmured, gripping the

steely supports of his shoulders tighter as he lowered in front of me. "I found a *Lepasterias*—"

"Aurora—"

"I'm sorry—a *brood sea star*," I mumbled, letting him lift one leg to remove my leggings. "They have light sensors, so they bury in the sand during the day and come out at night. And I found one. But then the wave..." I trailed off, trembling so badly my balance started to falter. "I-I'm s-sorry."

"Jesus," he cursed, pulling the black fabric. This time, he didn't go slow—or it didn't feel like he did. *Was time distorting, too?* "It'll be better in a second. Just have to get you out of those freezing clothes." His rough voice coursed over me, but for the first time, it didn't sound abrasive; it sounded husky with concern...and something else...but I was too foggy to put my finger on it.

I stared at him, kneeling in front of me. And then it hit me. *Freezing clothes.* I was still wearing clothes.

"I can help," I mumbled and maneuvered my lead-weight arms behind my back, my fingers fumbling for the hook of my bra.

"I've got it." He was focused on my feet, tugging the last of the fabric over my ankle.

I sighed as soon as the band loosened and exclaimed, "Me too." I shimmied my shoulders and smiled in triumph when my bra landed on top of my leggings.

It hardly made a noise when it fell, but the way his head cocked and he stared...it was like I'd dropped my severed head on the floor next to him. *Gross, Aurora.* But I didn't have subtle words to describe the shock on his face.

Slowly, he straightened. First, the curve in his back, then the angle of his neck, until he stared straight in front of him...*at my naked chest.*

This time, the aching tightness of my nipples had nothing to do with the cold. In fact, I couldn't really feel the cold at the moment. It was still there, but distant, trapped behind the hot wall of the man kneeling in front of me, his face only a few cramped inches from my breasts.

Air leaked slowly and unsteadily from my lungs. *Was I not supposed to take my bra off, too?* My mind swam. I just wanted to be warm, and he'd said to take the wet clothes off...but now...I tried to swallow. Now, my naked breasts hung in front of his face. My peaked nipples straining toward him. *Should I be embarrassed? Should I cover myself?* No one had ever been this close to my bare chest before. Ironic that the first time I was almost completely naked in front of a man, that man wanted nothing to do with me.

I shivered. "I-I'm s-sorry."

"Aurora..." He let out a low groan, his hot breath rushing over my skin.

I inhaled sharply. His stare...his exhale...*everything felt so warm.* It felt like heaven.

"Do that again," I begged, and his grip tightened on my waist. "Your breath felt so good...so warm."

Was it insane to ask someone to breathe on you? *Maybe. Probably.* But it was warm and that was all that mattered.

He didn't move. I wasn't sure he even dared to breathe. The only proof of life I had was that persistent tic on the side of his jaw, the muscle firing a rapid beat. And then his mouth parted, the heat of his exhale rushing through his lips and hitting my skin like a burst of heat.

"Yes, like that." I sighed. It felt so good. Goose bumps pebbled across my skin, my nipples pulling even tighter like they strained to get closer to his mouth. *Oh, that would feel good.* That would feel hot—the heat of his mouth on my nipple. Around it. The blanket on his tongue. "Again," I begged.

But I couldn't ask for that. Even fevered, I could still see that line.

Warm air spilled out once more from his lips. "Aurora..." He sounded like he was in pain, too.

"Closer." I pulled on his shoulders, and I heard his groan.

The room started to lose focus as I stared at him, my breath catching and waiting until I saw his head jerk forward in the tiniest of increments until there was hardly any space between his mouth and my skin—*only space enough for breath.*

But that was all I needed.

His shoulders swelled with each ragged inhale, and when he breathed out, I sighed in relief. Over and over, the heat of his exhale hitting my sternum chased the cold from my skin. *And maybe a little bit of the intensity of his stare, too.* If he just turned his head, his lips could touch my skin—my breasts. But where he was, he was trapped between them.

"More," I pleaded breathlessly, his breaths collecting like kindling low in my stomach, stoking a different kind of heat to life.

Slowly, his head turned, the heat of his exhale coasting down the slope of one breast. It felt so good, my knees threatened to shake. I slid my hands to the back of his neck, wordless encouragement to keep going.

And he did.

With that ragged, determined look he always wore, he continued to warm the curve of my breast all the way down to my nipple. When the first rush of his breath hit the sensitive peak, I couldn't stop the whimper that escaped my lips. It wasn't from the warmth or the cold, it was from the bolt of electric pleasure that fissioned out through my body and pooled between my thighs.

"More, Kit." I sounded like a drunken beggar as my fingers curled into the hair at his nape, sliding just a little higher onto his scalp.

I wanted his mouth on me. I wanted to feel his lips and tongue slide over my skin. Yes, I wanted that warmth, but I wanted something more. There was an ache that gnawed at my core, a kind of hunger the feel of his mouth would sate.

"Please."

His deep groan rumbled around the small room. His head drifted closer—so close. If I just bowed my back a little, my nipple would be in his mouth. *Just a little more.*

My hand speared along the back of his head, determined to pull him the last of the way. And I swore I felt the firm press of his lips—the kind of heat that only comes from skin on skin. I sucked in a breath, a moan swelling in my throat, ready to release. My fingers spread wider, bracing for the final impact, when they encountered a distinct ridge on the back of his scalp.

And then the bubble we were in burst.

"*Fuck.*" Kit stood so suddenly, it was a good thing

his hands were still on my waist to steady me or I would've toppled. His arm reached toward the small cabinet on the wall. A flash of white stretched toward the floor. And then I felt the towel being wrapped around me.

"Kit..." I was reeling—my emotions, my body— everything was spinning wildly out of control.

What just happened?

Why had he stopped?

"Stand still," he ordered so calmly, I started to wonder if I'd imagined the entire thing.

With almost painful efficiency, he patted the terry cloth over me. Chest. Arms. Legs. I must've still been wet from my clothes, but I couldn't feel it. Cold made everything feel the same.

"Don't move." He did his best to slip through the bathroom door without letting too much steam escape, but he was a little too big to make it without a rush of cold air hitting me and sending another tsunami of tremors through me.

A cry burst from my lips as I started to shake uncontrollably when he returned. My eyes squeezed shut as he forced the towel from my clutches and tugged my arms through something big and heavy. A sweatshirt. *His sweatshirt.* The fabric went all the way to my knees.

"Just a little more to get to the bed, all right?" he rasped lowly.

Bed. Blankets. *Warmth.*

I didn't know if I nodded or not. I wanted to. I definitely wanted to. But everything was really starting to go haywire.

The door opened and the cold hit like a slap to the face. I hardly registered the dip of the mattress as he guided me to the bed, but I definitely felt the blankets that covered me. *Cold.*

Colder.

"K-K-Kit," I whimpered, my teeth clacking together as I shook uncontrollably.

"Just give it a minute." He tried to tuck them closer. "Just one minute."

"C-can y-you h-h-hold me?" *You're so warm.* I wanted to explain, but I couldn't. My thoughts weren't translating. They felt trapped inside my head, my lips too frozen to speak them.

"Fuck."

Did he say that? Or did I?

"Please." The word whooshed out.

I cried out when the blankets moved, but then as quickly as the cold hit me, it was evaporated by the heat of him. Big, solid, *hot* male climbed into the bed next to me, his body engulfing mine. Like an animal starved for heat, I sprawled over him. My arms over his chest. My breasts pressed to his side. My leg flung over his. I was desperate for every burning inch of this man, and only then, when it felt like I was laid over a bed of hot coals, did my tremors start to subside.

"Kit..."

"Just relax," he urged, his voice sounding like he could do anything but that.

I let another exhale out, the breath sinking me deeper—closer to sleep. But it was the lullaby of his heartbeat that pulled me under—proof that Kit Kinkade wasn't as heartless as my captive sea stars.

CHAPTER 7
AURORA

The wave crashed over me from behind. It capsized my balance and pulled my feet out from under me. I went down, my head smacking on the rocks. And then the water began to pull me, like prey toward its hungry depths.

"Aurora."

The low rumble of his voice filtered through the water, and I whimpered. I loved how he said my name. I was glad I got to hear it one last time—

"*Aurora.*" The arm slung over me shook my shoulder.

I gasped, and my eyes flung open. I wasn't outside. I wasn't caught in the storm. And I wasn't on the verge of drowning. *But it was Kit who'd said my name, that much about my fevered dream was real.*

I tipped my head, a second passing before his expression crystallized through my glasses. So hard. So stern. But there was something else in his gaze as it raked over my face—the heat I'd felt in the bathroom was still trapped in his stare like a secret he refused to let out.

"Was I sleeping?" I murmured, my brain still very foggy even if the gutting chill in my bones was gone.

"Not well," he groused, his lips firm as he reached up and adjusted my glasses so they sat straighter on my nose. "How do you feel?"

Like a light switch, my body registered the hard stretch of him against me. The swell of his one arm under my neck, the other with his hand pinned to my hip. The rise and fall of his solid chest, a heartbeat still buried underneath all his prickly armor.

"Warmer." Definitely warmer.

He grunted, looking unconvinced.

"I need to feel your forehead." His strained voice sounded like he was preparing himself rather than me.

My eyes fluttered, watching his head drift toward mine. He was going to touch me...with his mouth. I shivered, anticipation sending goose bumps bubbling over my skin. It was all I wanted. To feel...to know...and then his lips touched down on my forehead. The slightest, most innocent touch, drove my inhale down to pierce the very depths of my lungs. Yet it was like a spark that set the whole of me on fire.

His lips were soft. In spite of everything else that was hard about him, including the harsh words that regularly left them, *his lips were impossibly soft.* And I wanted to feel them everywhere.

"Kit..." What did I say? How did I ask for that? *How did I convince him?*

He pulled back with a groan, like a little bit of him had fused to me in that touch. "You need to take some

Tylenol." His hand released my hip, and I tensed, clinging even tighter to him.

I'd studied countless organisms to recognize defense mechanisms when I saw them, and Kit's were as obvious as the warning headlight in the lighthouse. But I wanted to know why they were up around me. I wanted to know what possible danger he thought a plump, five-foot-one scientist who got excited over things called *nudibranches* could pose.

"Aurora..." He wanted me to let him go.

"This is how a sea star traps its prey," I blurted out, blinking up at my clammed-up prey. *As if Kit Kinkade would ever be prey.* I giggled at the thought. "It wraps its arms around the mussel, forces it to open up, and then pushes past the hard shell..."

"Aurora..." he said lowly, always using that warning tone with me.

My heart pumped faster. Just like in the bathroom, a warm ache pulsed low in my stomach, making me ache for whatever he had to give.

"Why didn't you kiss me the other day?" I murmured, clinging to the kind of bravery that a fevered brain gave.

There was no danger in kissing me. No danger in exploring whatever it was that pulled us toward each other no matter how he tried to avoid it.

He jerked, his eyes flashing with the memory even as they lowered to my mouth and then rose again. "Because I don't go around kissing strangers."

"I'm not a stranger," I muttered, offended. He called me a stranger while holding me to his side wearing nothing but his sweatshirt and my underwear. *And supposedly I was the one delusional with fever...*

Kit's eyes glittered, his jaw steeled, and his brow set. "You should be."

Should be...but wasn't.

Something strong and aching thrummed between my legs. I shifted my hips ever so slightly closer to him, trying to ease the discomfort, and pressed my core closer to the bulk of his thigh. With just a little more of an angle, I could rub myself—

His hand clamped on my waist, forbidding any more movement as he cursed, low and hoarse. "Dammit, Aurora."

"I wanted you to kiss me," I admitted so quietly that the sound of the rolling sea outside would've been enough to drown the words out if we weren't so close. What if I never felt like this again? What if I never experienced the *ache* to kiss someone ever again? I hadn't before now, so it was entirely possible. *What if this was an irreproducible environment?*

I had to know what happened. This was how I worked. Observation. Experimentation. Determination. *Aurora plus Kit plus fever equaled...*

"I still want you to kiss me."

The sound that escaped his lips made me think I was torturing him with the question, and for a second, I thought I'd miscalculated. That, of course, the man who had enough willpower to not kiss bare breasts that were less than an inch from his mouth could reject the idea of a kiss with much more ease.

But then a noise came from his chest that I'd never heard before. I was familiar with Kit Kinkade's dialect of grunts and groans of annoyance, frustration, and restraint...but this sound was something new. Something that came from somewhere I wasn't sure even he knew existed, the way it made not just his chest but the whole of him quake.

"Aurora..."

"Will you kiss me now?" I breathed, suddenly needing his kiss more than anything in the world. "Just as an experiment, so I know. Please, Kit."

His face could've been chiseled straight from stone for how hard it was. But there was a tremble underneath it. Like the rumble of an earthquake just below the earth's surface about to break free. Or the rise of a growing wave that he tried to keep from crashing.

"Please, kiss me," I whispered, my stare locked on his mouth and my breath captive in my lungs.

I watched his lips peel apart. I felt his hand leave my waist, and my lungs started to deflate in defeat. But then the heat of his palm landed on my shoulder. Weighted and determined. His hold slid to my neck, and he wrapped his big hand around my throat. I sucked in a breath as his thumb wedged under my chin, forcing my head higher.

The glint in his gaze darkened. Sharpened. Turning me from predator to prey. My heart galloped in my chest, beating so fast I swore he'd feel it and it would send him into a new spiral of concern. But he didn't.

Kit tipped my head with just the flat of his finger until my mouth was just below his.

"Do you ever heed the warning signs?" he charged, his voice husky.

Not when it came to him.

My throat bobbed hard against his hand. "No."

And that was how I got myself into trouble.

His mouth crushed mine—covered every inch with his own—and I was instantly swept away, caught up in the strong, warm storm that was Kit Kinkade. Any trace of coldness was obliterated—*incinerated*—by the heat of his lips. *And I was right.* How many times had I looked at his firmed lips—watched that mouth scold or frown—and wondered if there was any gentleness to them? *Now, I knew there was.*

There was so much demanding tenderness, it made the ache between my thighs border on pain.

Now, it was my turn to make sounds that conflated pleasure with pain. A whimper for more. A moan for relief. His hand at my throat held me steady, and his arm under me pulled me close. I was wrapped up in him—captive and captivated in equal measure. I wasn't the sea star. He was. And I was the prey ensnared in his arms, ready to be devoured.

Kit slid his thumb to the base of my chin, applying pressure as his tongue teased along the seam of my lips —*a promise for more.* My mouth opened without hesitation, welcoming the invasion of his tongue and the heat that pooled at my core. This was it. This was the thing I knew I was supposed to feel during a kiss but never had.

My heart tripped and stumbled, my body dissolving into complete chaos with each stroke. *How could this be just a kiss?* How could I feel a kiss all the way down to my toes? How could the swipe of his tongue make my core clench with need?

I gripped the fabric of his shirt, clutching and pulling at it to bring him closer. That seemed like the answer to everything. To being warm. To being safe. To being protected. *To being pleasured.* I let him angle my head and deepen the kiss, his tongue exploring every corner of my mouth with fervent hunger.

"Kit..." I begged, the ache bordering on pain.

He growled in response and pinned my bottom lip between his teeth, pinching just hard enough to make me gasp, and then sucking until I moaned.

This was nothing like any kiss I'd had before—nothing like any kiss that had ever existed, I'd be willing to bet.

No one kissed like Kit Kinkade.

And I wanted his mouth everywhere. On my mouth. My neck. My breasts. Between my legs. There was no chance my underwear would dry anytime soon, they were so slick with my desire. And now, without his hand on my waist, I could move my hips again. I tried to go slow—rocking just enough to give my core the friction it craved and hoping Kit didn't stop me again. But slow was practically impossible when he kissed me the way he did.

It scrambled my mind. My logical, rational, orderly mind became fevered with need.

"Fuck," Kit groaned, and I realized I'd been grinding harder and faster than I thought. For a second, panic injected into my veins, afraid he was going to pull away, but then he pushed his thigh harder against my sex. "You're so fucking wet, sea star, you're soaking through my jeans."

Sea star.

For a split second, I thought he'd called me sweetheart, and my chest squeezed. But realizing he'd actually called me sea star rearranged the very fabric of my heartbeat.

The pleasure building inside me grew like a wave cresting near the shore, one I desperately wanted to crash and drench me with a different kind of fevered fantasy. My mind was a flurry of instinct rather than thought; it made my tongue spar frantically with his. It made my fingers dig for more of his shirt as though I could reach his chest through the fabric. And it made my leg slide higher on his, giving myself a better angle to grind on him.

Higher and higher. *Harder and harder.*

I panted, my insides feeling as fevered as my forehead felt. I needed more. More pressure. More friction. *More pleasure.* So, I searched for it without thinking or knowing or paying attention—until my leg lifted so high that my knee rammed into something that was both impossibly hard and also incredibly sensitive.

Kit's sharp grunt of pain was followed by a swift inhale of reality and a sharp curse of consequence. *"Fuck."*

Crap.

I sucked in deep breaths, feeling the moment starting to unravel like a dropped ball of yarn. Kit pulled back and released my throat, and for some reason, the loss of his hold made it harder for me to breathe. He let out another deep groan of pain as he reached for his cock—*that I'd just kneed.*

Double crap.

"I'm sorry," I blurted out and reached down toward his groin. I had no idea what my hand was going to do when it got there, but I wouldn't get the chance to figure it out because he intercepted it, grabbing my wrist and swiftly yanking my hand away.

"Kit..." I exhaled tremulously.

I'd already begged for the kiss, was it too much to beg him not to stop now? I wasn't sure where to draw the line between sounding desperate and asking for what I wanted.

"You need to take some Tylenol," he ground out. "I need to get your temperature down." He practically threw my hand from his hold and sprung from the bed like it was a sinking ship, striding to the bathroom.

No.

My whimper was swallowed up by the blankets that I immediately pulled up to my chin. The loss of his heat reminded my brain that my body was still struggling. *And now wasn't the time to be worried about life-changing kisses or interrupted orgasms.*

By the time the fresh round of shivers subsided, the mattress dipped again with his weight.

"Kit—"

"I've got you." With one arm, he scooped me up and held me upright—held me to his chest to keep me warm. "Open," he ordered.

My lips parted and he pushed the pill between them, followed by the end of a water bottle, trickling just enough in my mouth so I could swallow. For a man who seemingly hated...well...people...he sure knew how to take care of them. His sisters were much younger, maybe that was the reason.

But why was he doing it for me?

And how could he pull back and toe this line so easily? Meanwhile, I was ready to rip the rest of these clothes from my fevered body and beg him to have his way with me.

"Kit..."

"I'm not going anywhere," he promised and then groused, "God only knows what the hell kind of trouble you'd get into if I left now..."

Kit would keep me warm. *Keep me safe.* No matter how prickly his defense mechanisms were, he was my reluctant white knight.

A smile coasted over my lips, but my eyes were too exhausted to open. I curled deeper into the heat of his body and headed for sleep.

One last thought filtered through the fog. He had towels on hand. A sweatshirt for me to wear. Tylenol in the bathroom. And a bed made to be slept in. Kit Kinkade didn't just work here as the lighthouse keeper; he lived here. *And he'd tried to hide it from me.*

A new dawn. A new day.

I stared at the sun creeping up over the horizon from my morning perch at the top of the tower. Whoever said yesterday's mistakes wouldn't ruin today's possibilities was full of shit. Yesterday's mistakes were lying in my bed. Warm and soft *and half-naked*. And the only possibility for today was trying not to let last night's *catastrophic* mistake do any more damage.

I tightened my hold on the rail for a second and then flung it from my grasp, stalking in front of the headlight and heading for the stairs.

Slowly, I descended from the tower, feeling less and less safe with each step, and went to the kitchen. The coffee machine rumbled to life as I shoved my mug underneath it and pulled out my notebook that I'd rolled and shoved in my back pocket.

Conditions: Rough seas. Moderate rain.

Events:

My pen pinned the blank space on the paper. The

dot of black ink felt like a black hole of all the things that had happened last night. Finding her with my damn sketches. Realizing she was sick. Fevered. Stripping her in my bathroom. *Those tits.* I groaned. The second my eyes shut, I saw them. Full and heavy. Her big nipples tight and red from the cold. Fuck, I wanted to feast on them. I wanted to lick and suck and bite until she was making all those damn sounds of surprise because of me.

And she would've let me. Hell, she wanted me to. The way she'd asked me to heat her—to fucking paint her with my breath. It was simultaneously the most erotic and most painful moment of my life.

But to kiss her.

Giant fucking mistake. To feel her full lips. To taste the sweet heat of her mouth. To hear the sounds of her moans. And god, to feel the way she wanted me. The way she rubbed herself on my leg like she couldn't help herself. It was entirely...Aurora. The woman could never help herself from going after what she wanted— even when that thing put her in danger. *And no, I wasn't talking about the wave that caught her and could've killed her.*

Kissing Aurora was the single-most catastrophic event of my entire goddamn, life which was saying a whole fucking lot considering...everything.

The coffee machine buzzed, and I pushed aside the thoughts. *Which unfortunately did nothing for how hard they'd already made my dick.* The empty section on the paper screamed at me for an answer, so with a low growl, I scribbled in my response and slammed the cover closed.

Events: Aurora.

"Kit?"

My head snapped over my shoulder. Aurora rounded the end of the counter into the kitchen... wearing only my sweatshirt. The sight of her bare legs instantly made me think of how they'd wrapped around mine, clinging to me like my very own vine.

"How are you feeling?" I returned my focus to my mug, filling it to the brim with coffee and wishing I could drown myself in the dark liquid.

"Okay...better I think."

I grunted. "Your fever broke about an hour ago."

The Tylenol had helped drastically within half an hour of her taking it, but she'd still been warm. I'd held her all night like a damn fool. Like a sailor who fell victim to my very own siren. I told myself it was so I could check her forehead every hour or so, but that was bullshit. One minute of that time was justified altruism; the other fifty-nine minutes were nothing but pure selfish desire.

"Thank you," she said, the husk in her voice killing me. Even in gratitude, the woman was pure temptation. "For everything last night."

Everything? My jaw clamped tight.

"Everything last night was entirely avoidable if you'd just been more careful," I snapped harshly and took two large gulps of coffee. "The water gets rough around the rocks—much rougher here than the rest of the shore—"

"I know—"

"I told you not to be out there when the ocean is even just a little unsettled. Do you know how much worse it could've been?" The fact that she'd walked away with wet clothes and a fever was damn near close to a miracle. She could've—I shuddered, unable to even handle the goddamn thought.

"I'm sorry. I just get so focused, but you're right..." She shuddered. "I didn't realize how quickly it could get bad."

I made the mistake of looking at her. Her face was flushed, her expression slightly stricken. For a second, I felt a twinge of guilt for berating her, but then I thought of all the other ways this could've gone—scenarios I'd mulled over during the hours I'd held her overnight. *But she could've died.*

My mug slammed onto the counter, and it was a miracle it didn't crack.

"Tell me what happened." I wanted the non-fevered version of events.

"I found two brood sea stars—" She paused with an unmistakable hitch to her breath. *Fuck, she remembered.* And now, talking about her work would always be a reminder of the endearment I'd given her. The one that tumbled from my lips before I had a chance to think or stop it because in that moment, nothing mattered except the soft woman in my arms—the one I was kissing without fear or panic or pain; *the one who'd let me feel normal again for a few fucking moments.*

"And..." I prompted, letting my anger radiate in my voice.

"They're a hard species to find because they're sensitive to light, so they spend most of their time living underneath the sand. But because it was later in the day, and the storm clouds—"

"So you risked your life for a brood?" I levied, staring at her over the lip of my mug.

"Even broods deserve to be understood," she replied

instantly, her glasses making her eyes appear even larger as they regarded me. *Like she was talking about me again.*

I made a low noise, and she blinked quickly and forged on. "I knew the water was getting choppy around my legs, but it really wasn't too bad, and then all of a sudden, the wave hit my legs and I went down. I don't know if it was the angle or what, but from there, another one kind of crashed over me, and that was what really soaked me."

I let out a slow breath, the course of events not seeming as dire as I'd imagined. *But still...*

"I came inside to get a towel or something to dry off. The bedroom door was unlocked, and when I went inside..." Her eyes went wide with recollection. "Your drawings...you drew my specimens." Her entire expression softened. "Why did you draw my specimens?"

Dammit.

"Trying something different," I offered with a grunt. And it was nothing more than that. *Definitely not for the look on her face now.* Awe. Admiration. *Nor for the swell of pride in my chest because of it.*

"They were beautiful. So detailed," she gushed. "Just incredible, really. I'd love—"

"They're going to my gallery," I said before I added new mistakes to the lingering consequences of yesterday's.

The drawings weren't for her. And I most definitely hadn't labored over them because she'd lamented about her lack of illustration skills when it came to her research paper.

She pushed her glasses higher on her nose, the movement lifting my sweatshirt and revealing another inch or so of thick, creamy thigh. *Goddamn, I wanted to feel those legs wrapped around my neck.*

"Oh." Her smile flickered. "I'd love to see them there. If you wanted to host an event, I could even explain to everyone about each of the species and what's special about them—"

"I don't do events," I said and drained what was left of the coffee in my cup.

"Of course." Her mouth snapped shut. "Can I have some coffee?"

I looked over at the coffeepot. There was plenty left. The only problem was what was in my hand; *I only had one mug.*

There were a *catastrophic* number of reasons why I should've said no. Apologized for not having another mug. And put an end to the conversation. Instead, I looked at her and said, "If you're okay drinking from my mug."

The smile on her face imprinted in my mind as I went to the sink to wash out the last drops from my cup and then refilled it with fresh coffee.

Our fingers brushed as I handed her the mug. Sparks flew from the contact, reminding me why she was dangerous. The things she made me feel—the intensity of them—was like pure voltage through a live wire. No shield. No grounding. Pure, unadulterated electricity that would kill me just as surely as it could bring me back to life.

"Kit, about last night."

Four little fucking words had the power of a bomb.

"A mistake. You were unwell. Fevered." I cleared my throat. *And I was a fool.*

"Right, but I wasn't entirely delusional." She

nudged her glasses higher and blinked twice. "I wanted you to kiss me." As if to prove her point, I swore she sipped from the exact same spot on the mug that I had.

My breath whooshed out. *Fuck, I couldn't talk about this.* Not so soon. Not with her half-dressed. Not with my dick completely hard.

"And I should've said no. It was a mistake." I widened my stance. Anything to try and relieve the pressure on my cock.

"But it was really good, wasn't it?" she asked earnestly. "I don't have a lot of experience for comparison, but I don't think kisses like that are normal, are they?"

"No." The word fled my lips like a damned traitor.

"So don't you think it's something worth experimenting with more?"

*Worth experimenting...*I stared at her. She wasn't being coy or flirtatious; she was being herself. Her open, blunt, heart-on-her-damned-sleeve self. And that was what weakened me. That kind of fucking honest innocence was as bright as a goddamn beacon that beckoned me from the shadows.

"Unless it wasn't that good for you." Like the flip of a switch, pink oozed into her cheeks. "Maybe it was the fever."

I teetered on the edge of the truth, but in the end, a lie would be better. *Her sunshine was no match for my storms.*

"Probably was the fever," I grunted and strode around her to avoid having to see the pain I knew would be written all over her pretty face. "I've got some errands to run. You should go back to your hotel. Rest. Recuperate."

I grabbed my cylindrical carrying case that I'd put my sketches in earlier this morning and then pulled my jacket off the hook. When I glanced back, I saw Aurora hadn't moved.

Dammit.

"Kit, do you live here?"

My breath whooshed out. *Double dammit.* I straightened and answered vaguely, "I stay here sometimes. It's just easier."

"But not since I've been here..." she inferred, moving toward me.

My jaw ticked. How this woman read me like one of her damn textbook specimens was infuriating. I wanted to be left alone. My life left in peace. My secrets left undisturbed. But at every turn, I only found her.

"I'm leaving. Don't go near the water today," I said roughly. There was still a chance of another storm in the forecast.

"Wait, Kit." She rushed toward me, and I went rigid. The more I saw her in my damn sweatshirt, the harder it was going to be to forget the sight. "Lou invited me over to your mom's house for dinner..."

I couldn't bring myself to do anything but stare, waiting for her question.

"Is that...okay?"

"With me?" I grit my teeth. "Not my house or my invitation. I keep a lighthouse...not my family's social calendar."

I SHOVED MY HANDS INTO MY POCKETS, MY ROUND artwork carrier tucked firmly under my arm, and jogged across Maine Street to the rich gold door that stood out from the navy facade: *The Kinkade Gallery*.

If it were up to me, I would've picked a place that stood out a little less—the blue and gold giving off an austere and elegant front that stood out from the rest of the buildings on the street. But Lou had been dead set on this one: perfect location, perfect size, perfect vibe— or so she claimed. So, I caved; I was already letting them down in so many ways, there was no reason to add something like this to the list. Plus, Lou was at the gallery more than I was, it should be her choice. I just supplied the art, nothing more—and definitely not a gallery show.

Another bitter scoff burst from my lungs. *Not a chance in hell.* I didn't do people. Or shows. I made art. Not even because I needed the money, but because I needed the escape.

I pulled out my keys, just fitting them into the lock when the door opened from the inside.

"Lou." I stared at my sister.

"Hey." She beamed. "I didn't know you were stopping by today." She stepped back and let me in. I wasn't even through the doorway before she grabbed for my carrier. "Please tell me this is what I think it is."

"Lou—" I tried to stop her, but there were times when she was as damn determined as Frankie. And she had the cap pried off, my drawings in her hands before I even had a chance.

"You did these?" She glanced at me and then went back to examining the drawings.

"Yeah." I pulled off my hand and speared my fingers through my hair. "I don't know if I want to exhibit them. They were just...an experiment." *Like that goddamn kiss.*

"They are..." Different. Not ideal for showing. Not consistent with my brand. *"Perfect."*

I jerked. I couldn't have heard her right. "What?"

"These are gorgeous and perfect, Kit." She couldn't seem to stop looking between them. "Don't get me wrong, your seascapes are beautiful and so popular, but this...the clean lines. The monochrome, black-and-white outline...it's simple and minimalistic and totally where the market is at right now."

"Is that so?"

She pursed her lips. "I do my research."

Of course, she did. Lou dotted all her i's and crossed her t's. Frankie, on the other hand...Frankie flew by the seat of her pants. Hell, sometimes Frankie flew by the seat of someone else's pants without them even knowing.

"So, you think—"

"Oh, these are going in the front window, for sure." She beamed. "I have to ask though...what are they? Well, this one is obviously a sea star."

I reached for the other drawing and quickly covered up the sea star. Apparently, the name was ruined for me, too.

"Some kind of sea snail." Telling her it was a *bushy-*

backed nudibranch would definitely draw way too many questions I was unwilling to answer.

"It's so...intricate," she said softly, staring for another second before she looked at me, and I tensed. "What made you decide to draw them? They're so different from your usual."

Didn't I fucking know it. But I wasn't about to confess to my little sister that the woman she'd befriended was the reason for the change.

Aurora was different. She'd made the lighthouse different. My routine different. My art different. God help me, if I wasn't careful, that damn woman would make everything so different that my life would never be the same.

"Got stuck with painting, so I decided to try something else," I said and turned away, my eyes glazing over the other paintings that hung on the light gray walls.

Storm after storm after storm. I didn't know the last time I'd looked around the gallery when I was here. Usually I was in and out. But damn, there wasn't a calm sea in sight. In fact, the only calm painting I could recall doing was the Christmas one that Lou said had been bid to an insane price.

"Well, I think they're going to be great." She beamed for a second. "Hopefully, they will be. For the both of us."

I angled my head toward her. "News on the inn?"

She bit her lip, always trying to moderate her excitement—her emotions in general. I think it came from living a life next to a twin who didn't moderate anything; Lou felt like she was Frankie's compensation.

"Yeah."

"Good or bad?" I folded my arms.

"Both?" She grimaced. "The owner was never planning on selling, but he passed away. The lawyer who was up here was sent by the estate to assess the property for the estranged son who's going to be the new owner once everything is all settled."

"So that's good news then?"

"Well, the old man died." She sighed. "It doesn't feel right to call that good news."

I let out a little chuckle. "Fair."

"Rumor has it that the son will want to sell as soon as the transfer of everything happens, which should be in two to four weeks. I guess he wasn't on good terms with his father."

"That's a pretty specific rumor..."

Lou blushed and then caved; she was terrible at keeping a secret. "You probably don't know her, but Frankie and I went to school with this girl, Adele Layton, for a year in high school before her family moved to Portland. Anyway, it turns out she's a big-deal lawyer in Boston and her firm represents the son. Since she's familiar with the town, he sent her up here to take a look at the property and give him an update."

"Interesting."

She bit her thumbnail. "It could be on the market in a month, Kit. A month. I don't know if I have enough savings—"

"We'll figure it out," I said and reached for her, wrapping my arm around her shoulders and pulling her close. "Whatever we have to do to get that inn, we'll do it."

I felt the weight roll off her shoulders as she sighed. "Thanks."

I grunted and pressed a kiss to the top of her head. "I should get going—"

"Are you coming to dinner on Friday?"

I tensed and quickly slid my arm back to my side so my discomfort wasn't too obvious. "Dinner?" I pretended like I hadn't already heard about this dinner once today.

"I invited Aurora over to Mom's for dinner to welcome her to town. I don't think she has many friends here, aside from me. And you."

I choked and quickly tried to disguise it as a cough. *We weren't friends. Not even close.* A friend wouldn't have a perpetual hard-on for her. A friend wouldn't fantasize about her perfect tits bouncing as I fucked her beautiful brains out.

I didn't have friends.

And I definitely didn't have...experiments. Or whatever the hell Aurora wanted to call it.

"Frankie said it was your idea," Lou added when I didn't respond.

I grunted. "One day, Frankie's...embellishments are going to bite her in the ass."

"Oh." Her face fell. "So, you're not coming?"

I inhaled deep, feeling my chest tighten as though a belt was lassoed around it. Everyone else at least masked their disappointment well, but Lou...Lou couldn't lie to save her life.

Before I could think better of it, I heard myself say, "No, I'll be there."

That would give me three days to figure out how to be around Aurora without wanting to kiss her and hold her and fuck her until all her sunshine bled life into my shadows. *If only that were actually possible...*

"Great." A smile exploded over her face. "See you Friday."

"Yeah," I croaked and backed toward the door. *If wanting Aurora didn't kill me first.*

"Hey, Kit."

My hand froze on the doorknob, and I looked back at my sister.

"I really love these." Lou ran her fingers along the paper once more. "Whatever caused the inspiration to strike...I hope it sticks around."

I attempted a smile—a feat considering my teeth were gritted underneath—and left without another word.

It was a who, not a what. And she definitely needed to go.

CHAPTER 9
AURORA

There was so much of them.

Not many—because there were only seven Kinkades at the table—but *much*. So much character and laughter and *family*. At home, it was just Dad and me...and our specimens. And I loved that. I loved our conversations about biology. About organisms and creatures and food chains and environments and global warming. I loved when dinner ended in experiments or fact-finding missions because that was us.

But this...this was something like I'd never experienced before.

I sat flanked by Frankie and Arlene. Opposite me was Lou, and on either side of her were Kit and Violet, who was Kit's older brother Jamie's wife. At the ends of the table were Jamie and their grandmother, Gigi. Truthfully, I struggled to remember if she'd given me her real name. I'd walked into a deluge of introductions, but I was pretty sure I was only given the name Gigi.

And to be fair, with her bright purple hair, I wasn't sure any other name was quite as fitting.

"I hope you're hungry, Aurora," Ailene said as she entered the dining room carrying a massive cast-iron pot. "I made goulash."

"Oh." My eyes went wide when she set the pot on the towel in the center of the table.

Their home was beautiful. A renovated farmhouse with rows of windows and clean decor. A fireplace crackled in the living room to keep out the chill, and the amazing aroma of the house—which I'd quickly learned was from candles that were handmade by Frankie— made it difficult to not feel at home here.

"Beef. Tomatoes. Pasta. Cheese." Ailene rattled off the ingredients, but the smell alone had me salivating.

"It smells amazing—"

"It's Kit's favorite," Frankie chimed in with a grin. Her smile might be the same as Lou's, but her eyes had a distinctly mischievous glint that I wasn't sure Lou was even capable of.

Kit's head snapped in his sister's direction, and I was pretty sure I heard one of his characteristic growls start to rumble through the room, but his older brother spoke up before I could be sure.

"So, Aurora, how's your research going?" Jamie asked as Ailene took everyone's plates one by one to serve them.

"Oh yes, tell us, dear. We've been so curious about what's been going on there," Gigi encouraged with a wide smile on her face, but there was something about the twinkle in her eye that made me think this woman with her bright hair was where Frankie got her cheek from.

"It's going really well," I began, handing Ailene my plate to fill. "I'm studying the marine species in the Gulf of Maine and what, if any, effects the local environment has on their populations. So, daily, I start with several water samples. I have a small kit that tests for different compounds as well as bacteria levels in the water to determine its quality. I also record the weather and some other characteristics about the water, but then I'll spend most of the day kind of roaming the rocks and tide pools, searching for different species, and then noting and studying whichever ones I find."

"Interesting," Lou said.

"What kind of species?" Frankie asked.

"Mollusks—so mussels and clams. Sea stars." Kit's eyes whipped to mine when my voice cracked. I cleared my throat and went on. "Sea snails. Whelks. I've been collecting specimens of anything and everything; Kit will tell you." I hazarded a laugh. "The kitchen counter at the lighthouse is covered with jars of creatures."

"Jars of them?" Lou turned in her seat, her interest flicking between her brother and me.

"Lou—"

"So that's where you've been doing all your new drawings from," she finished without heeding Kit's attempt to stop her. Clearly, he'd left out some details when he'd given her the drawings, and she was now putting the pieces together.

"Drawings? What drawings?" Frankie demanded, forgetting all about the bite of food on her fork in favor of finding out the answers.

"Nothing—"

"Not nothing," his sister insisted and then proceeded to gush. "Kit did these ink drawings of sea creatures from some of Aurora's specimens, and they're so incredible. Simple but detailed. Understated but elegant. I can't wait until they're up. People are going to go crazy for them."

"That's wonderful, Kit," Ailene praised, finally filling her own plate and taking a seat.

"They really are amazing," I chimed in softly. The memory of his drawings still hooked fast in my brain. The care he'd taken with them as though they were portraits.

"You've seen them?" Frankie asked.

My lips parted for a second. Was I not supposed to? No, probably not. They'd been behind the closed door of the bedroom.

"A few," I mumbled, my heart picking up its pace. The last thing I wanted was his family to think it was a big deal—or for Kit to think I mentioned it on purpose.

"I want to see."

"Here, I took photos because I'm deciding how to display them." Lou took out her phone, opened to a photo, and handed it to her twin.

"Christ," Kit grumbled, shaking his head and stabbing the food on his plate with a fork, clearly resigned to the conversation turning onto him.

"Oh my god, Kit." Frankie gaped. "These are so cool."

And then her phone made its way around the table.

I didn't need to look. The artwork Kit had done of my specimens was fresh in my mind. Maybe it was because of the fever, but the more and more I thought about them, the more I was convinced it was because of him. Because I'd been so shocked that the coarse and callous man who continued to push me away had taken the time and care to capture something that was so important to me.

And now, I sat back and watched his whole family react to those images. Their wide eyes, gasps, and praise. The way they admired him and his talent was as bright as the beacon in the lighthouse. And Kit...the expression on his face was one of pure pain as though every compliment or look of pride was another twist of a knife.

I didn't understand why, but that wasn't the problem. The problem was that I wanted to.

"I think the starfish is my favorite," Frankie said while Jamie and his wife looked at the photos.

I pulled my lips between my teeth, determined not to say a word because it really wasn't a big deal—

"They aren't fish." A low voice that was distinctly not my own sounded from across the table.

My eyes snapped to Kit, and air barreled to the base of my lungs.

"What?" Frankie blinked.

My throat tightened. *Oh no.*

"Sea stars aren't technically fish," Kit explained with a low, tense voice, realizing he couldn't take back what he'd said now. "They don't have gills or fins, so scientifically they're not fish, so they're called sea stars, not starfish."

It was irrational—illogical—no, it was most likely insane to be so affected by a simple fact. Except it wasn't just a fact coming from Kit. It was proof that he'd not only listened to me blabbering on about something I cared about, but he cared enough to remember; *he cared enough to now make it a point.*

"But you call them whatever you want," he

muttered under his breath and dug back into his food as though he hoped everyone would just forget he'd said anything.

But they didn't. Six sets of eyes moved in slow motion to me, staring as though I'd done something more to Kit than simply feed him facts.

"He's right," I said weakly. "Sea stars is the preferred name."

There was a second or two of complete silence, and I had a sneaking suspicion that it was a very rare occurrence in this family.

"And what about the other one with all the..." Frankie trailed off, using her fingers to mimic all the extensions of the nudibranch.

"That's a sea snail," Lou answered.

I nodded. "A bushy-backed nudibranch."

A ripple of laughter went around the table, the tension of the last few minutes broken as I explained the name, what it meant, and why the little snail was so interesting.

"I wish I could have this info by the drawings somehow," Lou mused out loud. "I think people would be so fascinated to learn a little about the subject of the drawing."

"You could do a little card or something," Frankie suggested. "Like underneath the frame."

"I could make some plaques to hold them if you want, Lou," Jamie chimed in, offering up his woodworking skills I'd learned about earlier when I'd complimented Ailene's dining table. She was quick to gush about the skills of her oldest son who had his own custom furniture business.

While his siblings went back and forth about his

drawings, Kit sat there in silence like a lighthouse watching the day go by.

I sank my teeth into my bottom lip, knowing I shouldn't say anything—knowing I'd hear about it another day when we were alone—but I couldn't stop myself. No one deserved to just sit and watch as life passed them by.

"I suggested a show at the gallery," I chimed in. "Then buyers could learn about the subjects...and the artist..."

Kit's furious gaze captured mine, staring like I'd just pulled a pin from a grenade.

Lou's eyes went wide like saucers, and then a smile slowly spread over her face. "That is...*perfect.*"

"No." Kit's fork clanged onto his plate. "Not doing a show."

"But we could sell tickets. Meet the artist. A behind-the-scenes look at the process and the subjects from the source."

My eyes bugged wide. That wasn't what I'd meant. I didn't want to put Kit on the spot, I just thought he would want that exposure for his work.

"No."

"You can't hide in the lighthouse forever," Frankie charged, her quick inhale of regret following a second later.

Everyone looked at Kit, his eyes glittering with the sharp shards of anger and pain. "Enough, Frankie," he warned with a voice I hadn't heard before—a tone so raw it sounded as though his vocal chords had physically bled over the words.

"We don't have to do a 'meet the artist' or any kind of presentation," Lou said, softly backtracking on the idea while trying to tamp down the tension. "I was only excited about the suggestion because I think a gallery show with the new drawings would put me so much closer to what I need for the inn."

The fight went out of Kit in a hot whoosh, hearing the despair in his sister's voice. I had no idea what inn Lou was talking about, but Kit's reaction told me all I needed to know about its importance to her—*and the lengths he'd go to help her*.

The muscle in his jaw bulged, one last protest before he replied, "Fine, but I'm not giving any presentations about the damn drawings."

Lou bounced with excitement in her seat. "Okay—"

"You could just have Aurora there to do it," Frankie added, her nonchalant tone carrying just a hint of something more. "Then Kit wouldn't have to say anything," she went on, looking at me. "You could just explain all the cool facts about the stars and snails to everyone."

"Not necessary—"

"It would be better anyway since she knows the most about them." Frankie barreled right over his protest, her eager stare making it practically impossible to deny her.

"Yes, that would be perfect," Lou agreed and reached for my hand. "If you can spare the time, I mean. It would be so hopeful, and I just know everyone would love it. Plus, just think, then you'd get to educate people in town about the animals that live along the shores; it's really an opportunity for you, too."

I stared at her, my mouth moving open and shut. "I...sure," I said with a weak smile, adjusting my glasses to block Kit's stare from burning a hole through my forehead.

"Wonderful." Gigi clapped her hands. "We'll make some special jams, won't we, Ailene?"

"Of course."

"Sea Star Strawberry," she envisioned, drawing a chuckle from the whole table except for Kit, the thread of his groan vibrating underneath the lighter rumble.

"Let me know what you pick, and I'll whip up some complimentary candles," Frankie added.

The way they all jumped in to help made my chest tighten. Don't get me wrong. I loved my dad. We were like two peas in a pod, having the same interests. The same preferences. And similar personalities. But it was always just us and sitting at this table with these people...it made me long for a family like theirs. So full of life and varied personalities—an entire ecosystem in itself.

The rest of dinner passed in a flurry of conversation about the gallery show which lead to insight on the local inn that Lou wanted to purchase and that spiraled to the furniture Jamie would make for the inn, the assistance Violet would give on growth and management since she came from a hotel-owning family though I gathered she didn't speak to them anymore, the custom candles Frankie would make to fill the lobby, and finally, circled back to Kit...and the paintings of his Lou wanted to hang on the walls.

"I hope he sells," Lou said when Kit and Jamie stood to clear everyone's plates. Gigi followed them into the kitchen to get dessert. "Whoever he is, I hope he sells to me."

"He will," Frankie said calmly, tipping back in her chair.

"You can't be certain."

"Sure, I can," her twin argued. "If he doesn't sell to you, he's a fool, and I will do whatever it takes to make him see the error of his thinking."

"And how will you do that?" Lou asked calmly, clearly used to challenging her sister's wild plans.

"Well, my first thought is that we could start squatting there, but I'd have to look up squatter's rights in Maine—"

"Francesca Marie, no one is squatting at the inn," Ailene chided.

I pressed my fingers to my mouth to try and conceal my laugh. I loved Frankie's determination. It reminded me of my own except hers had a reckless edge. I was sure Kit would argue that mine did too, but at least mine was unintentional.

"Fine." She huffed. "Well there's always bribery."

"And what do you have to bribe him with?"

Frankie paused as Kit and Jamie returned holding trays of jam-filled pastries, Gigi directing them to put one at each end of the table.

"Now, I made some puff pastry tarts. The tray on my end is cherry jam and the tray on Jamie's side is blueberry."

"Of course, it is."

Lou leaned closer to me. "Blueberry is Jamie's favorite."

For a few minutes, the discussion ebbed in favor of eating. I took one of each tart to try, and even though they were both delicious, I went back for a third one of the cherry.

"The cherry is my favorite, too," Gigi said with a wink.

"Maybe we could bribe the new owner with jam

and candles," Frankie said, shoving the last bite of a blueberry tart in her mouth.

"That's not much of a bribe."

"Fine, then we'll hold him hostage."

"My word." Ailene shook her head.

After several more equally egregious suggestions, all I could focus on was the soft tap of Kit's finger on the table as though he were counting down the minutes until he could leave. Until he could distance himself from me.

The thought shouldn't hurt as much as it did, and I only had myself to blame. I was the one who begged for the kiss. Begged for his touch. Begged for everything. I thought not knowing would be the worst fate, but as it turns out, having to forget the experience was far more painful.

"I should get going," I said somewhere in the middle of the conversation, but I couldn't focus. All I could feel was Kit's irritation with me—with my presence in his family's home.

"Oh, you can't leave just yet. I have to give you some jam." Gigi rose in a flurry of blue.

"Jam?" I looked at Lou who stood and ushered me up.

"Come with me." She hooked her arm through mine.

I looked over my shoulder, catching Kit's dark stare once more before I was led downstairs into the basement.

"Every few weeks, Mom and Gigi make a limited-edition batch of jam and we hand-label the jars," Lou said. "From those, Gigi will sometimes make a... special...label for people."

"Her Premonition Preserves," Violet said from behind me, the smile on her face indicating she'd been given one of these jars at some point.

"Premonition?"

"Think of it like a fruity fortune cookie," Frankie added.

"Come over here, Aurora." Gigi took my hands and led me to the worktable in the middle of the basement, the surface covered with fabric and ribbon and stacks of blank labels. Next to the table were shelves of small bottles of jam, the color a rich red.

She handed me a square of check fabric and a string of ribbon before grabbing one of the jars from the shelves. She placed it in my hands and then cupped hers over mine. Her expression softened as she closed her eyes, took a deep inhale, and held it for a second or two before her eyes flung open.

Leaving the jar in my hands, she grabbed a label and a Sharpie and began writing.

I looked to the other women in the basement—Lou, Frankie, and Violet—who all appeared far too interested in the result for this to be some kind of trick.

"There." Gigi beamed and handed the jar to me.

I blinked and read aloud, "Broken Brood." My brow furrowed. "I don't understand."

Gigi patted my arm, her smile making her eyes almost completely disappear. "You will."

When I turned to the other women for an explanation, they all shared a look among themselves like they already understood.

Broken Brood.

As we filed back upstairs, I took Lou's arm. "I don't understand," I said quietly. "Is this about the brood sea star? Is it predicting problems with the *Lepaste-rias* species? Or does brood mean family, like my family is broken?"

Lou hesitated, her eyes flicking around to make sure no one was listening as she said softly, "I can't say for certain—no one really can with Gigi's labels, but I wonder if in this case, brood means...someone who is...a brood."

My eyes went wide at the instant Frankie demand-ed, "Where's Kit?"

"He left. Said he had to check on things at the light-house for the night," Ailene said, her half smile weighted with sadness.

Everyone went about clearing and cleaning the table, but it was impossible not to notice the tightness in Jamie's expression, the shadow over Frankie's face, nor the subtle drop of Lou's shoulders when she realized her brother had left without saying goodbye.

"I'm sorry. It's my fault," I said quietly.

"No, it's not." Lou took my hands and squeezed.

I offered a brave smile but she could tell I didn't believe her.

"I promise it's not. It's...come with me," she urged and then guided me into the living room over to the bookcase. When we got close, my attention immedi-ately went to the shelf with all the photos.

Jamie. The twins. The whole family when Gigi had pink hair. And then...I squinted, looking closer.

"He hasn't been the same since he got back," Lou said softly as I stared at the picture of a Kit I just barely recognized without his beard, garbed in camo, and standing in the middle of the desert.

He was in the military.

"Something happened over there...it's not my place to share; I honestly don't even know enough of the details to say much, but he was injured pretty badly. They flew him back to the states as soon as he was stable but he was in the hospital for months."

"An injury to his head."

Her head tipped with surprise. "Yeah. How did you know?"

I brought my finger to my lips, recalling that moment in the bathroom when I'd tried to pull him closer, my hands buried in his hair...I sucked in a small breath. *A scar.* That was what I'd felt on his scalp...and as soon as I'd touched it, that was when he pulled away. I'd almost completely forgotten about it until she mentioned an injury, and it triggered the memory of the raised flesh under my fingertips.

"I just..." I swallowed. "Guessed."

She picked up the framed picture of the family and handed it to me. "This was before. When he smiled."

Even in a grainy photo, I could tell his smile was devastating. In fact, I was pretty sure that anything those lips chose to do, from smile to scold, kiss to curse, was devastating.

"So, it's not your fault. He just has a hard time being around people...letting them in. We've tried..." Lou bit her thumbnail. "Well, we're just glad to see a little change in him. Aside from one Christmas painting and the drawings of your specimens, I've never seen his artwork involve anything but storms. And I don't know the last time he came for dinner...it had to be around Christmas. He usually makes some excuse or another, but he came tonight." She flashed a small smile. "I think you know how important it is to notice small changes...to try and figure out what's causing them."

Her earnest look gave no room for misinterpretation. She thought I was responsible for the change in Kit. The ball in my throat inflated until it was impossible to swallow. I didn't know what to say. I wasn't about to confess to the kiss we'd shared or the way he'd pushed me away.

"Well, anyway." She replaced the frame on the shelf and we walked back to the dining room. "I'm glad you could come for dinner. You'll come to our birthday party, right?"

"Oh, yes!" Frankie clapped. "You'll get to meet our cousins, then, too."

Of course, I agreed. I wanted to be friends with this family, but I wouldn't do it at Kit's expense. After they hugged me and said goodbye, I got into my taxi and gave the driver my hotel information. As he pulled down the driveway, I stared at the jar in my hands.

Broken Brood.

"Wait, I'm sorry," I said as soon as we reached the end of the drive. "Can you take me to the Friendship Lighthouse instead?"

Retreating wasn't who I was. If I wanted to learn more about something, I observed. I made notes. I charted changes. And I asked questions.

There was no harm in asking, was what Dad always said. I wasn't sure Dad had ever met a man like Kit before, but the premise had to hold—and I had to ask.

I had to know how he could kiss me one minute and turn away the next. How he could tell me that our kiss wasn't normal but then not want to experiment. *How he could want to keep his distance and then turn around and champion my sea stars.*

The cabbie nodded, and my heart set off in a gallop.

I was going to get answers tonight whether I liked them or not.

"You sure this is what you want, miss?" the driver asked when he stopped behind Kit's truck.

Thank goodness, he was here.

"Yes, thank you," I said, tapped my phone to the payment terminal, and then hurried out of the car.

Aside from the headlight, only the faintest rim of light peeked out from the windows of the house, all the shades drawn tight.

I bundled my arms to my chest, practically jogging to the door. I rapped firmly on the wood over and over again without letting up. I knew he was in there, and I wasn't leaving without talking to him—without understanding what was going on.

Suddenly, the door yanked wide open, Kit's broad body filling the frame like some kind of godly giant.

"What are you doing here?" His glare was hot as fire, my neck burning as he watched me struggle to swallow.

I handed him the jar of jam like it was an answer.

"Even a brood deserves to be understood."

CHAPTER 10

KIT

There was no escaping her—and I wished that was a bad thing.

I'd slipped out of Mom's early specifically for this reason—to avoid having to walk away from her again. Day after day. Time after time. It grew increasingly hard to continue to walk away from Aurora Cross like she was nothing—like there was nothing between us. It was like the sun trying to walk away from the horizon. I only got so far before she was in front of me again.

Like right now.

My eyes raked over her as I gripped the side of the doorframe. "Aurora…"

She'd left her hair down for dinner tonight, a full storm of midnight rings haloed her head and danced against her cheeks, and she had worn these bright mustard yellow pants and an emerald-green blouse. So damn colorful, yet it didn't even come close to the vibrancy of her smile—and she'd smiled a lot with my family. Too much. She smiled like she belonged—like she *thrived* in their chaos.

"Take it," she urged.

In this light, shadows teased the edge of her shirt, taunting me with the creamy swells of her tits and the valley between them. And for a second, I envied my exhales. *What kind of fucked-up reality was it where I was jealous of my own breath?* The very air that entered into my lungs and kept me alive—I resented it because it got to caress the bare silk of her skin when I shouldn't. *Couldn't.*

That much was even clearer after tonight. The way my entire family looked at me and her, every interaction from her mention of my drawings and the damn gallery show to the way I hadn't stopped myself from correcting Lou about the fucking sea stars...I wished they'd looked at me like I had two heads, but no. There were flickers of recognition instead—of the man I used to be. *A man who was gone.*

"I want to understand." Aurora pushed the jam jar into my chest and I took it from her, reading the label.

Broken Brood.

"Dammit—" I shook my head. "Don't listen to this." *Sorry, Gigi.* "I don't need to be understood. I need to be left alone."

"I also wanted to apologize," she begged, her body rocking with a shiver.

Shit.

"Come inside," I ordered, cursing the cold night for making a fool out of my defenses.

"I wanted to apologize for bringing up the gallery show," she insisted as I closed the door behind her, the room rising in temperature. She tucked the wild curls of her hair behind her ears. "I didn't mean to put you on the spot. Lou was just so excited, and I thought..."

"Well, you thought wrong."

She winced, but then steeled herself and kept going. Christ, this woman was perpetually—genetically—undeterred.

"Why don't you want to promote your work? It's so good."

"Because I don't." My hand balled at my side.

"Is it because of what happened while you were in the army?"

Goddamn, this woman was bold. I stared at her, wondering if there was ever a time in the last eleven years since I'd been back, that anyone had dared to ask about what happened to me. Even Mom—hell, even Jamie—kept their distance, hoping I'd open up to them when I was ready.

But not Aurora.

She asked because...*of course she fucking asked*. That was what she did. She poked and prodded, watched and waited. She learned by unobstructed observation.

"I'm not one of your damn research specimens, Miss Cross," I snapped. "That's none of your business."

"Well, of course, you're not one of my specimens. You're not in a jar...and you growl."

I made the noise as if to prove her point. "Do you ever not ask questions?"

"How else am I supposed to learn?"

"Maybe there are some things that aren't meant for you to learn—things people don't want to talk about."

"Do you not want to talk about it?" *Another question.* "Because that's not what you said."

I opened my mouth like I was going to shout "*of course, I don't want to talk about it*" but nothing came out. No anger. No defense. No weapons or walls. I'd lived for a decade on the edge of the world, the lighthouse warning people away from my shores, but somehow, she carefully drifted close; she'd touched down and anchored safely along all my rocky edges, climbed into the remote corner of my life, and God help me, she never should've come here, but now that she was, I couldn't make her go.

"Where did the scar on your head come from?"

My spine steeled, and my lips narrowed into a firm line. I strode into the kitchen, grabbed a water bottle, and took several gulps, hoping the prolonged silence would prompt her to say something else.

It didn't.

She watched and waited, and meanwhile, I was convinced that she was made of more patience and perseverance than any person I'd ever met.

She wanted to know the truth? *Fine.* I'd give her the truth. Or part of it. Maybe that would stop this...experiment in its tracks. God knew pity had worked in the past to keep people away.

"I was put in charge of a special forces team assigned to covert operations in Pakistan after the Iraq War. We dealt with lingering insurgents, their leaders, and remaining camps as part of the War on Terror." I rounded the counter and set the bottle on the edge. "I was sent with a new team. Just the way things worked out. Some veteran special forces, but some not. The kinds of things we were tasked to do...they were the kind of situations where if we got caught, we'd be disavowed."

"Oh." Her lips formed a perfect circle, and my dick jerked. I shouldn't have stepped out of the kitchen. I should've left the counter between us, but like a fool, I hadn't.

"Shit ton of danger. Helluva lot more risk. Not everyone can handle it, and...I should've seen the signs." I dragged my hand over my scalp, feeling for the scar like it could tether me to the memory. "We'd just landed in country and had set up camp. The one guy on my team—Smith, he was new, and from the second we got off the plane, he struggled." I dropped my arm to my side. "I should've seen it. His agitation. Lack of sleep. Irritation. Inability to focus. But I chalked it up to it being his first time on a mission like this.

"We were in country three days in order to set up our base, gather and assess our intel, and decide strategy on infiltrating the insurgent camp. The morning of the op, Smith lost it," I rasped. I could still hear his voice bounce around inside my head. "Yelling. Pacing." I pinched the bridge of my nose, my eyes squeezing shut. "He went outside the tent, and I wanted to give him a minute—give him space to cool his jets. I turned for one second to grab my sat phone, and shots were fired."

She didn't try to hide her audible gasp.

"He'd come back in the tent and started firing his weapon," I said tightly, my head starting to shake as though protesting the walk down memory lane. "He wasn't aiming at any of us, he was just firing. Every-where. Crying. Shouting. Bullets flying—" I broke off with a sharp inhale when a small hand covered my fist that rested on the counter.

My eyes flung open. I'd forgotten I'd even closed them, the memory was so vivid in my mind. The smoke. The acrid smell of gunpowder. The shouts. *The pain*. My hand was clenched so hard my knuckles were white. But Aurora's touch...my fingers cracked open just a little. *Just like the rest of me.* What was it that made her touch feel like that? Like pure light rushing through me and breaking up my shadows?

"One bullet hit the back of my head, and...that's the last thing I remember," I told her. "Next time I was conscious, I was in a hospital bed at Walter Reed."

"Kit." Her breath whooshed out, and she inched closer to me.

Fuck. She was already too close. The heat of her. The comforting warmth that beckoned. The band around my chest began to tighten, and the scar along the back of my skull started to tingle. I didn't talk about this. *About then.*

"Was in the hospital for seven months before I was discharged."

"And then you came back here...to the lighthouse."

Every nerve in my body exploded with warning. "More or less," I croaked, and then cleared my throat. "They don't allow civilian lighthouse keepers anymore, so I reached out to a buddy of mine in the Coast Guard and asked for the position."

"And you've lived here...alone...since then?"

I wanted to be angry. I wanted to look at her, see pity steeped in her expression, and use that as a weapon to push her away. But with Aurora, there was never any pity, only understanding. She didn't just look around and see the world for what it was, she allowed the world to show her its secrets. *And I'd just shown her some of mine.*

Not the worst of them, though, but who the hell knew what would happen if I let her stay any longer.

"What are you doing here, Aurora?" I growled. "You should go home."

Color seeped into her cheeks like the finest pink gauze.

"Well, I did come to apologize," she said, her eyes dropping to where her hand still rested on mine, neither of us making a move to break the contact. "And then I wanted to ask if it's okay with you that I go to Lou and Frankie's birthday party because I won't be the reason you don't go. I can see how much they love you—how much they love when you're around. I won't get in the way—"

"Whether or not I go to their party has nothing to do with you," I interrupted her firmly, pinning her stare so there was no question. "Promise."

Her throat bobbed and my fingers twitched, recalling what that felt like when I'd caged my hand around her neck. Hot electricity spilled down my spine.

"Is that it then?" I demanded.

Her jaw slackened. The soft pink tip of her tongue slid out and swiped along her lips. Now I was painfully hard. Being this close to her...the heat of her breaths clashing with mine, the rapid flutter of her pulse as glaring as a neon sign...days of fantasizing about that night—about her—was quickly eating me up inside.

"No." She dropped the word like an anchor in our storm. "I also wanted to kiss you again."

Fuck.

My body turned to stone, every cell screaming yes—screaming for relief—but my mind refused to let go of its stronghold. "No."

"I want to know if it was a fluke—a fevered anomaly

that it felt like it did," she explained, her words coming out in a rush like she expected me to toss her out if she didn't talk quickly. "Don't you want to know, too?"

"No," I ground out, the pulse in my jaw tapping out L-I-A-R in Morse code.

Her eyelids fluttered, and her shoulders fell. "It's just all the other times I've been kissed, it's never been like that, and I just need one more experiment to know what to expect in the future."

"What?"

"I need to know what I should be prepared for—or looking for really." She rolled her bottom lip through her teeth, reddening the flesh like she was preparing it for me, and then let out an audible sigh. "What I mean is that when I kiss other men in the future, I need to know if what I felt the other night is possible again or if it was all in my imagination. It's important to have real-istic sexual expectations for potential boyfriends, so I'd just like to experiment with one more kiss if possible—"

Not a fucking chance.

I saw red, and then I saw her. Her face cupped in my hands. Her eyes wide and honest and filled with surprise. She'd rambled on like she always did—fucking oblivious to the warning signs: the flare of my nostrils, the steam emitting with my exhale, the growl clawing out of my chest.

She'd gone on about future boyfriends unbelievably unaware that the thought of another man touching her —kissing her—cut through the seams of my sanity like a hot knife through butter.

I was a protector. Always. In the army. For my family. And now. I warned of danger, of storms and destruction. But somehow, when it came to Aurora, I'd become her biggest danger, and I was doing a shit job of keeping her away from me.

I angled her head and dipped mine low, making sure I still had her eyes before I spoke. "No one will ever kiss you like this, sea star. I promise." *Not if I had anything to say about it.*

And then I forgot all the reasons I had for not kissing her and covered her lush, parted lips with mine.

CHAPTER 11
AURORA

I was a rational person. Methodical. Observant. Okay, maybe not when it came to weather and waves, but I rarely did anything without being relatively certain of the outcome. But when I begged for another kiss from Kit Kinkade under the guise of research, I—*rationally*—expected two things:

One, he wasn't going to agree. And two, if I ever did kiss him again, it would be exactly like the first time.

And I was wrong on both accounts.

As soon as I mentioned future kisses—a benchmark for future boyfriends—something snapped inside Kit and proved my first assumption wrong. His arm snaked around my waist like a massive steel chain, anchoring me to him, and then his mouth crushed mine.

And that was where he decimated my second assumption.

This kiss was nothing like the first time. I'd thought the fog of the fever heightened my senses; no, it had dulled them. This kiss was like being swept up in a sea of fire. Wave after wave of heat drenched me with pleasure and soaked me with want. My hands curled into his shirt, holding desperately to him like I was nothing more than a buoy in the middle of his storm.

Within seconds, he'd made good on his promise: no kiss would ever be like this. *Because no other man could kiss like Kit Kinkade.*

To be fair, my sample size was small. My body biased. And my brain a little frenzied. But I was confident enough to claim it as scientifically proven.

No one could kiss like Kit Kinkade, and he was kissing me again. In spite of everything.

The knowledge drew a moan from my chest, success doused by the hunger for more. His mouth angled along mine, and this time, I didn't wait for the probe of his tongue before I opened my lips and searched his out. Our breaths smashed together as our mouths tangled. My hands worked their way up around his shoulders, allowing my body to flush into his.

Our tongues slid and stroked, teased and tormented, the fire inside me burned so hot I was sure I'd disintegrate in his hold at any moment. But I didn't —couldn't—because the flame wanted something more. His hands moved, strong and deliberate from my hips. One snaked up my spine, cradling the back of my skull and imprisoning my mouth to his; the other moved lower. Over the dip in my back and onto the curve of my ass.

He let out a deep growl of hunger as he filled his hand with the flesh of my ass, and it sent the ache in my core into overdrive. My breasts weren't the only thing large about me. I was lots of large curves packed into a short frame. And when he pulled back, I had a split second to think about being self-conscious, but the pure lust in his gaze ripped that thought to shreds.

"What's the verdict?" he growled, nipping at my bottom lip and then my jawline.

"I think..." I sucked in a breath, lifting my hands to his cheeks, my fingers sinking into the soft pelt of his beard, holding him steady so I could catch his eyes. "I think you were right about the kiss but..."

One dark brow rose, and he grunted, "But what?"

My gaze roamed his face for a second, charging my courage with every evidence of lust in his expression, before I murmured huskily, "But what about everything else?"

For all my life, my brain has been my driving force —my strongest muscle. So strong, I'd been convinced for years that I didn't need to be kissed or touched—that I didn't need a man because I had my *men*—*my specimens.*

But when he kissed me, the strength of my thoughts retreated and let all my physical urges and aches run wild. My heart pumped in my chest. My breasts felt heavy—swollen for his touch. My nipples pearled into painful peaks. And low in my stomach...between my thighs...my core clenched and squeezed with want.

I needed to know what else was possible—what else my body was capable of with him.

"Aurora..."

I tipped against him, shivering at the feel of his hardness that stretched from the breadth of his chest to the taper of his waist...*and the thick rod of his erection wedged between us.*

"I need to know," I whispered, wanting more. "Please, Kit."

He stilled for a second, and then, with another low rumble from his chest, he lifted me and carried me into the bedroom. Before coming to Friendship—before meeting Kit—I couldn't remember the last time I'd been carried. When I was a child, probably, but definitely not in the last decade. And in the span of the last four weeks, Kit had carried me three times. First, to save me from the wave, then when I feverishly almost collapsed less than a foot from where we'd been standing, and now. And for being one hundred percent capable of moving myself, I was surprised how much I liked it.

I liked the things it did to his big muscles. I liked how it seemed like I weighed nothing to him—and I definitely weighed something. Several somethings plus whatever those delicious cider donuts I'd had every morning from the Maine Squeeze added. But mostly, I liked how it was his instinct when he knew how much I needed him—in whatever capacity—to haul me into his arms like a possessive brute and hold me.

I more than liked it. But there was no avoiding that now.

He kicked the door closed behind us, the wood rattling in the frame, and lowered us to the mattress. Him first, and me on his lap. My head spun in the current of his next kiss, as though this part of him had been locked away just as surely as he'd secluded himself in the lighthouse.

"Tell me what you need to know." He framed my jaw with his hand and began to kiss along the side of my neck.

My lips parted with a shaky breath.

"Say it, sea star."

My chest caved. "I need to know what an orgasm feels like."

His tongue swirled over my pulse, making it thrum harder. "And do you want that experiment to happen with my fingers or my tongue?"

I sucked in a breath. I wanted to experience it in every way—including sex—but it seemed like that was off the table. So, I asked for the next best thing. "Both."

He groaned low against my skin.

"I've never experienced it with either," I confessed.

His curse was cut off as his teeth sank into the side of my neck. I could feel the ridge of his erection swell thicker between my legs, and I was about to admit the rest of the truth that I'd never had sex before, but his mouth claimed mine once more.

Long, deep strokes of his tongue made my world start to tip on its axis. Pleasure pooled between my legs, and like the other night, I began to rock against him, needing more.

"Slow down, sea star," he cooed. "I'll give you what you need, I promise." His hands skated up the sides of my arms until they reached the top of my shirt. "But let me worship you first."

The fabric peeled over my shoulders. His fingers hooked the straps of my bra and took that with him, lower and lower until he'd bared my breasts and I whimpered, relieved that the fabric was gone.

He stared down at me, his hot gaze warring with the cool air, which pebbled my nipples harder. Meanwhile, I was mesmerized by his expression—the usual stone mask of distance and frustration gone, erased by much stronger emotions.

Desire. Hunger. Possession.

"Fuck, they're perfect," he groaned, and then pulled my head to his, stealing another kiss and sealing the compliment to my lips.

I hummed and said breathlessly. "You're good at compliments."

A hoarse chuckle pushed from his chest. "Are you searching for more?"

"N-No," I said tremulously when his hands slid down my shoulders to the outside of my arms, both of them pinned by my blouse that he'd left bunched down over my stomach. And then his hold tipped me back so he could stare.

"No?" His thumbs traced the underside of my breasts, painting fire along the skin and my breath hitched. I'd add this stare to the list of things I'd never experienced before. "Are you sure?" he growled and cupped my breasts.

Sensations exploded through me. The heat of his palm. The coarseness of his skin as it rubbed over the peak of my nipple. The stretch of his fingers—even his big grip wasn't enough to hold my entire breast...but it came close. And when he started to knead them—to weigh the aching flesh—I felt my eyes roll back in my head.

"No." I moaned and then shook my head. "I mean yes," I panted. "Yes, I'm sure." I didn't need compliments. Not with confidence.

His nose dragged over my collarbone, his next words making my heart trip. "Because you deserve them all." He swirled his thumbs over my nipples, the sensation making me shiver. "Smart. Determined." Another swirl. "Kind. Curious." My breath caught.

Was he sure he wanted to compliment me on that?
"Beautiful."

Beautiful.

To him.

"Kit." The room began to spin. The only thing left in focus was the press of his lips in a path along my breasts, closer and closer to where I needed him.

"I could spend a lifetime studying you, Aurora Cross," he said. "The curve of the dimple in your smile. The perfect pitch of your laugh or the sound you make when you find something new or exciting." He released my breast to trail a single finger down the slope. "The softness of your skin. The shape of your body. The taste..." he groaned. "Beg me to taste you."

Another time, I would've wondered if I should've been embarrassed by my whimper at his words—the amount of pleasure they had the power to cause, but not now.

He blew a stream of hot air over my nipple.

"Please, Kit," I wholeheartedly begged, urging him with the arch of my back because I'd lost the exact words to say.

But it didn't matter because he knew. He wanted it too badly, too. His hands tightened deliciously on my breasts, holding them higher and framing my nipples in the arch between his thumb and forefinger like he was presenting himself a feast.

And then the hot flat of his tongue swiped over one tip, and I lost my mind. I cried out—too preemptive in my pleasure—because his lips closed over the straining bud and began to suck.

Oh god.

What kind of experiment had I begged for if it killed me in the end?

"Impossibly soft and perfect..." He trailed off into a hungry growl as he moved to my other breast.

I searched for support in the thick strands of his hair, burying my fingers against his scalp—against the scar I knew I'd felt the other night, and held him to me. I felt his groans of appreciation rumble against my flesh just as surely as I felt the hot stroke of his tongue and the firm, steady pulls of his lips.

Pleasure pooled deep inside me, oozing through each of my limbs like a fountain of lust. But between my thighs...the ache was unbearable.

"Kit..." I breathed out, angling my hips until I found the spot where the hard ridge of his erection pressed to my core, and then began to rock. His eyes tipped up to mine, glittering with possessiveness and pride when they saw my face—saw how hazy with lust I was.

"I'd mark every flush and shiver," he said low, pressing a kiss to each peak of my breasts. "And every whimper—every sound I could draw from your lips just from these." And then he scraped his teeth over my nipple, soothing it instantly with his tongue, but not before the sensation caused havoc on my body. Heat flushed through me—drenched between my legs.

"*More*," I begged.

With a deep groan, he let my nipple pop from his mouth. His hand secured my hips, and then suddenly he pushed me off his lap so I was standing.

Panic crashed over me like icy rain. Had I done something wrong? Was that it? Was he pushing me away again?

His head tipped slowly up, and as soon as his expression swam into focus, my fears dissipated. *Hunger*. First, he reached for my shirt, taking it and my bra all the way up to the top of my head before I yanked it the rest of the way and threw it on the floor.

Next, wordlessly, he reached for the waist of my pants, the button and zipper giving way in an instant. There wasn't even a moment to hesitate—not that I wanted to—before the rush of cool air wrapped around my lower body as I stood completely naked in front of him.

And he didn't move—hardly even a rise in his chest to breathe. Time could've stilled on the steadiness of his brow as he regarded me. His eyes like twin pools of lust that surveyed me, staking an invisible claim to every inch of my curves.

"So fucking beautiful."

The compliment felt like it was tattooed straight to my soul—pinned forever to my psyche by the man who made me feel like no one else had before.

His lips closed back over my nipple, tasting and teasing the peak until I was drenched in goose bumps. "Kit..." I slid my hands around the back of his head again.

And then his hands started to lower. A featherlight touch over my stomach, tracing the soft curves of skin. "I want to taste you," he rumbled. "I want to know if all of you tastes as sweet as these." His head dipped, and he flicked my nipple with his tongue.

My eyes fluttered shut. My hands slid from his head down to his shoulders, about to coast onto the muscles of his back when his body tensed. I hardly processed it before my world went topsy-turvy. I cried out as he flipped us around, laying me on my back on the bed, as though I weighed no more than a feather.

I panted, staring at the bearded man who crouched over me like an animal, his shoulders heaving and his eyes dark with hunger. He bent closer, pressed a kiss to my sternum, and then moved his head lower. Air hiccupped into my lungs with every inch of descent over my stomach.

Oh god...was he...

"What are you doing?" I asked tremulously, feeling my legs tense, though there was no way to close them with him wedged between them.

His hands coasted from my waist to my thighs and gripped them tight. He lifted his dark gaze and captured mine.

"Experimenting," he growled and wrenched my legs wide, baring me to his open stare.

Protests crashed on the tip of my tongue like waves, uncertainty and embarrassment and want all colliding together. But none escaped. Not when he looked at me like that. *Not when he groaned like the sight was tearing him apart at the seams.*

He hooked his arms underneath my thighs and then slid to his knees at the base of the bed, hauling me to the edge. I couldn't breathe. The anticipation—the ache—stretched inside me like a band about to snap. Desire leaked from my core, I knew it by the way his lip twitched ravenously.

"Has anyone ever tasted you?"

"No one." My voice cracked.

His gaze reached mine, full of hunger and something else...*pride.*

"No one but me."

A different kind of heat bloomed inside my chest. Something that went well deeper than the physical reaction he caused in my body. But before I could think about it more, the heat of his expert tongue slid along my slit, and all rational thought evaporated.

He licked and lapped and groaned throughout, and it felt like all of me was reduced to the knot of pleasure between my thighs.

I grappled for his head once more, clutching him so tight that I would've worried about suffocating him if he wasn't already burying himself out of hunger. Within seconds, I couldn't even decipher what I was feeling—how his tongue was moving the way that it was or if it was his lips. All I knew was that it was the most incredible thing I'd ever felt.

"So wet for me," he grunted, his mouth moving like he couldn't get enough. "So creamy."

I gasped, my back bowing when his lips closed over my clit and sucked. I'd never felt such bright, intense pleasure before. It spiraled and seared and crashed through me like my own personal lightning strike, creating an avalanche of pleasure I couldn't stop. My core pulsed with the growing ache, spots flickering in my vision as my release began to claw at me. And that was when I felt him—his finger teasing my entrance.

"Kit—" I wanted to warn him that I was too close—too sensitive. But I had no chance before his big finger pushed inside my clenching muscles all the way until it hit that anatomical spot of nerves I only knew about in theory. Like he'd pushed on an *easy* button, my orgasm exploded through my body.

I cried out as my body went taut. *God, it felt so good*

from him. Was that reasonable? Was it possible? Or was I just imagining the difference between the orgasms I gave myself and the one he'd given me?

"Fuck, you're responsive," he growled, and before I could wonder about being insecure, he groaned and added, "I'm going to make you come again, sea star, you taste so fucking sweet."

Again? I didn't have a single second more to think about it before his lips embedded his growl into my swollen pussy. This time, it was lips and tongue and fingers that assaulted me. Layering pleasure like the finest delicacy through my veins. Vaguely, I heard my unabashed cries and whimpers for more. Vaguely, I registered that at some point, my legs had wrapped around his neck, pinning me to his face.

He tortured me with precision—the same precision he used when drawing my specimens. He traced every detail of my swollen clit with his tongue, shaped its pleasure with his lips, and then drew new pleasure from his fingers driving inside my pussy.

First it was one finger and then two that he pushed deep inside and then dragged along my front wall over my G-spot, reducing me to a puddle of pleasure. Literally. I felt my desire leak down to the seam of my ass, messy and wanton.

"Kit," I whimpered, desperate to come again.

"Shh," he cooed against my slick flesh. "I'm experimenting."

Torturing. He was torturing. Over and over he worked my body close to another peak with his fingers and his tongue, testing my limits and taking them higher without letting me come down.

Experimentation had become torture, and before long, torture had become master. My head lolled from side to side, willing to trade the oxygen of my next breath if he'd just give me the climax he edged me with.

"Please," I panted, trying to grind harder against his touch. "Please, Kit. I need you."

For a split second, he stilled, his head tipped so his eyes could meet mine. And then with a low, feral sound, his mouth sealed back over me, his fingers slamming against my G-spot as he sucked furiously on my clit.

I couldn't breathe. I was sure my heart had stopped beating and that I was going to faint any second, but then I heard him, his rough mutter keeping me conscious for one more moment.

"That's it, sea star," he said roughly, and then I felt it—the slide of his thumb along the seam of my ass before it pressed to my tight hole.

It wasn't a lot—it was probably hardly anything—but even the slightest touch on such a sensitive area was enough to whip me violently over the edge.

I screamed as my climax decimated me. My back bowed, and I came around his fingers and against his mouth so hard I was certain there was no room for him to breathe. And still, he didn't leave me to crash, he kept touching me—stroking me—guiding me with deep groans of pleasure through the most intense orgasm to ever exist.

Wave after wave of pleasure tore through me, and by the time it finally began to let up, I was convinced I'd lost limbs in the process—that I'd have to figure out some way to regenerate the pieces of me that Kit had claimed for himself.

"Fucking perfect," he said with a low rumble of appreciation as he lifted his head.

Heat flooded my cheeks. His face was soaked. His beard glistening...covered in...me. My desire. My orgasm. And when his fingers slid out of me, they were drenched, too.

"What just happened?" I whispered, my chest heaving to catch the beat of my heart.

His wicked tongue slid out and licked his lips first before he sucked his fingers clean. "Experimentation." His mouth quirked to one side.

Was erotic experimentation a thing? Could it be?

I pushed up on my elbows. "I made a mess of you."

The mattress shifted and he was over me in an instant, my chin pinned in his fingers. "No, sea star. I made a mess of you." His mouth crushed mine in a deep kiss. I could taste myself on his tongue and it was...interesting. Sensual. *Intimate.* "Don't move." And then he was gone, to the bathroom, and I could hear the faucet whoosh on.

I managed to sit up just as he came back into the room, kneeling back between my legs with a warm cloth. I caught his grimace as he stood—the reason for it stretching the front of his jeans to the point of bursting.

"Kit." I grabbed his wrist before he could walk away. His head jerked to mine, and I held his gaze as I pulled the washcloth from his hand and dropped it onto the floor.

"Aurora..."

There it was again...that warning.

"I'm not done experimenting," I murmured as I pressed my hand to the ridge of his erection.

His hips jerked and he hissed.

I blinked, a question forming on my tongue that was too strong to ignore. "When was the last time someone touched you?"

I didn't mean a handshake or a hug. I meant like this—intimate. Erotic. I palmed the massive ridge, want and curiosity dueling inside me to see it. Touch it. *Taste him.*

"Aurora..."

"How long has it been?" I pressed, my fingers finding the button of his fly and popping it free.

A hot hiss forced its way through his lips when I lowered the zipper, his answer finally coming out on a groan when some of the pressure released.

"Not for a long time."

I swallowed over the lump in my throat. It was a simple deduction to reason that it had been close to a decade. If the incident in the war had been a little over ten years ago, and if that was what sent him to live in the lighthouse...well, it was no stretch of the imagination to assume the seclusion he lived in now was the kind of things perfected over those last ten years.

So, a decade without being touched.

For a second, self-doubt flooded me. Was I the right person to be touching him after that long? My curiosity was off the charts, but my expertise was non-existent. I bit my lip, staring at my hand flattened to the front of his groin, and then lifted it over the most gorgeous man I'd ever met to find his gaze. My breath caught. I saw the truth written all over his face. He hadn't been warning me, he was begging.

For me.

For my touch.

Releasing his wrist, I hooked my fingers under the

waist of his jeans and boxer briefs, stretching and lowering them until his cock bobbed free right in front of my face.

My lips parted. He was so long and thick, and the veins that netted around his girth pulsed, bringing a bead of moisture to his tip. The urge to taste him was so strong, it made me gasp.

"Aurora..." He reached out and cupped my cheek, his thumb stroking the skin as he stared. And then I saw it—fear shadowing his eyes.

"I've thought about what you taste like, too," I murmured, bringing my mouth closer to him. "Wondered."

His jaw flexed. "Well, don't let me stop your research."

My small smile disappeared as I opened my mouth and licked the drop from his swollen head.

"Fuck," he growled, his hand tangling in my hair and guiding me to his cock.

I didn't need any urging. I closed my lips over him and pulled him into my mouth. The ragged groan that burst from his chest made me take him deeper until he hit the back of my throat and I instantly jerked back, gagging.

"Sorry." I coughed, and before I could get to them, his fingers swiped away the tears that leaked from my eyes.

"Don't fucking apologize, Aurora. Ever," he ordered. "But especially for this." He gripped his cock, his fist working from the base to the tip where he'd started to steadily leak.

It was so hot—watching him stroke himself right in front of my face. I was sure the lower parts of me would feel like Jell-O for days, but they started to quiver back to life at the sight.

But I wanted more.

I reached for his wrist again, halting him and peeling his hand away.

"I'm learning," I murmured and closed my mouth over his tip once more, sucking him slowly back into my mouth.

"Fuck," he hissed, and a thrill of victory swept through me.

Cautiously, I pulled him toward the back of my throat. I wanted to make him lose control the way I did. More than that, I wanted him to be free of all the weight and trauma he carried, even if it was just for a few seconds.

Closing my eyes, I sucked harder, my cheeks pulling tight to his length as I felt him bottom out against the back of my throat. This time, I'd gone slow enough to keep the urge to gag at bay, and the reward was more than I could've hoped.

"You feel so good, Aurora," he groaned, and I couldn't help but note how he'd said that *I* felt good, not a generic *that feels so good.* "So fucking beautiful taking all my cock."

I shivered with the praise, moving back and twirling the tip of my tongue around his head until he grunted and thrust uncontrollably into my mouth. *Yes.*

"Stroke me," he growled, rocking harder into my mouth, and I greedily slurped him in. "I want to see your tiny hand try to hold my big cock."

I gripped him firmly, my fingers unable to touch around his girth. I stroked near his base as my tongue swirled and sucked on his tip. *I wondered if...*his low curse and the tightening of his hold in my hair confirmed that my experiment of cupping his balls with my other hand was a success.

His breath was ragged now. Shredded over the sharp pull of pleasure as I stroked and sucked his cock.

"*Fuck, sea star.* Your mouth is killing me." He rubbed my cheek. The edge of my lips. Massaged the back of my scalp. Everything was encouraging me to do more.

I picked up my pace, my heart hammering just as hard as if I were the one on the brink of another orgasm. Over and over, I pulled him deeper into my mouth until he couldn't go any farther. Tears clung to my eyelashes each time my throat tried to swallow around him, saliva leaking from the corners of my mouth, but it was worth it.

To hear the noises of pleasure he made...to feel how his cock swelled even larger...to watch this immovable man become undone with pleasure...*it was worth every second.*

His hand turned to steel on the back of my head, holding it firm as he began to thrust hard and fast. I moaned and stroked him with my tongue, wanting him to know that I wanted more of this, even if my mouth was too full to beg for it.

"*Fuck,* I'm going to come," he hissed, his hips starting to pump frantically.

I moaned around him. It was all I wanted—to make this man lose his control. And I wasn't sure what prompted me—where the thought came from—except that it was what he'd done to me at that moment, but I slid my hand from his balls back toward his puckered hole.

He tensed. "Aurora—"

I didn't even push my finger inside, I only pressed it to the sensitive rim, but it was enough. He exploded like a storm unleashed, slamming against the back of my throat with a feral shout as his cock stretched impossibly thick and then erupted, the hot spurts of his release shooting straight down my throat.

A guttural growl ripped from his chest as he inched back a second later so I could breathe, his cock still filling my mouth with his cum. I continued to gently suck him, my tongue tracing and swirling around his length and head, trying to memorize every inch of him as his body came down from release.

Minutes later, his hands tightened in my hair, carefully pulling out of my lips with a low hiss.

I stared at his length, slick with my saliva, still thick, and cum still oozing from the tip.

"Aurora." His hands angled my head up, my jaw going slack when my eyes met his. "Push your tits together."

I obeyed, cupping my breasts and jamming my cleavage together. I didn't know what was hotter—his stare or the groan that escaped him. One hand reached out and began plucking my nipple where it protruded between my fingers. His other hand gripped his shaft, pumping the length with hard strokes.

I let out a little sigh of pleasure, watching him touch himself, and within seconds, his cock was jerking with another orgasm, hot cum spurting over my chest. It wasn't nearly as much as the first time, but the fact that there was a second time was impressive.

Again, the difference between experience and education: as a general rule, multiple orgasms were a female gift, but in this case, Kit Kinkade was the exception.

"It was my turn to make a mess," he said gruffly, grabbing the washcloth from the floor and wiping off my chest.

"That was part of my experiment," I murmured.

His eyes caught mine. "That was one hell of an experiment."

"Kit." I shivered.

"Here." He hauled my clothes off the floor and dumped them onto the bed. "I don't want you to catch a chill."

I looked at the pile. *If I put them back on, did that mean I was leaving?* When I turned back to ask, Kit was buttoning up his pants, his expression tight.

"I'll drive you back to your B&B."

Well, that answered that.

As I dressed, I thought carefully about what I wanted to say next. I didn't want this to be the one and only time this happened, but I also didn't want to pressure him into thinking that I'd just keep demanding more.

We rode mostly in silence back to where I was staying. He pulled up out front of the old colonial house just outside of town but didn't put the truck in part. *A subtle, silent goodbye.*

"Kit." I paused with my hand on the door handle and looked over my shoulder at him. "One experiment isn't good, quality research."

He stared at me so hard and for so long, I was on the verge of saying good night and getting out of the truck before whatever was building inside him crushed me. *Because it would.* The way he retreated so quickly and harshly into his shell was the kind of thing other species took centuries to perfect.

But then the low tenor of his voice oozed through the cab like a fire sparking to life on a winter day.

"Well, I wouldn't want you to be accused of doing poor research."

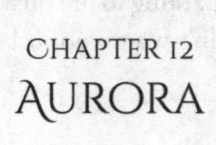

CHAPTER 12
AURORA

"*Kit!*" I clutched his wrist, his hand buried under the waist of my yoga pants, his fingers consuming my clit as we sat at the traffic light.

"Almost there," he rumbled, and for the life of me, he could've meant either to our destination or to my orgasm.

"*Do you need anything? I have to run into town and drop this drawing off at my gallery.*"

That was how today started.

"*Can I come?*"

And that was how it was going to end—his fingers working their magic on my body during the four-minute drive into town.

The light turned green, Kit hit the gas at the same time as his fingers tugged hard on my clit, and I saw stars.

"*Kit!*" I cried out, grasping his wrist and the handle above the door, my body trembling with release. It was wildly skillful and incredibly unfair the way he could bring me to orgasm in minutes.

It was partially biology—anatomy; the way I was made, made pleasure very easy to come by...when it was with the right person. Like most reactive things, I was relatively inert in many scenarios—like gasoline in your car or propane in a fireplace. But when the right spark was applied, I was...*on fire*.

And Kit was my spark.

I was panting as we drove through the intersection, the truck coming the opposite direction honking as we passed.

"Do you think they could see?" I gasped, embarrassment fusing to my cheeks.

"No." Kit chuckled low and slid his hand out of my pants, calmly bringing his fingers to his mouth and slowly sucking what remained of my desire from the tips. I bit into my bottom lip. It was so sexy when he did that. "That was just my cousin, Nox."

I slumped with relief. Friendship was a small town; in a matter of weeks, I'd learned just as much about its population as I had the coastal one I'd come to study.

The truck slowed, and I stole another glance at Kit. He sat calmly in the driver's seat, waiting for a break in traffic before turning the wheel with the flat of his palm and pulling into an alleyway next to his gallery.

Midnight blue with gold trim. A narrow door framed next to a large shop front window, the name *Kinkade's* swirled across the top. I'd passed it every day this week on my way to the lighthouse, more curious than ever to go inside. But something stopped me.

Four days, a dozen more experiments, and I was ashamed to say I no longer arrived at the lighthouse eager to learn about the creatures living on its shores but the one inside its house. And I wanted to learn about Kit through what he was willing to show me—share with me. That was why I'd kept my distance from his gallery—because I wanted to experience it with him.

"Ready?" he asked once he'd parked.

I licked my lips and nodded.

There was no side entrance; Kit led the way to the front, and my steps slowed at the window. The two drawings he'd already done were framed and displayed in the center. No prices were listed, just a small *Coming Soon* sign underneath.

"Aurora..."

My head snapped in his direction, finding him holding the door and waiting for me.

"I'm sorry," I murmured and snuck by, but I was hardly a step inside when I stopped again, my jaw dropping at the paintings on the wall.

"Shit—" Kit ran into me, his hand locking on my waist. There was no mistaking the hardness pressed against my ass or the grunt of pain he let loose when he touched me. "Aurora—"

"Sorry," I apologized again with a shiver and walked to the center of the gallery, putting some space between us before I was on my knees in front of him where anyone could walk by and see.

There I took a slow spin, drinking in the sight of every painting that hung on the walls. Scene after scene —*storm after storm*—from the vantage point of the Friendship Lighthouse. I imagined Kit sitting on his stool while the rain and the waves raged outside. *Alone.* But there was one painting on the wall on the right, large and hung high, that captured the lighthouse itself, waves crashing against its mighty tower. And when I saw it, that was when I really felt what the paintings were about—not Mother Nature's anger but his own.

Heat trickled down my spine, and I turned to find him watching me.

I'd recognized the sensation over the last few days when I'd feel that warmth when I was working outside, and I'd look up and see him checking on me through the window. His stare had the power to warm me through the cold, blustery ocean air.

And inside, we worked side-by-side, me making my notes and Kit working on his drawings, like embers waiting to ignite. And inevitably they always did. The catch of our eyes. The brush of our shoulders. That was all it took for my back to be at the wall, my hands pinned to my sides, while his mouth devoured mine.

Each day, I was tempted to look in his notebook—to see if his logs for the day before included all the ways he'd brought me pleasure. He had to be taking notes—studying each night—because every day the orgasms got more intense. Faster or slower, he commanded the storm inside me, deciding how much havoc it would create.

He had to be taking notes because I was, too.

I noted how he'd only let me pleasure him once he'd given me at least two orgasms. I noted which movements of my tongue along his cock made his big body tremble and which made his balls tighten. And I definitely made note of how intensely I could make him come by pushing my finger through the seam of his ass and teasing the rim of his tight hole.

But I also noted other things. Things like how his foot tapped when he drew something especially intricate. How he licked his lips and nodded to himself each time he got an area just right. How he never took his shirt off with me, which wasn't necessary, but the few times I'd reached for it, I'd been ordered to leave it. How he always managed to keep me from touching his back. It didn't make sense. He no longer shied when my fingers brushed the scar on his skull, but his back...there was still something he was keeping inside. Something he still wasn't willing to share.

Maybe that was why our experiments hadn't progressed to sex. Of course, there could be a variety of reasons for that, not the least of which was sex was another level. Something that would go beyond the idea of a test or trial.

"These are incredible," I said and faced him.

He looked away. Humility was one more of his shields. "They're all right."

"All right?" I laughed softly and shook my head. "There's a reason you have a gallery, Kit. You're amazing—*these* are amazing." I caught myself quickly. The last thing I wanted him to think was that our experiments would lead to emotion; I didn't need any kind of warning to know how that would end.

He made a low noise—the one I recognized and translated as his best attempt at a thank you.

"I just have to leave this for Lou. She'll handle everything else." He made his way to the aged desk in the back and set the carrier on top.

"What made you start drawing?" I asked and slowly wandered back over to the largest painting of the lighthouse, a wave erupting against the tower as dark clouds loomed above. The depth of character in the shadows. The flecks of detail in the lighthouse. It was no wonder the man's fingers could turn an orgasm into a work of art, they'd been creating masterpieces for years.

"The twins."

"Oh?" My voice cracked, and I moved to the next painting, giving Kit my back so he couldn't see how interested I was to know more.

"I watched them a lot when they were younger. Their dad was a piece of shit," he revealed, anger edging his voice. "Basically left when he realized Mom was pregnant, so Jamie and I stepped in. Jamie helped Mom and Gigi with the business, and I entertained Frankie and Lou. They liked when I drew pictures and told them stories."

"They still do," I murmured, recalling how both the twins looked when Lou passed around her phone with Kit's artwork on it. Everyone had looked with admiration, but the two of them...there was something more.

I felt Kit move closer to me, the tingles along my skin intensifying. And then came that grunt again.

"These are all storms you've seen?" The frame in front of me looked particularly frightening with the way the water crashed together, chewing up the shoreline like a hungry beast.

"Yeah."

"Are you afraid?" I wondered. "When it storms like this?"

"No. Not these ones."

But of others?

"I used to be afraid of thunderstorms when I was really little." I adjusted my glasses.

"You? Afraid?" Kit stood at my shoulder now, one brow arched, and underneath his beard, the faintest shadow of a smile.

I smiled back and folded my arms; the way his gaze dropped hungrily to my chest sent a warm burst into my stomach.

"Even the brave were once afraid," I replied wryly, the words ingrained in my mind for decades now. "I'd run screaming into Dad's room, my blanket over my head. He'd get out of bed and we'd hide out in the hallway, away from the windows. But there, he'd explain the storms to me."

"Explain them?"

I nodded and chuckled. "My dad's just like me—or I guess I should say I'm just like him. Stories and fairytales weren't going to cut it as a distraction."

"No, I don't imagine they would." Kit's gaze caught mine, making my breath hitch.

"He'd tell me that when warm, wet air rises and meets cold air, it creates atmospheric instability. Two different breeds of air colliding in the same space. The warm moisture condenses and creates the cumulonimbus clouds and the perfect environment for a... storm," I said, my voice turning husky thinking about how the lighthouse had created a similar environment for the two of us to collide. Clearing my throat, I went on, "The next storm, he told me about things like lifting mechanisms. After that, upward and downward drafts. And then electrical activity, and so on."

"After all that, you didn't become a meteorologist?"

I beamed. "No, I like living creatures too much for that." I shook my head, a strand of curls loosening from my headband. "*But,* after all that, I wasn't afraid of the storms anymore."

Kit hummed, and then I felt the brush of his finger along my cheek, the touch taking the bit of hair back and tucking it behind my ear. My stomach did a little flip. It was these little gestures that muddled things—that made the result of our *experiments* murky.

"It's easy to fear what we don't know," I said and angled toward him. "So, when you understand why something is happening. The reason. The mechanism. The purpose. It's hard to be afraid of it anymore."

His eyes narrowed almost imperceptibly. "I guess I'm lucky I was never afraid of storms then."

My lips parted, and I repeated his words back to him softly, "Not these ones."

His nostrils flared as his arm fell to his side, and he strode back to the back of the room. To the rest of the world, he appeared standoffish, solitary, and gruff. But after weeks observing him—learning bits and pieces about him—I understood. Or was starting to. He didn't pull back because he was angry or annoyed; he pulled away because he was wounded, retreating like an injured whelk back to his shell.

"Has there been interest in the two drawings?" I called over my shoulder, changing the subject.

"According to Lou."

I figured there had to be since Kit had done another inked piece; the portrait of the green sea urchin was what we'd brought over today to add to the collection.

"A lot of interest?" I probed, knowing Kit might hold back, but he wouldn't lie.

"Enough," he replied cryptically.

"You should draw Stuart."

"The three-legged sea star?"

"Are you judging him?" I teased and popped an eyebrow up.

"No. I'm just saying maybe he doesn't want to be

drawn. Maybe he's...vulnerable." Out of all my speci-
mens, Kit checked on my rescued sea star the most.
"Are you sure his legs are even going to grow back?
They don't look like they're doing anything."

I feigned a gasp. "Of course, they're doing something. He lost two legs. Cut him some slack," I teased,
sliding my gaze to him and adding, "There's a lot of
healing that has to happen behind the scenes before
noticeable changes happen."

Kit hummed.

"Even sea stars heal from the inside out."

Our eyes collided for a moment before he straightened and went back to the desk.

I'd gotten too close to...something. So, I retreated
back to the gallery exhibit. "I think the show is going to
be wonderful. For your work. And Lou."

"We'll see."

I walked over to him. "What are you worried
about?"

"Nothing," he said quickly—too quickly. "I just
don't like crowds."

"Is that why you don't want to go to the twins'
party?"

He shrugged off the question. "They won't even
notice if I'm not there."

"Kit." I caught his arm as he strode toward the door.
"They notice every time you're not there." It was
striking that night after dinner—coming back up from
the basement to find Kit gone; the look on everyone's
faces was somber.

The muscle in his jaw flexed, but before he could
say anything else, the door swung open and Lou
appeared.

"Kit!" she exclaimed, a wide smile breaking over her face when she saw him—and then it grew when she noticed me. "Aurora."

She came to me first, wrapping me in a giant hug.

"Hi." I squeezed her back.

"I wasn't expecting to see you here," she said as he pulled her close and kissed her head. Another thing I'd noticed about Kit Kinkade...for a man who didn't like to let anyone in, if you did make it into his atmosphere, the way he held you close rivaled the pull of gravity.

"I had another drawing to drop off. It's on the desk," he said.

"It's a green sea urchin," I chimed in excitedly. "You should see how he captured the spines."

"Oh, I can't wait." Literally. She rushed over to the desk.

"We should—"

"Did Kit tell you about the other drawings?"

"What about them?" My eyes flicked to him, catching the tick of annoyance in his jaw.

"Well, I put them up the first day without any prices. I wanted to gauge interest before deciding how to value them. Anyway, there were so many people who came in that afternoon, there was a line—*a line,* Aurora. In an art gallery."

"That's amazing. Kit didn't tell me any of that," I said, my narrow stare scolding his reserve as I walked toward Lou, wanting to hear more of whatever she had to say.

"Of course, he didn't."

"Wasn't important," he grumbled from behind us.

"Kit..." Lou let out a loud gasp followed by a long

pause of admiration, her fingers pinning the paper open on opposite corners while she examined the drawing.

"Incredible, isn't it?" I couldn't count the number of times I'd found myself forgetting about my own work in favor of watching raptly the way Kit brought the urchin to life on the paper. "The spines are so delicate, so you have to be very careful when you capture or harvest them."

"Harvest?"

"Urchin roe is a delicacy in Japan and Europe, so there's a huge fishing market for these guys in Maine because of their population here. I actually had to apply for a hand-fishing license to be able to take one of them by hand even though I'm going to put him back."

"Wow. I had no idea."

"If you damage a spine, it leaks sea water into the urchin and can affect the quality of the roe," Kit said, his voice reverberating behind us.

We both looked over our shoulders to find he'd moved closer.

"You've learned about them, too?"

"Everyone should," he grunted. "Their grazing habits are the reason there's a low number of algae and kelp along the coast."

Lou turned her focus to me, the look in her eyes making me feel like I was unknowingly responsible for some kind of miracle. "I'll have Jamie make a frame for it like the rest," she murmured, unable to contain her smile as she carefully rolled the drawing back up. "This is going to be amazing, Aurora. Thank you."

"Me?" I laughed. I hadn't created the drawings—or any of this; it was all Kit. "I didn't—"

"Because of the interest," she forged on, continuing

her story from earlier. "I decided that the new collection will only be available for sale at the gallery show, really funnel all of the interest into one afternoon."

"That sounds perfect." I glanced at Kit, who fought to keep his expression unmoving.

"We should get going, Aurora, if you want to stop at the store," he said, his weight shifting and his focus starting to fray.

"Oh, right." I nodded. "I broke one of my display cases for the shells I've been collecting, so that's why I came in with Kit; he offered to take me to the store to pick up a new one," I said, giving myself a mental pat on the back for explaining the reason we were here together before Lou got her hopes up.

"Okay, I won't keep you." Lou hugged me and her brother again. "Oh, you both are coming to the party, right?" There was no mistaking the way she held her breath and looked at Kit before adding, "Please?"

The tension coursing through him was palpable. *Crowds. He didn't like crowds.* But maybe if he knew more about the party, he wouldn't be so...worried. And that gave me an idea.

"Are there going to be a lot of people there?" I asked, pulling my lip between my teeth. "I'm awkward around a lot of people, especially people I don't know."

"What?" She gaped. "You're not awkward at all."

I cocked my head and blinked. "I relate everything back to sea creatures. And not the cool ones like sharks or whales either, but the weird, spiny, branchy, crusty ones that no one knows about."

"But that stuff is interesting!"

Tell that to...well, everyone I'd gone to school with for the first twelve years of my education.

"Not for everyone," I said softly.

"Only everyone with a brain," Kit grumbled, the low compliment making my cheeks heat.

"Well, it's just our family plus our cousins and a couple of friends—and they all have brains, so the ones who don't know you will love you, too, I promise," she assured me so warmly. For a second, I felt it soothe my insecurities, too, even though the reason I'd asked was for Kit. "We're going to do dinner—Mom's making our favorite lasagna—and then Jamie is going to build a bonfire."

"So, not too many people?"

"Oh, not a lot," she promised. "But we're a lively bunch...especially when Frankie and our cousins get together, so I can't promise there won't be any shenanigans."

I laughed. "I'm okay with shenanigans."

"So, you're coming?"

I nodded and then turned to Kit, my breath lodging deep in my chest, waiting for his answer.

"Yeah," Kit replied after a long beat. "For a little."

Maybe by then, I'd understand a little more about why he avoided crowds...and if there was anything else I could do to help him understand it.

CHAPTER 13
KIT

"You're here!" Lou wrapped me in a giant hug. I squeezed her back and let out a deep exhale. "I said I would be."

I'd keep my word, even if it killed me.

As I hugged my little sister, my eyes surveyed the surroundings. I'd been in Mom's house a hundred thousand times, but with the living and dining rooms rearranged and the steady, solid furniture replaced with loud, living people, it was a different scenario. Lots of people meant lots of noise and commotion. Lots of places for panic to surprise me.

And the cold tap of fear on my shoulder begged me to wonder if I'd made a mistake.

There were more people than I'd expected. The list of family and friends I'd conjured up in preparation was overshadowed by the number of faces milling around.

"I'm sorry," Lou said as she stepped back, her lashes fluttering. "Frankie added a few more people to the list I wasn't aware of."

"It's fine." *For now*.

I inhaled slowly and let my gaze drift to her. Aurora. She had on a long, loose skirt, the shade of rusty autumn leaves, a cream blouse that hugged her chest in a way that made me want to rip it off of her, and a bright blue bow tied like a headband. She was deceptively captivating. The kind of woman who thought she didn't draw any attention but captured the whole room the moment she walked into it.

Lou pulled her in for a hug, the two of them bouncing as they embraced as though they'd known each other for a lifetime rather than a couple of weeks. Maybe that was how my family was, but it was also Aurora. She was just so damn warm and inviting and honest...it was impossible to not want to get close.

A hand clapped me on the shoulder, and my head turned so fast I was surprised my neck didn't snap. Adrenaline pounded my heart. *Panic*.

"Hey, Kit." Nox grinned at me, and I swallowed down the bile in my throat, willing my heart to steady. *Dammit*.

And in that split second, her words swept through my mind like a stroke of fresh paint. *Even the brave were once afraid*. Bright white brilliance to cover up the inky dark shades of fear.

"Hey," I rasped.

"So good to see you, man. Really."

I managed a grunt in agreement. Nox Hamilton was our cousin on Mom's side. He was thirty, his older brother, Max, was a year older than him, and Harper, their younger sister, was only twenty-four. Nox worked with his dad, our uncle George, and Mom at Stonebar Farms. Max owned MaineStems, a flower delivery service, up in Stonebar Harbor, and Harper...was still figuring out her passion in life.

If I thought the zing of adrenaline was startling when he'd come over, it felt like nothing compared to the electric burn that pumped through me when Nox turned his attention to Aurora.

"Hey, I'm Nox, Lou and Kit's cousin." He introduced himself before anyone else had the chance and extended his hand.

"Aurora Cross." She slid her fingers into his, and my world started to narrow.

His smile widened. "I've heard a lot about you. You were in the truck with Kit the other day." He pointed a finger at her, recognition dawning.

Aurora's cheeks stained red. *My very own warning.* "Y-yeah." Her head bobbed, her curls shifting around the bow in her hair. "He was giving me a ride to the hardware store. I needed another container for my samples."

"Frankie was just telling me that you're researching at the lighthouse for a semester? That's pretty cool."

Her eyes lit. "Oh, you have no idea. The ecosystem in the Gulf of Maine, especially along the coastline, is so unique, I could spend years cataloging all the details." Without hesitation, she delved into her studies of coastal marine life, the excitement on her face drawing everyone in.

On any given day, I'd wager with decent certainty that Nox Hamilton didn't care about waved whelks, purple sun stars, or green sea urchins, but like the rest of my family—*and me*—it was impossible not to be interested when Aurora spoke about them. Her energy was contagious. Warm, bright, and infectious. Like the sun, it was impossible to not crave her glow.

Nox's easy smile canted higher on one side. "I don't think I've ever been so interested in biology before. Or urchins." *Or her*, I could practically hear as he folded his arms, stared at Aurora, and then turned to me, the look on his face making the hair on my arm stand on end. "So, are you two a thing?" he asked nonchalantly.

Goddammit.

"No," I growled, just as Aurora looked to me for an answer.

"No," she echoed, but there was no mistaking the slight quiver in her voice.

"Nox!" Lou swatted his arm.

"What?" He flinched and laughed. "A man's got to know if he can offer the lady another drink." I'd never wanted to punch my cousin more than when he extended his arm toward the kitchen, inviting Aurora to lead the way.

She looked at me first, waiting to see if I'd say or do anything to stop her, but I didn't because I couldn't. It would send the wrong message to her and my family. It was bad enough we'd rode over from the lighthouse together—something I justified because we'd both been working all afternoon.

"Keep an eye on him. He pours heavy," was all I could manage.

Aurora's eyes fluttered like they could sweep away the flash of pain in her eyes, and I pretended like they did.

"Not me. That's Max." He looked at Aurora and explained, "My older brother. He's in the kitchen, so I'll introduce you."

They walked off together, each of Aurora's steps feeling like a swift kick to the gut.

It didn't matter, I told myself, repeating the words like a chant in my head. It didn't matter that I'd left my mark over her lush curves earlier this morning when I'd painted her breasts with my cum. It didn't matter that I'd had her ride my face until she'd drenched my beard and screamed my name. We were just experimenting, and in a few weeks, that research would be over.

She would be gone. Things would be normal again. Dark and lonely and normal. And that was why it didn't matter if she went off with my cousin right now. The more reminders I had that she wasn't mine, the better.

"You shouldn't have let him do that," Lou chided softly once they were out of earshot.

"Why not?" I grunted, unable to take my eyes off of them.

"Because it's all clearly part of Frankie's plan," Lou said, jerking her chin in her twin's direction. Only then did I notice Frankie was watching me...watch them. "She's matchmaking again. So, first, she had Nox come over to ask if you two were together; if that answer was a no, her contingency plan was this...to see if you'd get jealous."

"I'm not jealous," I snapped.

"Well, your scowl says otherwise."

I drew a tight inhale and faced Lou, making it impossible for me to see Aurora at all.

"One of these days, Frankie is going to plot herself right into a corner and the rest of us are just going to sit back and watch her squirm," I muttered.

Lou laughed. "I hope you're right."

She glanced at her twin, the look in her eyes one I'd seen plenty of times before. *Longing.* For as much as she agreed, there was a part of her that envied the... boldness...of Frankie's personality. Her sister took no prisoners when it came to what she wanted. When Frankie was sixteen, she decided she wanted to make candles. Not even a year later, she was selling them under the brand *Frankie's Scents,* a cheeky play on the word *frankincense.* By the time she was nineteen, she'd had enough money put aside for the down payment on the cabin; the whole family chipped in to renovate, and a few months later, the Candle Cabin opened. When Frankie wanted to do something, she made it happen no matter what it cost—money or otherwise.

But while Lou might've been woven from the same genetic fabric, she was cut differently. Just like Jamie and me. But sometimes, I could see the way she felt like she wasn't enough—hadn't done enough.

It was amazing the kind of things you picked up when you lived on the periphery, assessing rather than engaging. *Observing rather than living.*

"Any news on the inn?" I pushed my back harder into the wall, partially wishing I could dissolve into it instead of facing the crowd of family and friends milling through the house; at some point, I'd have to talk to them, but for now, I could seclude myself in conversation with my sister.

Her attention snapped back, eyes brightening. "Not yet, but I checked in with my friend, Adele, the other day, and she said it will probably be soon. I guess he's been putting the word out in the real estate investment community about the sale."

Which confirmed she'd be competing against some big fish for the purchase.

"Christopher!" Gigi hurried over, her hands full of Mom's appetizers.

"Hi, Gigi." I leaned in to hug her, and she tipped back.

"Don't you 'hi, Gigi' me."

"What?" I mumbled, unable to stop my gaze from darting back to Aurora as soon as I heard the wisps of her laugh. Her head was tipped back, throat exposed, as she laughed at something Nox said. Instantly, the dangerous urge to sink my teeth into the skin of her neck and mark her exploded inside my chest, and I almost let out a snarl as my stare narrowed on my cousin.

"First, eat this. You haven't eaten since you walked in." Before I could act on...whatever it was raging inside me, Gigi aimed one of the prosciutto-wrapped brie bites at me, not leaving me much of a choice except to fit the whole thing in my mouth.

"Gigi!" Lou laughed.

"Here, this one is for the birthday girl." She shoved one at Lou; they were one of Lou's favorites, so, of course, Mom made them. Between the saltiness of the prosciutto, the creamy brie, and the sweetness of Stonebar's fig jam layered in, they were pretty damn delicious.

A second later, Frankie appeared and barreled into me for a hug. "I'm so happy you're here," she said softly. Heaven forbid anyone hear that Frankie Kinkade knew how to be vulnerable.

"Are you?" I grumbled.

"Of course I am." She smiled at me, the twinkle in

her eyes devious. "There's no better present than seeing you give Nox the death glare for the last ten minutes."

I turned that glare on her, and when she saw it, all she did was laugh.

"It's okay to like her," she whispered loudly.

"So, I guess you don't want your present then?" I changed subjects. "If my expression is enough for you."

"What? Of course, I want my present." She pressed her hands together, begging.

I drew out the second and then reached behind me where their gifts sat wrapped in deconstructed paper bags. Aurora had been the one to wrap them this morning, but I'd keep that to myself.

I handed them their gifts, noting how Gigi, while curious, was far too interested in when she was going to get to say what she'd come over here to say, her knobby fingers tapping on her arm.

"Thank you," Lou said before she'd even opened it.

Frankie tore at the paper, shredding it to get to what was underneath while Lou carefully peeled the tape apart at the seams, keeping the paper otherwise intact as she pulled out the frame.

"Kit..."

"I love it," Frankie gushed, staring at her drawing. "What is it?"

I chuckled.

"Oh my gosh, it's a shell, Frankie," Lou murmured under her breath.

"Obviously, it's a shell." Frankie rolled her eyes. "I know what a conch shell looks like."

"Not a conch shell," I began, grabbing the edges of both their frames and lowering them flat so they could see each other's. "They're Dog Whelks—or Dogwinkles."

They laughed.

"They're the same?" Lou murmured, peering closer at the drawings I'd finished after my conversation with Aurora earlier in the week. "They look different though. These lines. Even the shape of this one is a little wider..."

"Yeah. Same species, but each one is unique." I nodded. *Just like they were.*

They both looked at me, then the drawings, then at each other.

"Was this Aurora's idea?" Frankie broke the silence, always searching for a way to keep the conversation light when her emotions got too much.

I tensed. "No. She just collected the shells." *And then told me about them.*

They both looked at me disbelievingly, but neither stare was as strong as Gigi's.

"Girls, I think Jamie is ready to do the toast. Why don't you start ushering your guests outside?"

They both hugged me with a quick thank you and then vanished, leaving me with the formidable purple-haired matriarch of the family.

"Gigi." My chest rumbled.

"What are you doing over here?"

"Well, I was talking to Lou—"

"Why is Aurora in the kitchen with your cousins?" she demanded, giving her foot a small stomp.

I tensed. "Because Nox offered to make her another drink."

She stared at me for so long, I wondered if she'd had

a stroke, but I knew there was no chance I was getting off that easy. "What is wrong with you, Christopher?"

My teeth locked. "You don't have enough time for that answer."

"No, I don't have enough time for your horseshit," she huffed, and then pointed a knobby finger in Aurora's direction, unmistakable to everyone in the room. "You should be in there with her. She came here with you."

"No, we rode over together from the lighthouse where we both work." I wasn't having this conversation right here, right now, or with her.

Gigi's arm fell and she shook her head in dismay, sadness shining bright in her eyes when she looked at me. "Why don't you want to live, Christopher?"

"Excuse me?" I practically choked.

"What did your fortune say?"

I fought not to roll my eyes. "Chasing dawn."

Her head bobbed. "You have to chase the light, Christopher. You know how important it is. The light." She paused and then slowly turned, looking at Aurora and then back at me. "Chase the light. She's right in front of you."

And then, like a switch, her serious intensity flicked off, and her bubbliness switched back on.

"Ailene! We need the champagne!" She patted my hands and hurried over to Mom, leaving me standing there, steeped in the urgency of her words.

I knew how important the light was...for the lighthouse. For the ships. For the shore. For safety. *For shelter from the storm*. But that wasn't the same. *Or was it?*

Aurora laughed again at something Max said to

Nox, her whole face brightening. Like everything else she did, when she smiled, her happiness consumed every inch of her expression. From the wide white of her smile to the dimples on her cheeks, I'd noticed her biggest smiles made the swells of her cheeks bump the bottom of her glasses. Only once her smile dimmed did she realize they weren't sitting right and she'd have to reach up and adjust them.

I'd noted that in my logbook two days ago—a journal that had gone from a few brief mentions of her presence and studies when she arrived to daily notations of the numerous things I learned by watching her. Talking to her. Touching her. *And then there were the sketches.*

I wasn't a portrait artist by any means, but I couldn't...*not*...try to capture her. Small, rough sketches in the margins of my log. I knew I was an idiot for doing it, but at some point, she'd leave the lighthouse, and those notes would be all I had to remember.

My eyes flicked around the room, looking for anything else to focus on. Mom and Gigi were talking to Violet, Harper, and some of Lou's friends from town. Jamie and Lou were discussing something by the door before Lou hurried off. No sign of Frankie now, so I assumed Lou had been sent to find her sister so Jamie could give the birthday toast. But inevitably, my attention worked its way back to the kitchen like a yo-yo, unable to wander far from the woman who I tried to pretend I wasn't attached to.

This time, when Nox gently touched Aurora's elbow to claim her attention, it pushed me over the edge. I stalked from the very edge of the room—from safety—over to her.

Maybe Gigi was right. Maybe Aurora was the light, and all I wanted was for her to drown out my darkness.

"Aurora." I said her name even though she'd turned to me as I approached, like she could sense me coming. I purposely put myself between her and Nox, my body blocking him from any further contact.

"Kit. Good to see you." Max extended a hand.

I shook it quickly and then pulled back. "I think they want everyone outside by the fire for the toast." My hand went to the small of Aurora's back, her shiver only adding to my unwarranted sense of possession. I didn't wait for their response before guiding her toward the back door.

"YOUR FAMILY IS SO NICE," SHE SAID AS I LED US down the steps to the paver patio off the basement where the fire pit was.

"Too nice," I muttered, stopping near one of the main beams that supported the deck above, needing to have something at my back.

"Thank you, everyone, for coming," Jamie said, putting a stop to whatever she was about to say as he stepped forward, a beer in his hand. "Frankie...Lou... I've always said there was a reason you were due on April Fool's but arrived the day after, and no, it wasn't to give you a pass for all your pranks." Everyone laughed, and Frankie faked a pout before winking at him. "You brought a lightness, laughter, and a level of love to our lives that never would've existed otherwise.

The things that the two of you have accomplished and will accomplish make me not only proud to be your brother and excited to see what the future holds...but also a little bit sorry for whichever men try their luck for a chance with you." He paused, let the laughter start to rumble, and then added, "Especially you, Frankie."

My sister's mock gasp quickly dissolved into a wide smile, but it was Aurora's soft laugh that caught my attention. Like she knew I was looking, her head tipped toward me, a breeze catching the ribbon in her hair and loosening the bow.

"Shit," I muttered, snagging the fabric in my fingertips before it blew off altogether.

Her eyes lifted to my face. I focused on the ribbon—on tying a new bow in her hair—and not what it looked like. *Or the flicker of warmth I felt.* My fingers worked the ribbon securely onto her head, holding it in place while I formed the bow. Years of doing this for the twins should've made my fingers move deftly, instead, they worked clumsily and slowly, clunking around like the stupid thing that beat in my chest—thrown off by her nearness.

"Happy birthday, Frankie and Lou." Everyone raised their drinks and cheered, the sound ringing painfully in my ears and snapping me from the moment.

The cheers. The chants. The runners. The lump in my throat swelled. *Fuck.* I squeezed my eyes shut and chugged all the water in my paper cup, trying to block out the memory that wouldn't leave me in peace. My heart pounded. I could feel the rumble of the runners. The excitement in the air. And I knew it was coming... something bad. The chill in my spine was the same as

I'd felt before Smith came back into the tent and unloaded his weapon.

"Kit..."

My eyes slammed open. Aurora swam into focus in front of me. Her big, warm brown stare searching mine with concern. *Breathe, Kit. Fucking breathe.* My hands slid to her face, holding her like she was my life raft—my way back to the shore of sanity. *Breathe, and it'll pass—*

Boom.

Boom. Boom. Boom.

Instinct trumped everything.

"*Get down!*" I roared and hauled Aurora to the ground, covering her with my body.

There was shouting. Curses. A few more bangs as I shielded myself over her, my back on fire. *Shit. Fucking shit.*

Not again.

Not another bomb.

Not again.

"*Kit!*" Jamie's voice cracked through the wall of adrenaline. He shook me violently, and my eyes flung open. Aurora stared up at me, tears glistening in her eyes.

"Kit..." It was the softness of her voice that shattered me—that brought reality crashing down through the flashback. She was okay. No one was in danger. *The noise wasn't a bomb.*

"Fuck." I shoved up off her, Jamie's grip on my arm helping lift my weight.

"It was fireworks," he rasped low. "Nox told Richie not to, but he didn't know—he wanted it to be a surprise—"

I heard what he was saying, but all I saw were the stares. Dozens of eyes looking at me, almost all filled with pity. The hum of concern buzzed through the silence.

My head whipped toward Aurora. I reached down and helped her stand, acid burning up my throat. "Are you all right?" I demanded, scanning her for signs of injury.

"Oh, just fine," she said, but when she went to nod, I felt her sway.

Fuck, I was an idiot. Careless. A fool. *Broken.*

I knew better than to come here, but I was selfish. I thought I'd be okay. I thought it would be okay. *What could possibly go wrong in a few hours?* Everything. The answer was everything.

This was what happened when I got close.

"I have to go."

"Kit—"

I jerked out of Jamie's hold and stormed around the house. Bile worked its way into my throat with every beat of my heart. Sweat started to soak through my shirt, the wind feeling like whips of ice on my chest. But better that than the burning. *Better sweat than scars.*

"Kit!"

I spun when she grabbed my arm, hating the way it made her gasp. I closed my eyes for a second, but instead of relief, I flashbacked to that day, the smell of my own burning flesh filling my nostrils.

"I'm leaving." My voice sounded like it had been hit with a pipe bomb, all its smoothness blown to bits. "I have to go." I yanked open my truck door, nausea rolling through me.

"Let me drive you," she insisted, one hand holding the door, the other extended for my keys.

I glared at her and clutched the keys until the metal bit into my palm. I wished like hell I could hold onto them and refuse her, but not only was she right—I shouldn't be driving like this—behind her several yards back stood Jamie, Mom, my sisters, Nox, and Gigi, all ready to jump in if Aurora couldn't get through.

Fuck, I wouldn't take their pity. I'd already taken enough.

"Fine." I dumped the keys in her hand and stalked to the other side of the truck.

"JUST TAKE IT. BRING IT BACK…WHENEVER," I ordered gruffly, slamming the passenger door and heading toward the lighthouse.

She needed to take my truck and go back to her B&B. Back to town. Back to anywhere that was away from here. *From me.*

I wiped the sweat from my brow, my heart still slamming into the front of my chest. Every time my eyes shut, I saw the dust. The smoke. The debris. *Fuck. Fucking fuck.* I walked faster toward the water— desperate to drown out the sound of screams with the crash of the sea. *God, there were so many screams.* I reached up, my fists pressing to the sides of my head as I forced myself to focus on breathing.

In and out. Just breathe. *In and out.* It was over. *In and out.*

The whip of the breeze hit me in the chest, sinking salt air into my lungs, the brine burning in the open wound of my memories. It welcomed me back to the edge. Back to where nothing and no one else could stand to be...where the only things that survived were covered in hard shells just to survive...back to the only place fit for a man like me.

I reached the house, the door swinging wide as I stumbled inside. The scent of her hit me first. Orange and vanilla. *Since when had she become so infused into my home?*

My life?

"Kit!"

Shit. I hadn't even noticed she'd shut the truck off—that she'd followed me.

"You need to leave." I whipped around and ordered like a snarling beast.

Aurora stood in the doorway, her cheeks stained with pink, her eyes glistening beneath the rims of her glasses. The wind took her dark curls and sent them fluttering around her face. The bow I'd fixed in her hair was long gone.

She shook her head. "No, I'm not leaving—"

"You have to!" I roared and grabbed her upper arms, hauling her right to me like a glutton for punishment.

"I'm not here to study you, Kit. I'm here to support you. Stop pushing me away." She fought back with her brave words.

"Pushing you—" I broke off with a bitter laugh, lowering my head so our noses just touched. "There is no supporting me. No fixing me. *No understanding me,*" I declared with a low, raw voice and then covered her mouth with mine, spearing into her soft warmth like I could scorch every inch from ever having wanted my touch.

I kissed her like a lunatic, lust and loathing whipping through me with gale force, not caring that the door was open. Not caring that the wind howled through the house. Not caring about anything except her warmth.

Her tongue met mine, tangled and dueled, stroked and seduced. She was smart. Weeks of steady observation and dozens of kisses meant she knew how to be just as punishing as I did, but in a way that was deceptively alluring. The heat of her mouth drew me in. Soft and warm, she drew my tongue to every corner, letting me uncover moan after moan of pleasure.

I crowded her back toward the door even as I held her tighter, at war with myself whether to send her away or pull her closer.

Her small hands clutched my shirt, the heat of them sinking through the damn fabric.

Fuck.

I pulled back with a deep groan. Removing my lips from hers was like peeling the flesh off my bones. *How had she become so necessary? So vital? How had she become the only thing that kept the darkness at bay?*

"This isn't an experiment anymore, Aurora," I rasped, my forehead pressed to hers, our heavy breaths colliding into a fog between us. I searched for her eyes. Wide, bright, wanting. "You need to go." And she needed to have the strength to do it because I, apparently, didn't.

"No."

A shudder cracked through my big frame, my voice

coming out even more hoarse than before. "If you stay, I won't stop."

Her eyes opened a fraction wider, understanding the implication. *The warning.*

"If I leave, I'll never know," came her soft reply.

A groan ripped from my chest. "You should be afraid." *Of me. Of this.*

I'd just thrown her to the ground, dragging her into my own personal nightmare without warning. *How many ways did I need to spell it out that I was dangerous?*

"I was once." She slid her arms around my neck, her fingers curling into the hair at my nape. "I'm not anymore."

And then she pulled my mouth back to hers, braving my darkness like the sun charges through the horizon to fight off the night.

I'd warned her. So many fucking times, I'd warned her of the danger. But she got close to me anyway. Closer and closer to my sharp and craggy shores, braving the swells of my stoicism and solitude.

I'd warned her. It couldn't be my fault that she didn't heed my warning.

CHAPTER 14
AURORA

I wouldn't let this man go back into his shell. Not when he had so much to give. So many people who cared about him. So much life that he deserved. *So much light he brought to the world.* I didn't know exactly what happened back at Ailene's, but logical deduction gave me a pretty good idea. Fireworks weren't a good idea around someone who had PTSD.

Tomorrow, I'd wake up with some bumps and bruises from having been less-than-glamorously tackled to the ground, but none of that mattered compared to how much I would hurt if I couldn't reach him—if I couldn't be with him now.

I grabbed hold of his arms—his shirt—anything to hang onto and let my grip dig deep. I'd take whatever he had to give, no matter how sharp and shattered it was, no matter how many cuts and scrapes I'd leave with. I wasn't going to walk away from the chance to know all of him, including every broken piece.

"Aurora..." he growled, slanting his mouth over mine.

He kissed me like the oxygen in my lungs was the source of his survival. His hands cupped my face, angling my head until the kiss became so deep I didn't know where I ended and he began. It seemed impossible, but it wasn't. All the logical foundations in my brain crumbled against Kit's touch.

His other kisses had been fervent. Demanding. Ravenous. But this one was desperate—as though my kiss was the only safe place for him right now. *As though I was the only safe place for him now.*

Again, he lifted me, and I felt that same thrill—that my curves I loved so much, curves that weren't the standard of beauty—made no difference in how he treated me...wanted me. If anything, they made him want me more.

In the short steps to the bedroom, I pulled my blouse over my head and let it land somewhere on the floor.

His hold on me didn't loosen as he lowered us to the edge of the mattress, keeping me on his lap. My skirt bunched as my legs widened around his hips, the hard length of him sitting against my core.

His hands roamed my back, flicking the clasp of my bra open and groaning as my breasts spilled free. I heard the material land...somewhere...but I couldn't focus on anything when his mouth latched over my nipple.

I arched and moaned, his hand sliding to claim the other weight, thumbing the hard peak as his mouth laved the other one. Everything about me was so sensitive. And it only seemed to be that way with him, as though Kit had unlocked a pleasure switch in my brain that set all my senses in overdrive.

In minutes, I was rocking against him, needing the friction against my clit.

"Kit..." I begged, my fingers sliding along his beard, through his hair, my nails scoring his nape.

I wanted him naked. Me naked. I wanted the hardness I felt underneath me to finally be inside me. I wanted it so badly, my inside muscles clenched and released to the point of pain.

But Kit...Kit was both the lighthouse and the storm, thrashing me about on the waves of pleasure even as he guided me toward the warm beacon of release.

His mouth slid to my other breast, the tip so sensitive from the torture of his fingers that I cried out at the warm suction, a wave of wet heat rushing between my thighs.

I felt his groan against my skin. "You have no idea what you do to me.".

My mind scrambled. Did he not see what he was doing to me? I was practically melting from his touch.

"Kit, please," I whimpered and grappled for the fabric of his shirt.

He tensed, everything stopping, and I realized what I'd done—where my hands were: his back. Slowly, his head tipped up, my nipple sliding free from his mouth as he searched for my eyes. Panic settled into my bones like a cold chill. *He couldn't stop now*.

"Show me," I pleaded. "Show me what I do to you." I drew a ragged breath. "Show me everything."

Pain lanced the depths of his eyes, spearing through the last of his walls and sending darkness bleeding into their orbs, and then his chin dipped ever so slightly. Resignation. Acceptance. *A plea*.

Slowly, I gathered the fabric in my fingers. His

mouth returned to my breast, not to distract me—though it was impossible to fight the waves of pleasure that began to lap along my skin—but to distract himself as I bared his torso.

All those experiments, and I'd never seen him without his shirt. I'd never pushed the limit because I wasn't willing to lose whatever we had. *I was afraid.* But after today, I couldn't be afraid anymore—*I wasn't afraid anymore*—to risk what we had in order to know if something more was possible.

When the tips of my fingers touched down on his bare skin, he shuddered so violently that it felt like I shuddered, too. Cautiously, under the guise of gripping the fabric, I gently charted the quarter inch of skin available to me...and realized two things. First, his skin was so warm, burning up under my fingers. And second, it didn't feel like normal skin. It was smooth—too smooth—and then broken up by unnatural ridges.

Scars. My palms flattened on his back, his shirt forgotten. *His entire back was gnarled with scars.*

My cry of distress died in my throat when I realized Kit was frozen—his entire body as hard as stone. The knot in his jaw thrummed, and the heat of his breath blew in ragged bursts against my skin. *Touching him was torturing him...and I didn't want to torture him.*

I slid my hands back to his shirt and pulled it up, his arms moving to comply. Once it was gone, I framed his face, savoring the feel of his soft stubble, and pulled his mouth to mine. The kiss broke his trance, and heat ignited like gasoline on an open flame, a different kind of hunger eking into every corner of the kiss.

His mouth traveled back down to my breasts, and I moaned at the way he worshipped them. Licked and sucked...but it was the soft bites that drove me insane. Little marks of possession. Pain mingled with pleasure. His big hands roamed the sides of my legs, bunching the bright fabric of my skirt even higher until one hand coasted underneath it.

A whimper pressed through my lips when his fingers traced the seam between my leg and hip, back and forth, each time getting closer and closer to where I wanted him most.

"Kit, please," I begged, my hips rocking with a mind of their own.

His teeth locked on the peak of my nipple, holding it tight enough to make me gasp as he sent his hand gliding along the edge of my underwear and then sank it between us. As soon as his fingers hit the knot of my clit, his teeth released my nipple, and the flood of sensations made me see stars.

"Kit!" I bucked against his hand, those skilled fingers gliding through my slick folds all the way to my entrance and back.

My body sizzled and sparked. My core clenched, aching for something more than before—something close to everything.

"You're drenched, sea star," he groaned appreciatively, pinning my clit prisoner as his thumb rubbed it again and again. "So wet for me. So fucking responsive."

He'd said those words a dozen times to me, and each time, it sent a thrill of desire spiraling through my nerves.

"I'm going to come," I breathed, my eyes rolling backward at the next stroke of his finger. Another stroke, and the hunger of my orgasm started to sink its teeth into my body.

I held my breath, waiting for the next touch that would let it devour me, waiting for the exquisite relief that release would bring. I waited right on the brink, and then his hand disappeared, sending my senses tumbling back down.

"Not yet," Kit cooed as I tried to catch my breath. Slowly, I watched him bring his fingers to his mouth and suck them clean, staring at me the whole time. I knew what he saw. Flush cheeks. Parted lips. Desire-drunk eyes.

"I need you," I murmured, unashamed.

His jaw tensed. "Aurora—"

"I need you, Kit. Please."

There was no thinking. No stopping. *No warning.*

In an instant, I was on my back on the bed, my skirt and underwear nothing more than a flutter of colorful fabric floating to the floor. I gasped in a breath in the same amount of time it took for him to undo his pants and shove them below his cock—the thick, straining length seeming even larger than before.

I reminded myself that I'd fit him—*or part of him*—in my mouth. Promised myself that he was going to fit and I wasn't going to be torn apart. But before I could believe all my rationalizations, he was there—the blunt tip that I'd licked and sucked, memorized with teeth and tongue, was pressed to the seam of my core, my slickness letting him sink inside.

"Fuck, you're so wet for me. So needy for my cock. I can't—" Kit swore like a man who'd lost his grip on the shore, the waves of want dragging him into the deep, and then he plunged inside me. Fully. Irrevocably. With a single stroke.

It was only the slight prick of discomfort that

reminded me of the truth I'd forgotten in my desperation to feel him—*that I was a virgin*.

Explanations and apologies charged to the tip of my tongue. I'd forgotten. Sort of. Not really, but it just didn't matter. My virginity wasn't a variable I wanted included in the equation. It didn't even hurt anymore; there was...too much of him to hurt. I'd thought fitting him in my mouth was a feat, but this...my body felt stretched to the seams. Stuffed and full in a way I'd never felt before—in a way that made me realize how empty I'd feel without him.

I dragged my eyes slowly upward, drinking in the sight of his taut abdomen and muscled chest. The delicious smattering of hair that darkened his golden skin. The cords of his neck drawn so tight, I could see every beat of his pulse slam against the skin. And his face...his face was equally strained, but his eyes...his eyes bored into mine with an intensity I felt all the way to my bones.

Air dumped into my lungs. *He knew*. It was the only reason he looked like he did—like he was on the verge of exploding. *I had to explain*.

"Kit—" I wiggled.

"Don't," he ordered and grabbed my hips so tight, I knew I'd find shadows of his fingerprints on my skin tomorrow morning. "Don't move."

My mouth parted. Was something wrong? Had I done something wrong? *Aside from not telling him that this was my first time*.

"You're so fucking tight, Aurora," he ground out, and I could almost believe it was a bad thing. *Almost*. "*Fuck*," he swore again.

"I don't understand..." My throat bobbed.

His glare sharpened, and he forced an exhale through his drawn lips. "You're so fucking hot and wet and tight around me..." He took a slow inhale, his eyes squeezing for a second. "I haven't done this...in a decade. And your sweet little pussy feels so fucking good..." Another groan interrupted from the depths of his chest. "So fucking good that if I move—*if you move* —I'm going to come."

Understanding hit me like a spark to kindling. It wasn't me—he hadn't stopped because I was a virgin.

"So...it's good?"

"Too good. Too fucking good, sea star." He breathed out a sound that was somewhere between a laugh and a groan. "I'm so hard...so close...I'm fucking leaking inside you. Dripping cum because I'm so damn close to bursting."

I shivered, my skin pebbling with desire. Here I was, the virgin, and he was the one hardly able to control himself. Years of pent-up sexual longing hauling him to the brink of sanity and control.

Meanwhile, I had years of wondering—of knowing in theory what this was supposed to be like. Testing it a few times with various toys. But it never felt like this. Firm silicone was an entirely different sensation than this hard, heavy flesh that stretched me to the point of splitting.

"Christ," he groaned, and I felt his cock pulse inside me, the sensation so strange and delicious at the same time.

"Kit—"

"Weeks," he snapped, holding me steady. "Weeks I've dreamed of nothing else but sinking my cock inside you. Every time my fingers...my tongue...touched you...

tasted you...I've wanted this. Every time I fucked your mouth—stuffed myself down your throat—I thought about this, but it's nothing—*fuck*," he swore when my inner muscles flexed around him, fury glinting in his eyes.

I sucked in a breath. I hadn't meant to do it, my body was just responding—*wanting* more.

"I'm sorry—"

"Touch your tits," he ordered low, fire swirling in his eyes.

I licked my lips, and my hands slid to my breasts like they were entirely under his command.

"Knead them for me," he growled, and I complied, the caress oozing warmth low in my stomach. "That's it. Push them together."

I started to shiver and his grip doubled down on my hips, his lips curling in warning.

"Touch your nipples like I do."

I bit my lip and framed the sensitive peaks with my fingers.

"Pinch and then roll," he ordered. "That's what sets you off—what makes you so fucking wet..." He trailed off with a groan, and I knew it was because my body was milking him, but there was nothing I could do to stop it. "I need you to come for me, Aurora. Come all over me."

My lips parted, understanding dawning. He couldn't let go of me—of my waist—because anything more than this would send him over the edge too soon. All of this—he could let go at any moment and put an end to his torture, but he wouldn't because he wanted my release, too.

He gave his hips a small rock and made both of us

shudder. He was right. He was so big—so thick—he rubbed right along that spot his fingers had found, the one that set me ablaze.

"Now touch your clit," he ground out.

Like a freed anchor, my right hand sank like a lead weight between my thighs. I bit down hard into my cheek, feeling the way my sex was spread wide to fit his girth, my swollen clit sitting exposed just begging for touch.

"Rub hard the way I do."

At the first press of my thumb, my body started to shake. His too, if I was seeing it right.

"Faster." The command was deadly low. "Show me how I make you come."

"Kit..." I trembled, my body at war with itself, part wanting to break apart, the other desperate to hold myself together for him. My fingers moved clumsily, chasing pleasure just as furiously as it distracted me from claiming it. "Kit, please." My pleasure stumbled. "I need more—I need you, *please.*"

"I warned you," he said low, so low and so strained the words were almost incoherent, as he released one hand, shoved my fingers out of the way, and then drove my clit over the edge with one deft rub of his fingers.

I screamed and bucked as my orgasm took me, and Kit went wild.

His roar filled the room as he pulled out and slammed into me with such force the bed—maybe even the very ground underneath—began to shake. One thrust was all it took—one thrust through my spasming muscles to make him come. His cock erupted inside me, warmth flooding my already slick pussy. But one release didn't stop him...it wasn't enough.

I knew I wasn't the only one capable of multiple orgasms, but this time was different. He wasn't going to come again just because he could. He needed a second release like it was the only thing going to keep him alive.

Bright spots flickered in my vision, pleasure swelling all of my cells from my release, but instead of floating down from the high, the friction of his drives pulled me higher. My head spun, and I grabbed into the sheets, twisting and turning the fabric, clinging to anything as he pummeled against my G-spot, the sensation using one orgasm to build to another, even bigger one.

"*Fuck,* you feel so good." His ragged curses filled the space between the slaps of his flesh against mine, driving me into the mattress with the force of each thrust. He stared between us, watching his cock sink all the way inside me over and over again. "Look at you taking my cock. So beautiful." I was already melting, my limbs held together by nothing but skin, but his words made me dissolve.

"Oh god, Kit," I panted. Begged. Cried. My heart beat so fast, it felt like it was going to trip and stumble straight out of my chest, but he didn't stop.

I forced my eyes open and was met with the sight of his massive body glistening with a sheen of sweat. His muscles moved with a kind of fluid beauty I wished I was artistic enough to capture.

I didn't last. I couldn't. Not when I looked up and saw him like that—so beautiful. So strong. So commanding yet vulnerable. Reality exploded around me, and in that instant, the thought that I'd never get enough of this—of him—swept through me so powerfully, I thought I might shatter.

"That's it, sea star. Come again so I can fill you up," he growled, angling his hips so he hit harder on my G-spot.

My head swam. Spun. *Sank.* My second orgasm stacked on top of the first, my G-spot thrumming for another release, my core pulling him deeper—harder. I felt my nails dig into my palms through the material of the sheets. I stopped breathing. Thinking. Nothing existed except the pressure of him inside me, and my release swept me under.

My scream pierced my lungs as I came again with his name on my lips. My eyes slammed shut, and my body bowed like a fish out of water, bending and tensing as pleasure replaced the very oxygen in my cells.

He followed me over the edge a second later with a low, guttural noise, leaving the two of us as a tangle of loose limbs and gasping breaths.

"Wow. That was..." I didn't have a word. I hoped he did, but instead his response was to swipe his thumb across my overly sensitive clit. I bucked, pleasure slicing through me like the sharpest of knives.

"Kit," I whimpered, my head lolling to the side as I searched for his gaze. "I can't."

"If you can talk, you can come," he grunted, the side of his mouth quirking up ever so slightly.

I opened my mouth, thinking to quip back with something, when the fullness inside me disappeared. His heavy cock hung in front of him, *hard* evidence that he wasn't done with me yet. But then his smile disappeared, the whole of his expression turning ashen.

My brow creased, and I tried to follow his gaze. He

lifted his cock, angled the massive length, and then I realized...my heart plummeted into my stomach.

Between the mix of our desires, the distinct color of blood streaked his length.

I pushed up on my elbows, my heart racing. "Kit—"

His eyes snapped to mine, furious. "You were a virgin?"

CHAPTER 15
KIT

A virgin. She was a virgin.

Her soft "yes" only confirmed the truth smeared along my dick in red. *My bare dick.* I looked between her legs, her pussy swollen and puffy from how I'd fucked her, and leaking, leaking because—

"We didn't use a condom."

I was broken *and* an idiot. A couple of fireworks, a decade without sex, and a woman I couldn't deny were all it took to eviscerate what brain cells I had left. *"Fuck."*

"It's okay." Aurora sat up taller, reaching for me.

I was an asshole the way I jerked from her touch. But I couldn't think when her hands were on me—not about anything except wanting her. My eyes dropped to her pussy, a different broken beast inside me still hungry for that third orgasm I'd been about to chase with her.

"I know you've never had sex before, but please tell me you understand what it means for me to fuck you unprotected?" I said between clenched teeth.

She glared at me and charged, "Of course, I understand. What I'm trying to tell you is that I...track my cycle, and I'm not ovulating right now. I can show you my app—"

"No." I held up a hand. I believed her. I also didn't need to see calendar proof of how many more days she wasn't ovulating...how many more days I'd have to take her like this.

But a virgin.

"Why didn't you tell me?"

"It didn't matter."

My brow arched.

"I'm an adult, Kit. I should've stopped being a virgin long before now"—she adjusted her glasses—"but I haven't."

"Why didn't you tell me?"

Her throat bobbed. "It didn't hurt."

I hissed out a breath. That confession soothed something inside of me—something that hated myself for hurting her. For not making her first time...whatever it would've been if it hadn't been with me. Instead, I'd taken her like a beast who'd been starved for a decade and was just given a feast.

"Kit...it did everything but hurt," she promised huskily, her gaze sliding down to my cock, which still hung heavy and loaded in front of me. *A beast that was still hungry.*

Slowly, I kneeled down in front of her, my hands reaching for each knee and gently stroking the soft skin there before sliding my fingers higher to gently trace along her seam. She was slick. She could take me again. But it would hurt.

Bile rose in my throat. She'd never had more than

these fingers inside her, and tonight, I hadn't even given her those to stretch her. All I felt was her softness. All I saw was her light. And all I could do to keep the darkness at bay was to bury myself in her. Without warning. Without a warm-up.

"Why didn't you tell me?" I asked again, softer this time, my fingers gently teasing her clit, savoring the almost instant response from her body. "I would've..."

Would've what? Stopped? Sent her away? I gritted my teeth. I was honest enough to admit that wasn't a possibility. As soon as I closed the door to the house, the only way she was leaving was if it was by her choice.

Her hand cupped my cheek, jarring me from my thoughts. Twin blue eyes pierced mine, compassion eking from every corner of her gaze.

"I didn't want you to," she said softly. "I didn't want you to do—to be anything but who you are."

I grabbed her wrist and turned my face into her palm, pressing my lips to its center and inhaling deep. Orange and vanilla.

"I want you, Kit," she breathed. "Please, don't stop."

I swallowed through the tightness in my throat. I wasn't going to stop—not for her at least.

"Lie back," I commanded low.

I turned my head and pressed my lips to the inside of her knee. And then the inside of her thigh. Higher and higher, I lined her skin with the marks from my lips until my face was in front of her pussy.

"Kit..."

I blew a stream of warm air over her, reveling in the way she shuddered.

I gently pushed two fingers inside her, giving her

body something to clench as I lowered my mouth to her pussy, swirling my tongue over her clit.

"Oh, god," she cooed, and I felt myself smile a little.

I might not have hurt her, but she still deserved better.

"Kit." Her hands clutched my scalp. "I'm going to come."

Yes. I knew she was. I could taste it, the way she was slick and sweet on my tongue. The tremor of her cunt around my fingers. I growled, setting my tongue in a pattern over her that didn't take more than half a minute to claim another climax, the rush of her release soothing the guilt I had for the way I'd made her come the first time.

But I didn't stop there. If I didn't bring her to the brink of exhaustion, I knew Aurora—I knew she'd want to take care of me, too. And she'd already done more than enough of that—too much of that—already. So, my tongue lapped. Lapped her desire and mine where it leaked. And then when she stopped trembling, I started to lick her again. Firm strokes of my tongue over her swollen bud, dragging her to another peak.

"Kit..." Her voice was weak.

I hooked her legs over my shoulders and set my tongue harder to her, swirling and flicking, until she quivered and melted again to the tune of my name.

"Please..."

"If you can talk, you can come," I reminded her somewhere between orgasms two and three.

On orgasm four, she drenched my face with her release.

Orgasm five...orgasm five I claimed with barely a press of my tongue on her overstimulated nerves. The flutter of her inner muscles wasn't as strong, and I knew I could only give her maybe one more before she needed a break.

Her head lolled to one side and then the other, and when I pushed her to that sixth orgasm, she hardly made a sound, her body sagging in defeat against pleasure.

She hadn't passed out, but one more, and she would. Her eyes barely tracked me as I went to the bathroom and warmed a cloth, returning to carefully clean her and myself before tucking her under the covers, her limbs completely limp with exhaustion.

"Don't leave," she murmured so softly that I should've pretended not to hear her. Should've pretended it was never said and walked out of the room to let her sleep—to spend the next several hours counting all the ways I'd fucked up tonight and trying to figure out how to right them all.

But I didn't pretend.

I didn't even hesitate before sliding under the covers. I'd add climbing into bed next to her—*naked*—as one more problem I created for myself tonight. One more problem I didn't know how to solve.

"I won't," I rumbled and pulled her to me.

I couldn't. That was the real answer. I couldn't leave her. And that was the biggest problem of them all.

I WOKE BEFORE THE ALARM THAT I HADN'T SET— before the dawn I knew was coming. I looked down at the sleeping woman on my chest, her softness stirring my dick, that was still begging for that last release. *And that was the last thing she needed.*

Carefully, I slid from the bed, yanked on a pair of sweats, forgoing a shirt because I was afraid the creak of the dresser would wake her. I took one more long glance at her stretched naked in my bed—my own personal siren—and then stalked toward the tower.

Emotions. Urges. Memories. They ripped me apart inside. I shouldn't have let her stay last night. I should've forced her to leave. But I was so fucking... *fucked*...that I didn't even have the strength to save her from myself.

I grabbed my notebook and climbed the stairs to the lamp room, searching for the solace I found every day in these tasks. I checked the battery and the light. Wiped down the windows and the rest of the glass. But as I started to make notes in my journal for the previous day, dawn bled along the horizon, and before I realized what I was doing, words turned into lines—into curves. Full, luscious curves and tight rings of dark curls among the rumpled sheets of my bed.

"Kit."

My eyes snapped up, my hand closing the pen inside the notebook at the first sound of her voice. I saw her in the reflection in the glass; her hair was wild, and she wore one of my shirts—*the one I should've been wearing,* I noted grimly as her attention immediately went to my back.

I swallowed over the ball of acid in my throat.

I knew what she saw. The inhuman tapestry of scars that mangled my back.

She stepped closer, and the urge I thought I'd feel to

pull back—to turn around—never came. I held the rail tight like a wounded animal unable to move—unable to do anything except exist at the mercy of her touch.

"Can I..." She searched for my eyes.

Gritting my teeth, I nodded and braced myself. Like earlier, the first brush of her fingertips was like straight electricity to my skin. The scarred skin didn't... work like the rest. It was tight. Uncomfortable to move in certain ways. And the nerve endings...they hadn't healed the same either. Nothing had.

"Sorry."

"Don't stop," I ordered when she began to pull away.

It wasn't painful. Not like it used to be, I realized with more than a little surprise. Her fingers skated along my shoulder blades, retracing her first touch at the border of the marred skin before moving lower.

The skin used to be so sensitive, it would hurt to even wear clothes, the softest fabric feeling like it was knitted of nettles. *So don't wear a shirt.* Simple solution, right? *Wrong.* No shirt meant constant reminders to my family of what I'd suffered—how I was still suffering— and that made it even worse. So, I stayed in my room at Mom's house and bore the pain of clothes when I did come out. *But that didn't fix the problem either.*

I shivered, and Aurora paused. "Are you sure?"

"Keep going," I rasped.

When her fingers moved again, I let my eyes drift closed. I let her touch guide me through the darkness— to its center. After everything, she deserved to know.

"After I was discharged from Walter Reed, I came back here—back home," I began, my voice hoarse, like the memory lane I walked down was made of rocky gravel rather than smooth pavement. *One more thing to deter me from venturing down it.* "After months in the hospital, all I wanted was to get back to life—a new life." I swallowed hard and clung to the feel of her touch. "I wanted to start over. Do something... completely different. I painted a lot while I was in the hospital. Small watercolors of places from my deployments. One of the nurses saw them—told Mom that her uncle was a veteran who owned a gallery in Boston that only displayed artwork done by enlisted or retired servicemen and gave her the number."

Tension rippled through me, and Aurora paused again, finding my eyes.

"Don't stop," I repeated, now unsure if I was talking to her or myself.

Her eyes softened, and she flattened her whole palm to my back, claiming much more of the scarred skin than just her fingertips had.

"At first, I wasn't sure. Wasn't sure how things were going to go when I left the hospital or what I wanted to do," I went on. "I came home eleven years ago yesterday."

I heard her inhale in surprise. "On their birthday?"

A brief smile took hold of my lips. "They said it was the best gift they ever got." My voice cracked at the end, recalling the emotion in theirs. I cleared my throat and continued, "After that, I just wanted to be normal—didn't want to worry them. They loved my paintings, and begged me to call the owner of the gallery to show my work. So, I did. Martin Bruce. He was just about to get on a plane when I called, but he didn't miss a beat. Told me to gather my best pieces and meet him at his gallery in two weeks when he was back from vacation; I said I'd be there."

I stared at the glass, watching her brow start to pull together like her brain knew there were pieces to connect but couldn't.

Meanwhile, all the pieces were together for me, their edges sharp, cutting through all the armor I'd layered on top of the memory for over a decade.

"I drove into the city that day. Traffic was crazy, so I had to park a ways away. I remember walking to the gallery, wondering why the hell it seemed so crowded." I made a sound that sounded like a mangled laugh. "I realized why when I reached Boylston Street."

Like dominoes, I could see the facts topple over in her mind one after another—*Boylston Street. Boston. April. A decade ago.*

"Kit." Her lip trembled over my name.

"The gallery was close to the finish line—closed for Patriot's Day to observe the race," I pushed on with a voice that felt prosthetic—as though my real one was lost that day, too. "I don't even know what it looked like —the gallery. Never made it." My head throbbed like my brain was trying to fall on its own sword rather than try to go back. "I remember the finish line. The runners. The crowd. And then the blast."

But then I felt her hands. Both palms were on my back now. On the burns and scars from the bomb's explosion and shrapnel.

"I didn't—I didn't even feel my back at first. All I saw were the other injured—all I saw were battlefield wounds." I blinked back tears like I could still feel the smoke in my eyes. "Shrapnel and mangled limbs and blood. Lots of blood."

Tears streamed down her face, but I didn't stop. She'd wanted to stay—wanted it all. *I warned you,* I wanted to remind her. *I warned you from the start.* But even if I did remind her, I knew it wouldn't make a difference. She'd still stand here, patient and observing, waiting to hear whatever I was willing to tell. *Waiting to understand.*

"I was trained in emergency medical care for these kinds of situations. Homemade explosives—IEDs—are common currency in the Middle East. The key is pressure—to stop the bleeding. So, that's what I did. What I told everyone I saw to do. First responders aren't the paramedics, they're the people. The crowds. The laymen who were already there and able to help."

"Who helped you?"

My chin dipped. "I don't know." I gulped. "I didn't realize how bad my back was—how much blood I lost until I passed out. The next time I woke up, I was in the hospital. Again."

My head started to spin. The memories were like a tornado trying to tear me to shreds. And then her hands were on my arms, turning me to face her, and I had no strength to fight. *I didn't want to fight,* I realized. I wasn't afraid of the story, I was afraid of the things it did to me.

"Kit..."

"Two and a half months in the hospital. Two skin graft surgeries for the burns on my back—some of the worst out of all the survivors. The hearing loss—that took the longest to recover. The doctors weren't sure it would. While I was in the hospital, they'd have to write everything down—I would, too—in order to communicate. Even after..." I let my head sway. "It was close to six months before I could hear like normal again."

Her lip quivered. "Is that why you're here—why you live at the lighthouse?"

Always observant. Always questioning.

"It was easier."

"For you?"

"For them."

Understanding widened her gaze.

"Between what happened in my unit and this...I wasn't...I wasn't okay. I felt..." I sighed. "I felt like I'd been broken into a thousand pieces of sand—sand that my family kept trying to help and shape back into a man, only for another wave of pain or memories to wash it away again. They loved me. Would've done anything to help—wanted to do anything to help. But there was nothing to do. I wasn't...fixable," I rasped, my voice cracking. "When I found myself wishing that my family loved me less, I knew I had to leave."

She ducked her head for a second, and when she lifted it back up, a tear had landed on the inside of her glasses. "So, you moved here and shut yourself away."

Carefully, I reached up and slid them off her nose, taking my time to wipe away the droplets and then replace them.

"I'm not the only creature that lives out here," I murmured lowly. "You of all people know that best."

"But don't you want more?"

"More what?" My jaw locked, pain whipping the words from my lips before I could stop them. "I have my life, which is more than some walked away with that day. I have family. My art. My lighthouse. There is no more."

She flinched—ever so slightly, but the impact of my words was unmistakable.

"There's no more I can give," I clarified. Of course, there was more to life than those things, but not my life. I was barely able to offer the remains of a son, brother, a grandson to my family. *What could I offer her?*

I sucked in a breath, the thought cinching me like the warnings of a trap. *This was how it started.* Wondering what I could offer her when the only thing I had that wasn't broken, damaged, or uncertain was a warning.

I was nothing more than a lighthouse in the storm. A lonely tale. A persistent caution. *Come close at your own risk.*

"You should go back downstairs."

Her tongue slid along her bottom lip. "I'm not going anywhere."

"Aurora..."

"Tell me you want me to go, and I'll leave."

I groaned. "You should. You'll be sore."

"Should isn't the same as want," she countered with a husky version of the tone she used to correct me when I'd called sea stars starfish.

My nostrils flared, watching as she gripped the hem of my T-shirt and lifted it over her head, leaving her standing naked in front of me. Instantly, my dick was solid again. Throbbing. Beating against the front of my sweats, telling me that it still needed more.

I reached up and framed her chin. "And what do you want?"

She took my other wrist and pulled my hands between her legs, shivering when my fingers slipped through her slickness. Her sigh melted into a sharp whimper as I thumbed her swollen clit. *Yeah, I bet the pleasure was painful after how many times I'd made her come.* My jaw locked. She shouldn't want this. She was too sensitive—too sore.

"*Fuck,*" I hissed as my fingers worked through her cunt in slow, sweeping strokes, unable to stop myself from drenching them with her cream.

"I want the rest of you," she pleaded softly. "Whatever part you locked away earlier downstairs, I want it let loose. I want to know it—to know you."

"*Fuck.*" I crushed my mouth to hers, kissing her hard until she trembled, her knees giving way. I grabbed her hips and spun her in front of me. "Hold on to the rail." As soon as her hands gripped the iron, I pushed her forward. "Aurora..."

I said her name, but all I really thought was *mine.*

I trailed my finger down the seam of her ass all the way to where she was pink and slick and swollen from last night. The sight was nothing short of magnificent. I fought the urge to drop to my knees and make her come by just blowing on her clit.

But my own need overtook me, like a different kind of darkness that I'd forced into hibernation for all these years. What was sex but passing pleasure? A fleeting release from a future I couldn't escape. So, what was the point? Especially when any kind of touch was painful.

But not now. Not with her.

It hadn't hurt when she touched my back—my scars. It hadn't hurt to tell her what happened. And, god help me, but being inside her felt like more than just sex.

I dragged my throbbing cock along her seam, coating the tip. "Don't say I didn't warn you."

"You know I'm not good with warnings." She moaned and wiggled back, the movement notching me at her entrance. "Please."

Spots erupted in my vision. My cock swelled to the point of pain, anticipating the tight heat of her. *Needing the tight heat of her.* A need that consumed me. A groan ripped from my chest as I gripped her hips and drove forward, sinking in. And in. And in. One sure thrust took me to the hilt as her gasp filled the small room.

"Are you all right?" I focused on my hands—where they held her. Where her pink flesh dipped from my grasp. Anything to draw my attention from the hot clutch of her cunt—from the physical pain it caused to hold myself back.

"*Yes.*" It wasn't an answer as much as it was a plea.

I pulled back and slammed into her, the force making her rise up on her toes. I saw the way her eyes widened in the window—the way they went round when she realized just how effectively I hit her G-spot from this angle.

"*Yes,*" she said again, and I repeated the thrust.

Over and over, my body moved to her command. I thrust to the tempo of her husky pleas. When they came faster and more forcefully, so did I, her drenched pussy welcoming each drive, though those muscles would regret her neediness later. I was too big to be fucking her this rough, this many times. But her moans and pleas of encouragement were like a knife straight to the heart of my chivalry.

"Oh god," she whimpered, her body instantly priming her path to orgasm.

"Fuck, you feel so good." I drove into her. "Look so perfect."

But it wasn't enough. I'd never get enough of her sweet cries and soft warmth. Her undaunted truth and eager lust. I'd never get enough of her.

I pulled out, groaning as my cock protested, and spun her to face me. I kissed her hard, letting her take the air from my lungs for her gasp, and then lowered us to the floor. I laid on my fallen shirt and kept her above me. She rose up on her knees, forever my Venus rising from the sea, her dark curls sweeping over her sloped shoulders. Her full breasts heavy and marked with red. The soft curve of her stomach, and then lower.

Lower to where she kneeled with me poised against her. Our eyes met. Without words—without questions—I knew she was observing. Understanding. She knew why I wanted her like this. My hand on her hips tightened when her body lowered down on mine. Inch after inch back into her tight pussy.

In this position, she could take me deeper. So fucking deep into her light, I hoped the darkness would just let me live there. Let me be.

As she slid all the way down, a rich moan drew from her lips. My cock thickened at the profound fit, pulsing when she settled all the way to my root.

I drew a tight breath and captured her gaze. "Don't stop."

Fucking me. Questioning me. Pushing me. *Don't stop fighting for me.* But I didn't say any of those things because I wasn't her burden to bear.

Aurora rose up and sank down, slowly at first as she adjusted to the position—to me. But then faster. Never ashamed. My woman was never ashamed of her truth—her pleasure.

"Hold the rail," I ordered, my fingers curling into her fleshy hips.

She tipped forward to reach the handrail, a small cry tumbling free when the angle put me right back against her G-spot, a rush of her desire soaking me on contact. She didn't need more instruction after that. Desire drove the movement of her hips up and down along my length. Faster. Wilder. *Recklessly*.

My fingers curled into her fleshy hips, wishing for the strength to try and slow her—stop her from fucking me so hard she'd hurt herself, but I couldn't. I couldn't control myself around her—even to just keep her away, knowing I would hurt her in the end, too.

"Aurora." Her name repeated from my lips like waves crashing on the shore.

Over and over, she sank down onto me, each time hitting that sweet spot that made her cry out. I knew I was sinking too deep—hitting delicate parts inside her that deserved more care—but she was so slick, there was no avoiding it.

I found my hips thrusting into the downward drive of hers as release barreled through me. I watched her, feeling like I could die from the pressure building inside me, from the pleasure of being inside her, but I needed her to come first. And I knew she would. The way she pounded me into her G-spot didn't take long to send her spiraling over the edge.

The handrail supported her as she fractured with a loud scream, and I followed her over the edge, pinning my cock so deep inside her that it felt like my release pumped all the way into her stomach. Her chest. Her throat. I filled her with everything I had...and for a moment dared to wonder if it could be enough.

Her eyes peeled open, and she looked down at me, blissful exhaustion hazing her features.

I reached for her arms, peeling them off the rail, and pulled her to my chest. Our heavy breaths collected in the lamp room, the windows fogged from the heat. Thankfully, dawn had broken, so the light no longer needed to beckon through the glass.

"Is it always like this?" She curled against me.

I gritted my teeth. "No."

"I didn't think so."

CHAPTER 16

AURORA

Technically, there was no comparison. I'd never had sex before, so logically, I had no other experience or data to compare. But still, I couldn't stop myself from believing wholeheartedly that Kit wasn't like any other man that existed. And that sex with him...well, I just knew I'd never experience anything like it again.

Maybe that was why we were ravenous. Because we both knew it wasn't normal. Maybe it was his not having sex for a decade and me not having sex...ever... that made us unable to stop.

For a week after that night, we'd hardly left the lighthouse. I'd say we barely left the bed, but that wasn't true. We left the bed. We just didn't stop having sex.

On the floor. Against the wall. In the stairwell. On the kitchen counter. In the shower. In the lamp room at midnight, the beaming silhouette of our tangled limbs all the way to the horizon.

Each time, I thought *this* would be the time the pleasure finally killed me. But it didn't. I'd shatter—

wholly, trustingly—in his skilled hands, and then he'd carefully put those pieces back together.

And that was all I wanted to do for him.

I found myself drawn to the sight of his back—his scars. Not because the injured flesh was jarring, but because the knowledge of what he'd endured and survived was mesmerizing.

He was afraid of pity. Afraid of disappointment— for himself and those he cared about. But I didn't pity him. Just like I didn't pity the sea star that had regenerated a leg. Yes, maybe it didn't look the same as the others. Maybe it didn't quite function like the original leg had. But it had created something wholly new from a position of extreme trauma.

Just like Kit.

I wondered if maybe he'd just let himself embrace what he'd been through—embrace the darkness rather than trying to fight it—he could understand his wounds. Heal himself. *Be with me.*

I bit my lip and slid the coffee machine forward on the counter, hearing Kit stride from the bedroom into the kitchen.

Neither of us talked about the future. About what sex meant. About relationships or complications. We avoided it like we had our very own lighthouse warning us away from the shores of that conversation, warning that the rocky crest of reality could obliterate the amazing...*thing*...we had right now.

But every day, we drifted closer, no matter how hard I tried to ignore it.

"We're out of coffee," I murmured, staring at the empty bag of grounds. I'd used the last of it yesterday but avoided mentioning it because leaving the lighthouse felt like it would be the first pinprick in our fragile affair.

Kit came up behind me, his hand snaking around my middle.

"I don't need coffee to get up," he muttered against my neck, his hand sinking between my legs.

I let out a weak laugh and grabbed his wrist. "I need coffee." I turned and found his gaze. "And to get some things from my B&B. And you have more sketches to bring to the gallery before Lou comes out here to hunt you down."

She'd texted him every day since the party. Everyone in his family had. And he didn't ignore them, no matter how hard it was to face what had happened. He responded so they wouldn't worry—so they wouldn't try to take care of him. *So he wouldn't be more of a burden.* And my heart ached to watch him hurt himself in order to spare them pain.

His jaw tensed, and his eyes darkened. "I don't—I'm not—" He broke off and stepped back, driving a hand through his hair.

"Why don't I run them into town since I have to go anyway?" I offered, needing no more explanation than the strain on his face to see he wasn't ready to be around people—other people—yet.

"Do you have to go?" He folded his arms, his eyes roaming hungrily over me. This morning was the first morning all week that I hadn't woken up to some part of him inside me. I'd been up early, wanting to make some semblance of progress on my actual research, before the day tempted me with his presence.

"I need coffee to function," I said firmly.

He stepped closer and reached out for the counter

behind me, caging me between his arms. His head dipped, his low voice teasing my lips.

"You don't need coffee to fuck," he rumbled, nudging his hips forward so I could feel the hard length of him press to my stomach.

I shivered, heat pooling between my thighs. "No. But I need to function a little today, and you do, too. That shutter needs to be put back up," I reminded him. There'd been a thunderstorm last night that knocked one of them off the window.

His stare bored into mine for a long second before he grunted and pushed himself back with a curse, palming the front of his sweats to adjust his cock but making no (futile) attempt to hide how hard and heavy he was.

"You're right," he said low and nodded, and for the first time, I saw flickers of his former walls start to rise back up.

Instantly, I wanted to take it back—to pull him back to me and kiss him until we both forgot I ever mentioned leaving. But I couldn't take it back any more than I could wipe away the scars from his back. Reality was coming for us, whether we wanted it or not. Better to drift toward it slowly rather than hope we'd survive a sudden crash.

"I'll get the drawings together. You can take the truck."

"Aurora!" Lou was around the counter, pulling me in for a hug, before I was barely through the door. "Thank God," she muttered once she was close enough that only I could hear.

She hugged me too tight, and my glasses were askew by the time she pulled back. I could read the worry in her eyes even before her next words left her mouth.

"How is he, really?"

"Okay," I answered as honestly as I could. "Not ready for people yet, which is why I'm here. I need some ground coffee. The big container. And I have some drawings for the gallery, too."

The flicker of excitement in her eyes was brief before it fizzled.

She let me over to an open end of the counter, leaving me for a second to place a tin underneath the grinder and start the machine.

"Is he really okay?" Her eyes glimmered with unshed tears, and my chest squeezed.

I understood why Kit wanted to be alone. I understood how looking at a face like this every time something broke him only magnified that pain a thousandfold, knowing he was hurting those he loved most. But I also knew that while seclusion might be an answer, it wasn't a life. And after everything he'd been through, Kit *deserved* a life.

I nodded and took her hand. "Yeah."

She sighed, hesitating a moment before saying, "He told you?"

Again, my chin dipped.

"It's always the worst around this time of year...the anniversary."

April 15th was a week away.

"I was there when Mom got the call." She stared at me while she spoke, but I could see her eyes going into a trance as she stepped back into the memory. "Jamie, Frankie, and I were standing in the kitchen talking about the shelves Jamie was making for Frankie's candles. Mom and Gigi had just come upstairs from the basement where they'd been wrapping jars when the phone rang. We were laughing because Gigi had just given Frankie her label—the one that said *Chandler*. Jamie answered the phone and handed it to Mom..."

I held my breath. A tear leaked down her cheek.

"I'll never forget the way Mom just collapsed. Like there were no bones left to hold her." The grinder beeped, jarring her loose from the story for a moment as she wiped her cheek and finished sealing the tin for me. "Let's walk to the gallery," she said.

"Are you sure?"

Her heavy nod was all I needed to know that she needed some fresh air right now, too. She went over to Lauren, the two of them talking softly for a second before the other girl nodded, releasing Lou on a break.

The weight of her unfinished story hung like a low cloud as we walked down Maine Street. We passed the Stonebar Farms shop, and I caught sight of Nox inside. Lou walked a little faster so he didn't see us. Then there was the chocolate shop, the scent of sugar fused to the air that rushed out when the door opened. Next, we passed the inn. The old building was set back behind a row of lampposts that stood like iron sentries along the fence. Another block of silence, and we reached Kit's gallery.

Lou unlocked the door and let us in, but she didn't

turn on the bright lights. Instead, only the muddied daylight streamed in from the big window, its fingers barely stretching to the back of the room.

We wandered in separate directions from the entrance. Her to the back to set the case with the new drawings on the desk near the far wall, and me to the giant storm painting I'd stopped in front of before. Somehow, the painting looked entirely different.

The two waves that crashed into the lighthouse tower from both sides were no longer waves; they were the two traumas he'd endured. Unlike the other paintings, there was no sign of the town in the periphery. No lights. No trace of civilization. *Because he was alone.* Kit was the lighthouse—a lone, battered sentry at the edge of the world. And the light...my jaw went slack. There was no light shining from the top of the lighthouse. How had I not seen it before?

My hand went to my chest and then slid up to my throat. *No light.* Just the tower. Just a hollow shell. *Like he believed there was no life left for him.*

"I'll never forget her scream," Lou continued softly next to me. My hand went to my face, feeling the damp remains of tears I hadn't even felt fall. "This was the second time Mom got that call. The first time...I can't say she was prepared because I don't think you can ever be prepared for a call like that, but she was...braced. Kit was overseas. Fighting in a war. She knew the risks. We all did. But this time..."

There was no bracing.

"He was home. Healed. Safe. He was just going to an art gallery. No danger in that, right?" She let out a broken exhale. "Thank God, Jamie was there. He held her and took the phone. He listened to the rest. He told us what happened. Got us in the car. Got us to the hospital."

Now, I didn't bother to wipe the tears that flowed down my cheeks or try to steady the broken inhales that ebbed into my lungs.

"He had so much blood loss, they told us they weren't sure he was going to make it—he almost didn't make it. Again." Her shoulders started to shake, and so did mine, and without thought, I turned and hugged her. I wasn't sure how long we hugged, standing in the middle of her brother's paintings, caught up in the aftermath of his own storm.

"We almost lost him twice, Aurora," she finally said softly, and we pulled apart. "And now, every time he's hurting...every time he pulls away...it's like that moment all over again. Like we're losing him all over again." She looked at me desperately. "How do we stop losing him?"

My jaw went slack. How was I supposed to answer that? To know? Pain lanced through my chest, and a small cry pushed from my lips. I didn't even know how to stop myself from losing him.

"Lou, I don't know—"

"You're the only person he hasn't run off from the lighthouse," she revealed. "The only person who... unsettles him. Who gets behind all the walls he's put up."

"No, I don't—"

"He's never come to the house for dinner when anyone other than family has been there. He'd never care—never bother to know whether it's called a sea star or starfish if it weren't for you. He never would've done any of these drawings—anything other than his seascapes..." She exhaled loudly. "He only came to our party because of you. And the way he watched you in the kitchen with our cousins...he let you stay with him after the fireworks. You're the only one he didn't push away."

"He tried."

"Did he?" she charged.

My mouth opened, but nothing came out. *Had he tried?* No. When I thought about it, he hadn't. Not really.

"You're the only one who's reached him, Aurora," she said, her voice just above a whisper. "How do we reach him, too?"

I swallowed over the lump in my throat, my mind spinning to try and weave together what seemed like an answer to an impossible question. *Did I know how to fix this? To help him?*

My mind flipped through what I knew. He loved his family. I knew he loved them. I watched him endure pain and discomfort, risk ripping open old wounds, just to see them happy. And I knew he loved the lighthouse. It's solitude and solace.

But I didn't know about healing from trauma or PTSD. I didn't know—I sucked in a breath, my gaze catching on the framed drawing of the sun star that hung brilliantly in the center of the wall behind Lou.

And then I thought about how sea stars regenerate. How the miraculous creatures could lose more than a limb—how they could lose everything *but* a limb and regrow the entirety of their being.

"Did you know when sea stars regenerate a lost limb, they don't grow it from the inside out? They start by recreating the farthest tip of the lost arm and then slowly filling in the middle part—slowly extending that tip farther and farther away from the body," I said quietly, knowing this probably sounded like it was coming out of nowhere to her, but Kit had lost a piece of him—a piece he was trying to grow back.

"I didn't know that."

Maybe that piece wasn't long enough yet to comfortably...safely...connect to the people who loved him. Maybe he couldn't reach them yet. *But that didn't stop them from coming to him.*

"Why don't you come to the lighthouse for dinner?" I rasped, the idea blurting from my mouth. "On the fifteenth."

Her eyes widened. "Are you sure?"

Maybe sea stars and broken soldiers had nothing in common. Maybe regenerating a limb wasn't the same as regenerating a life. But if I managed to reach Kit with how I thought...who I was...then maybe, just maybe, this would help.

"Yes."

I wasn't sure, but I had to hope.

IT SEEMED LIKE I BLINKED AND THE REST OF MY errands were done. Too lost in my own thoughts, I'd grabbed almost everything from the B&B rather than waste time trying to sort out what was necessary and what wasn't. Then, there was a brief stop at the grocery store. Kit might be able to survive on the most basic canned goods, but I didn't want to. I always cooked for

Dad when I was home, so I gathered up the essentials for all my favorite dishes.

It wasn't until I turned onto the gravel drive to the lighthouse that I realized even after all my thinking, I still hadn't come up with a plan for telling Kit that Lou was coming over for dinner.

I wasn't afraid to tell him. Weeks and weeks of observation meant I could perfectly envision his instant wince, the flare of his nostrils, the knot of his jaw muscle. I could picture the pain he'd prepare himself for. The fear and uncertainty that would cloud his gaze. But I could also see his solemn nod of agreement because he'd always put others before himself.

I was afraid of what the conversation would reveal —that this was no longer an experiment. No longer a deniable fling. I was afraid of having to admit wanting something that I'd classified as impossible for me before: Attraction. Affection. *Love.* My rationale had been sound; my former experiments with kissing had been failures, so why would I continue down that road of research? It was safer to shut it off. To hypothesize that I wasn't made for kissing or relationships or sex. *Or love.* I shuddered. But now...

The lighthouse came into view.

A haven.

A safe harbor.

A place where I'd found a part of me I hadn't known existed, and I was afraid that part of me only existed because of him.

CHAPTER 17
KIT

"I can't," she gasped and tipped forward, her body trembling above me as my tongue swiped over her clit.

"If you can talk, you can come." The familiar refrain muffled against her slickness. Somewhere in the last two weeks, that saying had become a favorite of mine. "Now grind on my face."

She panted and shook her head. "I'll suffocate you."

I growled and sucked on her clit hard, the bud so sensitive that her hips bucked against me.

"I've almost died before, sea star. Trust me, I'd rather go when some part of me is buried inside you." I curled my fingers forward, reminding her that my mouth wasn't the only thing eager to please her.

Her chest caved in, air whooshing from her lips. And then she settled on my face, letting me feast on her hot honey. My hands roamed the flesh of her hips, guiding her onto my mouth. I stared up as her head tipped back, pure pleasure overtaking her every limb. I memorized the sight of her beautiful body moving above me. The soft swell of her stomach. The heavy weights of her tits. The sweet taste of her pussy on my tongue. Within a minute, my deep, rough licks tore a strained cry ripped from her lips as she collapsed forward, limp from release.

I groaned in deep satisfaction, knowing this was the most important part I would memorize—the taste of her pleasure as she came apart for me. Always. Without abandon.

Gently, I moved out from under her, letting her tip forward onto the mattress.

"Good?" I rumbled, pressing a kiss to the flesh of her hip.

She moaned deep, making me chuckle.

"Maybe I should start calling you jellyfish," I teased, moving behind her, my gaze drawn to her full ass perched in the air and her wet center on display.

She made another intelligible noise as I traced her entrance, carefully probing one finger back inside her. Her muscles quivered around me, sore and pushed to their limit. Reverently, I repeated the movement. A slide along her seam. A slow push inside her cunt. And with my other hand, I gripped my shaft, working myself in hard, rough strokes.

"Kit..."

I bit back a groan. I knew that tone. It was fucking carved into my goddamn soul for how many times I'd heard it in the last two weeks—that voice that begged me to take more even after she'd given everything.

And I was too fucking weak to deny it.

I moved my hand to her ass and fed my cock inside the heat of her body, a tremor breaking me with how fucking good it felt. I moved slow—painfully slow because she was so sensitive. Slow, punishing strokes until we both ached for that next thrust. Panted for it. But even going slow, it didn't take long for the pressure in my spine to build and my balls to tighten.

"More, Kit," her soft voice whispered.

"My greedy girl," I groaned and moved faster. My thrusts shorter and harder, careening us toward the edge.

"Don't stop," she panted.

"You're so beautiful," I murmured, staring down where we were joined. "So perfect." I steadied her hips, making sure I hit her G-spot with each thrust. I felt her go tight. Her back bowed and her muscles fluttered around me, and all I cared about was giving her pleasure—giving her what she needed. I was determined to give her *more*—desperate to give her everything.

I reached around, my fingers just above her pussy, so that my next thrust pushed her clit against them, and she flew apart, moaning my name into the sheets as she came hard around my cock. I held my breath—clung to it like I could hold back the passage of time for just one second longer—to feel the tight heat of her cunt ripple and milk along my length. But one second was all I got before I couldn't hold it any longer. I pulled out of her with a feral growl, worked myself with my hand, and after two rough strokes, was coming in long, thick ropes all over her back and ass, painting that fair skin with my cum.

Fucking hell.

Two weeks of this, and every time I was inside her, it still felt like *I* was the one who remained a virgin.

"Don't move, jellyfish," I rumbled, giving her delicious ass a light tap as I climbed off the bed, went and grabbed a warm cloth, and returned to clean us both.

She turned over, stretching out fully on my bed with a sated sigh. Her dark curls inked over my pillow. Her sinful curves on full display.

Goddamn, I'd never get tired of this. My breath caught in my chest at the idea. Never was a long time— longer than I had with her.

"You are the most beautiful thing I've ever seen," I said without thought.

Her eyes fluttered open, staring up at me. I kneeled on the bed and slowly lowered myself next to her, placing kisses at random spots of skin along the way. The top of her knee. The corner of her hip. The valley between her breasts. The slope of her shoulder.

When I reached her ear, I pulled the lobe between my teeth and murmured, "I'm going to keep you in bed all day."

She shivered, but surprised me when she drew back, turning on her side and propping her head up on her palm. "Kit..."

"What?" My blood hummed. "What is it?"

I noted the column of her throat bob as she swallowed.

"I...invited Lou over."

"Today?" I choked on the word. Of all days, today was not the day.

"Tonight. For dinner."

I couldn't stop the shudder that went through me. Today was the fifteenth. The anniversary. The hardest day. And that was why all I wanted to do was keep this beautiful siren in my bed, losing my mind—myself—in her body over and over again until there was nothing left for my demons to find.

I sat up, feeling the band around my chest tighten.

"I don't know if that's a good idea."

Aurora rose up, too, her hand coming to rest on my back—on my scars, I shivered—not because her touch wasn't familiar by now, but because it was still unnerving for me to feel it and for it to feel good.

"She wants to see you—wants to be with you," she murmured, her fingers tracing slow circles over me.

"Here?"

"Here," she confirmed.

My jaw clenched. Not at Mom's. Not in town. Here at the lighthouse.

"And if I say no?" I turned my head, capturing her gaze.

"You won't." Her full lips pressed against my shoulder, her eyelashes fluttering. "You love them too much not to try."

I shuddered once more, looking away from her as I rasped, "And if I can't? How many times do they want to torture themselves seeing how broken I am?"

Her warm hands framed my face, turning me as she moved to straddle my lap.

"You're not broken, Kit," she said with no doubt in her eyes. Like she'd seen, observed, studied every inch of me—of my soul—and concluded it to be fact.

"How are you so certain?"

"Because broken men don't fight—don't care enough to try." She lowered her head. "Broken men don't feel." Her lips gently brushed mine. "Broken men don't love."

Her mouth sealed to mine, and no matter how I tried to convince myself she was still talking about my family —about how much I loved them—part of me wondered if she meant something else. *Meant something more.*

Her tongue slid along my lips, and I opened for her —let her inside. *Something I couldn't stop myself from doing.* Not today. Not yesterday. Not last week. Not last month. Not from the moment she'd intruded my lighthouse.

I hadn't been able to keep her away from the start, no matter how harsh a warning I'd given. But now, looking back, I realized she was right. She hadn't been destroyed by getting too close. *I had.* Irrevocably, unalterably wrecked by having her in my life. My walls. My solitude. *My hopes.* For the rest of my life. *For the rest of time.*

THE LATER IT GOT, THE MORE I EXPECTED THE nerves. The tingling. The elevated heart rate. The break of sweat. It happened every time I was around other people—even my family. My hands stilled under the running water in the sink, the thought hitting me that it didn't happen around Aurora. *Maybe that was why it wasn't happening now.*

No. I soaped my fingers rough and quick. It had to be because I was at the lighthouse; this place was my own bubble of safety. The reason why I didn't like people to come here was because I was afraid if the bubble popped, I'd have nowhere else to go.

But then Aurora showed up.

I grabbed a towel and bumped off the faucet, turning to watch as Aurora bopped along to the music playing from her phone that sat in a cup on the counter while she cleaned the living room.

I wanted to tell her it was just Lou—and that there wasn't much to clean. But I couldn't stop her—not when she looked so damn adorable. *Nor when the sway of her hips looked so fucking inviting.* She kept wearing my shirts around the house—*and nothing underneath them*—which was becoming a hazard for both my dick and my laundry policy. *Once a month to Mom's: wash. Dry. Retreat.* But God help me, I didn't want to see her wearing anything else.

I thought I'd at least keep us in the bedroom—distracted—until it got close to dinnertime, but Aurora had other ideas. We'd spent the day cleaning the house. Tidying all of her books and papers and notebooks on the desk. Organizing all the specimen jars on the shelves I'd bought at the hardware store the other week; I'd grumbled some excuse about the containers taking over the space on my counter and wanting them out of the way. The truth was Aurora was running out of space, and she kept having to sift through all the jars to find the one she wanted.

Those specimens had given me an outlet—they'd given me back the spark to draw. To create. And I wanted to give her something in return. Something that made her comfortable here. Something that made it easier to stay. Something that might tempt her to never leave.

There was a soft rap on the door. I glanced at Aurora and then went to it. I took a deep inhale, bracing myself for the next few hours of needing to convince Lou I was all right, but when I opened the door, it was more than Lou on the other side.

"Kit." Lou was the first to barrel into me with a hug.

I hardly got one arm around her before Frankie launched for me, too. I stepped back, both my sisters in my arms, as Mom and Gigi filed inside next, their arms filled with baskets and blankets.

"What is...I don't have..." Room. Chairs. Space... anything.

"We do," Jamie said lowly, the last to enter with wooden folding chairs under either arm. "We've got you."

I turned slowly, like I stood in the eye of a tornado, watching my family fill the house, bringing with them everything I needed. Two chairs for Mom and Gigi. Loads of blankets for the floor. *A picnic,* someone said as the space transformed in front of me. Frankie dispersed a bag full of candles that she'd clearly stocked up to bring. Mom, Gigi, and Violet unloaded baskets of already-prepared food onto the counter. Aurora and Lou took out paper plates and silverware.

Within minutes, it no longer looked like the bare-bones barracks from earlier. The candles glowed. The aroma of baked ziti and garlic bread filled the air. And everyone crowded around Aurora's shelves, mesmerized by her creatures.

"Time to eat before it gets cold," Gigi declared, ushering everyone to the open trays.

The house was small. It was frustratingly small when it was only Aurora and me inside, and I'd been trying to avoid her. It was impossibly small once I'd had her and tried to stop myself from reaching for her at every moment. And now, with my family crammed in the space, I thought I'd feel claustrophobic and panic—the press of bodies too similar to the crowds at the race that day. Instead, I felt calm. Protected. Like the love and laughter around me were too strong and a thick buffer to let the darkness creep in.

"You okay?" Aurora checked in with me softly while we waited for our turn to fix a plate.

"Yeah."

"I didn't know..."

"It's okay." I reached for her hand, tucking it into mine for a quick squeeze. "I should've known Lou wouldn't show up here on her own. Not how my family works."

She smiled with relief.

"Aurora, you never told us. Do you have siblings?" Gigi probed with a wide smile on her face.

"No." She shook her head and filled her plate with the ziti. "It's just my dad and me. My mom passed away when I was pretty young."

From breast cancer. Aurora had only been six. Her father had explained what happened the same way he'd told her about thunderstorms. *It's hard to be afraid of something when you understand why it's happening.*

"Oh, I'm sorry to hear that." Gigi maneuvered to the open chair in the room. Meanwhile, Aurora sank onto the floor between Lou and Frankie like it was the most normal thing to have a picnic inside a lighthouse.

"Thank you, but I don't really remember her," she admitted.

"Your dad never remarried?" Frankie wondered.

There was space on the floor near the corner of the room by Mom and Violet, but I chose to stand near the edge of the counter instead. Not because I was worried about sitting over there, but because it was farther from Aurora.

Her midnight curls bounced as she shook her head, swallowing her bite before gushing, "Oh, no." She smiled. "My dad loved my mom beyond...understanding. She was...his world. When she got sick and passed, a part of him died with her, and after, he threw himself into science."

Mom hummed, Aurora's words striking a chord. "When you lose someone you love, you throw yourself into anything...anyone...who will distract you from what you've lost."

"Once she was gone, that was it—I was it for him, and it's always just been the two of us since."

"That's lovely," Mom said, trying to carefully swipe a tear from her cheek, and I knew she was thinking about Dad. "Heartbreaking but lovely."

"Where does he work?" Lou wondered as we ate.

"At Tufts University. He's a professor."

"Is that where you want to work when you finish school?"

"Oh, no." She smiled. "While that would be fun, I don't really want to work in a school setting. I want to be..."

"In the wild," I heard myself finish for her before realizing I'd been about to speak.

"In the wild in Boston or in the wild here?" Frankie asked, the innocence in her voice so manufactured it was impossible not to hear it.

"Francesca," Jamie warned like she was twelve instead of a newly minted twenty-seven.

"What? I'm just wondering what her plans are

when the semester is done," she returned and then slid me a look. "I'm sure I'm not the only one."

At no point had I felt a sense of panic. Of dread. No band around my chest or ringing in my ears. No elevated pulse or the chill of sweat. At no point had the darkness crept in with its blanket of fear until now... when Frankie brought reality to the forefront of my mind.

That Aurora's semester was going to end in a month, and then what? Would I let her leave? Would I beg her to stay?

"I'm open to anything," Aurora answered without a hiccup. "The kind of research position I want isn't too common. There are some companies in Boston and then all along the coast of Maine, but I think..." She rolled that bottom lip through her teeth, thinking over her next words carefully before speaking them. "I guess it will ultimately depend on who's willing to have me."

Me. The word surged through my veins as though it had replaced my blood. *Me. I wanted to have her. To keep her.*

In an instant, I imagined the room without her. Without the orange and vanilla scent. Without her books overtaking my desk. Without her specimens lining my walls and counters. Without her enveloping curiosity. The warmth of her in my bed. And the light in her eyes when she looked at me. *Her light. Everywhere.*

Air vacuumed into my lungs so loudly—the thought so painful—it drew the attention of the entire room.

"Well," Frankie forged on, simultaneously saving me from the attention and skewering me with hope. "I hope *someone* around here wants you because we like having you around."

Fucking Frankie.

"And how about you, Frankie? You think someone around here will like having your trouble around?"

She stuck her tongue out at Jamie.

"Chandler," Gigi blurted out and pointed her fork at Frankie.

Frankie groaned. "Yes, my candles want me, and my candles are all I need," she quipped with a smile, but there was something sharp in her words. Not like a knife but like a pin. Something tiny and subtle that both held her together but barbed at anything or anyone who got too close.

"It's not the candles." Gigi shook her head but went back to enjoying her dinner.

Lou grinned and shook her head.

"What are you smiling at?" Frankie demanded of her twin and then set her eyes on Gigi. "What about Lou, Gigi? She's the only one who hasn't gotten a label."

"Not her time."

Frankie snorted. "*Bull—*"

"Frankie!"

"*Crap.*" She set her empty plate down, eyes twinkling. "I know what's going to happen."

"Oh, yeah?" Everyone watched Lou play along.

"Yup." Frankie licked her fork and then poked Lou in the knee with it. "The inn is going to go up for sale. You're going to put in an offer, and lo and behold, the new owner is some fancy Park Avenue Prince who's going to take one look at you, feel your...*passion*...for turning his dad's property from a lump of coal into a diamond, fall head over heels, and voilà."

"That's not going to happen." Lou rolled her eyes so hard I was surprised she didn't tip backward.

"I'm going to make sure it happens."

Lou groaned. "I honestly don't know where you get this from. Mom, are you sure we came out together? Gigi, are you sure her label shouldn't read '*crazy*' instead of '*Chandler?*'"

Everyone laughed while Frankie playfully swatted her sister. "Rude."

"Me? If you set me up with someone, it's going to come back to haunt you," Lou mumbled, rising and grabbing every empty plate in sight.

Frankie moved to help her sister, followed by Aurora, and then Violet and Mom. Before I knew it, everyone was huddled back into the kitchen, squeezing and bumping, joking and laughing. For the first time in a decade, my lighthouse was filled with laughter. With love.

And it was all because of Aurora.

"You didn't have to do this," I said to my brother when he came to stand by my side; the rest of the crew had migrated back to Aurora's shelves, admiring and probing about all of her specimens—*especially Stuart*.

"I can't believe that's going to grow back," Frankie gaped. "So freaking cool."

"It looks just like Kit's drawing," Lou added.

Meanwhile, Aurora's face was pure light. Brilliant. Warm. Glowing. She was pure light as she picked and pointed, happily sharing with anyone who would listen to the life stories behind her collection.

"Yeah, we did have to do this," Jamie replied, drawing my attention back to him. "We've been broken for far too long."

"We?" I shook my head. "It's me." My throat bobbed. "I'm the one who's fucked up." Even as I said the words, I didn't feel them like I normally did. Their sharp teeth seemed dull, skating over the surface of my skin rather than sinking deep.

Jamie shook his head. "No matter how hard you try, no person...no animal...no organism...exists on its own." He nodded to Aurora and our sisters, a few words like *ecosystem* and *symbiotic* and *environment* filtering over. "Even all the way out here...even after everything you've been through...you don't exist on your own. We all were broken by what happened to you. Mom still hesitates every time her phone rings. I still have nightmares that this family is going to lose one more person it loves. Frankie...remember when Frankie burned her finger badly a couple months ago and I took her to the hospital?"

I nodded. Hazards of candle making.

"She had a panic attack when we walked through the doors. Froze up. Cold sweat. I took her right back to the car because that was worse than the damn burn on her finger."

And then I thought about that tiny sharpness I'd heard from her earlier and wondered if that little pin in Frankie's armor was there because of me. To poke a hole in any hope of love that inflated too quickly.

"It's all my fault." The pain in my chest deepened.

"No, Kit," he swore, his tone one that he hadn't used on me in a long time—the one he grew when Dad died and he stepped up to take care of the family. "It's not your fault because none of us live in a vacuum. Not those creatures from the sea. Not the sea from the shore. Not the sun from the horizon. Not the ships from this lighthouse. We're all affected—we're all in this together. We have been from the moment you came home."

My teeth gritted tight, and then my brother handed me a scrap of paper.

I took it, confused, and unfolded it. There was only a single number written on the sheet. A single—large—number.

"What is this?"

"The only way we've been able to help," he said lowly. "When you came back from the hospital and then moved into the lighthouse, Gigi..."

My head snapped to him. "What about Gigi?"

"She was devastated. She paced the house for weeks, trying to figure out how to help you. She saved dozens of articles. Cut out albums of newspaper clippings. About what happened. About the survivors."

My chest felt like it was ripping in two, hearing about my grandmother who had always been a pillar of strength. Of happiness and mischief. All these years, I thought I'd been sparing them the pain of what happened to me.

"She couldn't just do nothing. None of us could. But since you needed space, we decided to help who we could," he rasped. "Every year, Gigi picks a charity started by one of the marathon survivors and donates all her income from Stonebar to it in your name. Mom and I match it, and Lou and Frankie, Max and Nox, and Uncle George chip in." He cleared his throat. "That number is how much we've donated in the last eleven years."

A number that crested over a million dollars.

My shoulders caved as emotion crashed into my chest like a charging wave, rushing over me and pulling me under. I couldn't see. Couldn't breathe. All these years, I thought I was sparing them the pain. I clung to that *fact* like it was my shield and sword and savior.

"We're all healing, Kit," he finished lowly. "Not like you are, but with you. Always with you." He reached up and squeezed my shoulder, then moved for Violet, leaving me alone to process.

I stood almost in a vacuum, the sights and sounds of my family happening all around me but feeling like they were at a distance. I watched them congregate around Aurora, watched her arms animate to describe something about sea stars, watched the array of comical expressions on her face—unafraid to be silly, unafraid to be smart, unafraid to be strong—and in that moment, I realized I'd fallen in love with her but was too fucking scared to admit it. Too fucking scared after everything that happened to me that I'd do something to push her away. That loving her wouldn't be enough to make up for all of...this.

"*Kit.*"

It wasn't until Lou jolted my arm that I realized she was trying to get my attention—and had been for a little while from the look on her face.

"Yeah? What's up?"

She looked nervous. Concerned. And then she looked back at Aurora, who nodded—*encouraged*.

"Is the...do you still want to do the gallery show?"

For all the people in the room, it suddenly went eerily silent. Quiet enough that I wondered if everyone was holding their breath.

My gaze moved from my sister's upturned face to the warm, steady stare watching me from behind her glasses. The stare that had watched me for months.

Learned. Observed. Carefully questioned. The stare that had held strong when I pushed back and opened herself to me in spite of every warning.

And it hit me. Like a wave against the shore. Or the sun to the horizon.

She was my lighthouse. Her glow was not a warning but a guide. A guide to safety. A guide to shore. A guide to warmth. A guide to love. And I'd chased her light until she'd led me here, led me home.

Chasing Dawn.

Loving her had made me stronger. Loving her had made me braver. And I needed to prove it to her. I needed to show her how I'd changed because of her before I asked her to change her life because of me.

"Yes," I said and nodded slowly. "The gallery show is still on."

CHAPTER 18
AURORA

"**A**re you okay?"

I blinked twice, pulling myself from the trance of the painting and turning to Kit. I brushed a strand of hair back behind my ear and smiled up at him.

"Yeah." I nodded and then couldn't stop myself from asking, "Why hasn't this one sold?"

I'd been inside Kit's gallery at least two dozen times, most of those visits in the last two weeks as Lou asked me to help her start preparing for the show, and every time I was here, I was drawn to the painting of the lighthouse, its darkened tower peeking through the waves of the storm.

Kit shoved his hands in his pockets. "I can't...bring myself to sell it."

I pulled my bottom lip between my teeth and turned. "Is this how you see the lighthouse?" *Was it how he saw himself?*

The cords of his neck tightened and his throat

bobbed. "It...was," he said, and then instantly shifted his weight and changed topics. "Lou wants your help arranging the last of the drawings. Something about how you would know which animals should go next to which."

I took a moment to look at him. The strong angle of his jaw. The short stubble of his beard. The prominence of his brow. Even the way he stood—legs separated, arms crossed—he mirrored the stance of the lighthouse. Strong and stoic, but no longer solitary.

Kit had been different these last two weeks. Since that picnic at the lighthouse, there'd been a shift. Subtle but perceptible. At least to me. The way he looked at me. Touched me. *Took me.* There was a deeper charge to it all. Like before he'd been caught up in the storm, and now...now, he was the storm.

In the day to day, there were the constants: How we woke up together and shared breakfast. Then I'd go back to my research and Kit to his work. Eventually, we'd both end up around the kitchen counter. Me, making my notes. Kit, sketching. I'd talk about what I'd uncovered that day or what Lou and I were thinking for the show, and he'd listen, taking it all in.

But then there were the last three days, when it was Kit's suggestion to grab coffee and a pastry at the Maine Squeeze. A quick trip into town, but more than he'd ever suggested before. There was the way his conversations teetered on the edge of discussing the future. *What happened when my semester was done? Did I have to stay for anything else? Where was I thinking of applying for a job?* And finally, there was the gallery show.

Before, his sense of obligation—his need to help Lou —defined his demeanor. But now, his diligence in his drawings and his desire to come to the gallery each day to check on the progress, everything screamed different. Everything screamed change.

And I watched, hopeful that what I was noticing was the beginnings of a kind of regeneration.

"Aurora!" Lou called from the other side of the room.

I smiled. "Coming."

I felt his gaze follow the sway of my hips as I headed to the back of the room where Lou hunched over the desk, Kit's drawings scattered on top, where she arranged and then rearranged their positions.

"Does the sea star look best next to the periwinkle? Or the nudibranch?"

I smiled. "We probably should start referring to the nudibranch as a sea snail, otherwise, your brother is going to be in for some very interesting questions."

Her lips quirked, and she glanced at Kit. "Interesting questions might loosen him up a bit."

I looked over the options and then the empty spaces on the walls, thinking for a second. I was about to give her my first suggestion when I felt the brush of his fingertips on my low back, and my breath caught.

I turned, thinking Kit might have a thought of his own, but his attention was elsewhere. *His hand purely to tease me.*

"Let me see the two of them," I said weakly, trying to ignore the slow circles of his fingers—*and the way I'd grown to love his constant need to touch me.*

For someone who'd spent most of my life trying to

be hyperaware of my brain rather than society's standards of beauty, I loved how his attention—possibly borderline obsession with my body—brought that part of me to life, too.

Heat zipped along my spine, his fingers moving lower. And lower. *Too low.* I practically skipped forward to go stand by Lou.

"Why don't we try this one with it?" I traded the frame in my hand for one in hers, shooting Kit a glare over my shoulder.

The slight tip of his lips was the sweetest victory.

The door opened and Frankie charged through, beelining for her twin with hardly a glance at anyone else. "The inn is going up for sale this month!"

In an instant, the plans for the gallery show were forgotten while Frankie shared all of her news.

"I just got off the phone with Adele. She was in a meeting with the new owner this morning. He said his realtor is doing photographs next week, and then the listing will be posted."

I could practically see the blood drain from Lou's face as she swayed.

"Lou!" Frankie shook her. "Don't fade on me now."

"Right, no." Her twin tried to pull herself together, but I understood her swell of emotions. It was one thing to have the idea—the plans and hopes and dreams—but the moment you had to take that leap...it was frightening. "I'm here. That's great. Really great." She didn't sound anywhere near convinced. "I just..." I took the frame from her hands, watching her cover her face for a second. "Sorry, it just got very real. My whole life could change at the end of this month."

I wasn't prepared for the way her words hit me. Suddenly, she wasn't the only one thinking about where her life would be—could be in a few short weeks. *Four short weeks.*

The end of the semester. I'd have to go back to Boston to finish my program. But what then? Would I look for a job back here? Would Kit want me back here? Would I be able to leave Dad—leave Boston?

Sure, he'd probed a little about my future, and yeah, I didn't have any clothes remaining at the B&B, all of them stuffed into the dresser at the lighthouse. *But he hadn't said anything about me staying.*

"This is exciting." Frankie took her sister's hands, giving them—and my thoughts—a little jostle with the movement. "You'll finally be back on track to your dream."

If there was one thing—one moment—that gave the perfect snapshot of the breadth of differences between the twins, this was it. Frankie, practically bubbling over with excitement, and Lou, stunned and worried into silence.

Frankie babbled on for another minute or two before she apologized for the intrusion and then dashed back out because she was in the middle of a delivery.

"Lou..." Kit reached for his sister's shoulder. "Are you all right?"

I turned to give them a moment, pretending to thoroughly examine the blank wall.

"Yeah." I heard her small voice. "Just nervous. The gallery show isn't for another two weeks. What if it gets sold by then? What if I don't have time to place an offer?"

"Hey," he chided. "These things take time. You

think they're going to take photos of the inn as it is? The yard overgrown with weeds? The one sconce hanging askew? Not a chance. If this guy wants to unload it, he's going to make sure it's marginally presentable before taking those photos."

Lou didn't reply at first because Kit made a good point. Especially since this new owner was looking for a bigger return on the asset than his half brother had gotten when he'd "sold" it to Ailene and George.

"I'm afraid," Lou said softly. "What if I lose it?"

"I might not know a lot, but I know things happen for a reason. If you don't get the inn, you'll find something else—something better," he assured her.

"Really?"

"Promise."

"I wish I could be as brave as you," she said with a wistful laugh.

"Even the brave were once afraid."

My breath caught, and when I turned, Lou was heading for the back desk and her phone, and Kit was right in front of me.

"We should go," he said lowly. "I want to stop at Jamie's shop to pick up the frames he finished for these so Lou doesn't have to, and then I want to get you home."

Home.

Before he could hear—or read too deeply—into the catch of my breath, I said, "But we didn't finish—"

"The only thing that's getting finished right now is you finishing yourself off on my cock," he growled. "So, that can happen here, but the kind of questions it's going to draw are going to be much more than interesting."

My jaw slackened, and then I squeaked, "Okay, let's go."

WE STOPPED AT HIS BROTHER'S WOODSHOP, TAKING a grand tour of the massive barn and all the projects Jamie was working on before Kit finally took hold of the five new frames for his drawings.

I almost suggested that we could stop and see his mom on our way back, but the second we were back in the truck, his delicious fingers reached over the console and began teasing me through my bright blue pants in the truck.

I was panting heavily by the time he pulled up to the house and parked, and I'd just made it out of the truck when my phone vibrated.

"It's my dad," I said, biting my lip with an apologetic look as I mouthed *"one minute."* I swiped to answer, watching Kit head inside. "Hey, Dad."

"Hello, is this Miss Aurora Cross?"

I tensed, my stomach dropping like a stone. "Yes, speaking?"

"Hi, Miss Cross. This is Dr. Fucarile at Mass General. I'm calling because we have your father here. He's okay—stable, but he's had a massive heart attack."

A cry pierced my lips, and I sank to the rocky ground.

I DIDN'T REMEMBER FALLING TO MY KNEES. I didn't remember Kit coming back outside and lifting me. But those things must've happened because suddenly, I was inside the house, held tight to Kit's chest, the knees of my pants stained with dirt.

He carried me into the bedroom and set me on the mattress. It wasn't until he kneeled in front of me and cupped my face that I realized I was crying and shaking.

"What happened?"

"My dad had a heart attack."

"Jesus—"

"He's unconscious. Stable but unconscious. I have to go. I have to go to him—to the hospital." I shook my head wildly, unsure where to even begin. "But all my things..."

"Aurora." Kit squeezed my shoulders. "Breathe. In and out." I did as he said. "Again."

"I have to be with him—be there when he wakes up. They said he needs another surgery—another bypass." I shook my head. "I have to get back to Boston."

Kit looked like I'd just twisted the knife buried in his chest, but it wasn't my choice. I couldn't change where my father was—where I was from—any more than I could change the state of his health.

"I'll drive you to the B&B to get your things, and then Jamie will take you back," he declared, his statement like a bucket of ice water over my head.

My things? I didn't have any things left at the B&B, so the only reason he was taking me there was so that Jamie wouldn't pick me up here.

And that brought me to his brother. I watched in a daze as Kit stood and fished for his cell, calling Jamie and asking him to take me. *Of course, Jamie said yes.* The Kinkades were the kind of family you could count on at a moment's notice, day or night. I wanted to argue—to protest. Hell, I wanted to beg him to take me. To come with me.

But as soon as he faced me, I knew I couldn't.

Back into town was one thing. Around people he'd grown up with was one thing. Back to the place where he'd almost lost his life...that was a whole different kind of thing.

I could never ask it of him, not because I knew he'd say no, but because I knew he'd say yes. He'd take me without batting an eye. He'd help me like he helped the other victims of the bombing that day—without even realizing his own injuries were on the brink of killing him. And it would undo everything he'd worked so hard to overcome.

"Kit." I reached for him, and he pulled back as soon as my fingers landed on his hot skin.

"I can't," he rasped low. "I can't...go back there." Slowly, his head lifted, the pain in his eyes just as heartbreaking as the truth—the one we'd avoided this whole time.

My place wasn't here, but his was. My home—my life—was in Boston, somewhere he, understandably, couldn't go. Like a bird and a fish, we were from two very different worlds. And the lighthouse...these months at the lighthouse were nothing but a bubble that had lifted this fish into his sky.

I'd stay.

I'd come back to him...if he wanted.

But one look in those eyes, and I knew he'd never ask. No matter how much had changed, no matter how far he'd come, he still saw himself with missing pieces while I saw the whole picture.

"Kit..." Tears exploded down my cheeks.

"You have to go." He cleared his throat and looked over to my shelves. "Grab what you can, and I'll ship the rest to you."

Our time had been severed. These last weeks of the semester that should've given us time to explore our future had been cut short. Amputated. The shock alone made it hard to breathe. The pain...I knew the pain wouldn't fully settle in until later.

"Wait, please, I have to tell you—"

He took my hand from his chest and brought it to his mouth, kissing the center, his eyes darker and more tortured than the day we met.

"Don't," he said. *One last warning: don't tell me you love me.* I saw it as clear as day—clear as the beam from the tower in the middle of the night. "You need to be with your dad. He needs you."

The lump in my throat wouldn't go away. It was filled with so many words—so many feelings—I wanted to say, but for maybe the first time ever, I couldn't bring myself to say them. *For the first time, I heeded his warning.*

"Kit..." His name was hardly anything above a whisper, and my pulse slowed to hard, heavy beats, afraid of what the next one might bring.

"You need to go. Be with him. Finish your semester. Your masters. Get your degree and the job of your dreams."

My lips parted. "And you..."

His big body shuddered. "I'll be here. Where I've always been." *Alone.*

"And this?" I wanted to scream. *What about us? What about love?* Instead, all I could offer was every inch of my heart as I stared up at him and hoped it was enough.

And then his jaw flexed. A flex I'd observed and then studied and finally *understood.* It was never anger or frustration that triggered the muscle, it was always restraint. Holding back from what he wanted. What he deserved.

"This was only an experiment," Kit said lowly. "Now we know."

His words pierced my hope—piercing my heart.

Now, we knew how it could be. What we could have. *And that it wasn't meant to last.*

We stood frozen for a moment, our eyes locked in some kind of tailspin that both felt like forever and ended too quick.

"Now we know," I repeated thickly and let my arm fall to my side. "I'll get my things."

I held back my tears while we took ten minutes to pack what we could from the house. I held back my pain on the silent drive over to the B&B, where there was nothing to do but wait a few minutes for Jamie to pull up. And I held back my heartbreak when I turned to say goodbye and Kit pressed a kiss to my forehead.

"Goodbye, sea star."

My throat was too tight to respond as he bundled

me into Jamie's truck, muttered something too low to hear to his brother, and tapped on the trunk.

I watched Kit in the sideview mirror for as long as I could, and when I finally couldn't see him anymore, a sharp inhale sank into my lungs, feeling as though I'd lost a piece of myself in leaving him.

Unfortunately for me, I wasn't a sea star. If I were, I wouldn't feel this kind of pain. Not because I could regrow the missing piece, but because sea stars didn't have hearts.

CHAPTER 19
KIT

It was for the best.

With every passing minute of the last twenty-four hours, the thought cemented into my bones. I hadn't pushed her away, but when reality took her back to her real life, I'd let her go and told myself it was the right thing to do. The honorable thing. Just because I could make her come didn't mean I could keep her. She'd be better off without me. A broken man who lived in a lighthouse.

I'd watched Jamie's truck drive off from the sidewalk in front of the B&B in shock. In pain. The inside of my body responded in a way I hadn't felt in over a decade. *From trauma.* My heart raced. Sweat beaded. My skin buzzed. Every instinct screamed to run. Run after her. Rip the door open. Haul her back here and lock her in the damn lighthouse. But I wasn't a beast any more than she belonged here.

So, I held onto my thin thread of control—its strength fueled only by the memory of Aurora collapsing in the drive and the cry that whipped through my bones—and told myself it was for the best. Because it was. It had to be. And when I finally did move from that spot on the sidewalk, the weight on my shoulders was so great, I was surprised my feet hadn't left permanent impressions in the concrete.

I'd returned immediately to the lighthouse, gravel kicking as I sped down the drive toward my home. My haven. The only place that would feel safe at a time like this—when it felt like a part of my life had been ripped away once more.

By the time I'd made it through the door, I was desperate for shelter, heaving breaths from my lungs like they were made of water. But inside—inside the place I'd taken refuge for a decade, shelter from a life it seemed impossible for me to have lived, I found none.

Instead, I only found her.

Her things. Her books. Her clothes that had once been mine, I now hardly recognized with seeing them on her lush form. Her specimens. Shelves of colorful, interesting creatures filled...well, it no longer felt like my space. It felt like theirs. Hers. *Ours.* I'd walked over to the shelf and picked up a container, staring at the damn sea snail inside.

Bushy-backed nudibranch.

Pain lanced through my chest. I didn't know why I thought this place would be better. She was everywhere here. And the pain was suffocating me.

Bare minutes I'd lasted inside the house before I was back in my truck, driving toward town. I needed boxes. Packing material. Tape. I needed to get her things out of my lighthouse.

And that had been my sole focus for the last

twenty-four hours. Packing everything of Aurora's in sight to send to her in Boston.

I'd started with the specimens she'd told me could be released back into the ocean. One by one, I opened the containers and carefully dumped the creatures into the rocky tide pools around the base of the lighthouse. With each one, I told myself that was what she was. Something beautiful and fascinating that I'd kept in my lighthouse for a time but belongs back in her natural habitat. A stupid analogy, but it kept the pain at bay.

I'd spent the night in Jamie's barn, knowing better than to think I'd get any sleep in the bed she'd been in only the night before.

It didn't matter. I didn't get any sleep anyway, tossing and turning, wondering how she was doing—how her dad was doing. Wondering who was holding her if she needed to cry? Who was taking care of her while her focus was elsewhere?

Not me, came the harsh answer. I could hardly take care of myself.

When morning rolled around, I was back to the lighthouse before dawn, clinging to the tasks that sustained me before her. Checking the light. The battery. Cleaning the windows. I willed it to be the same as before. I *needed* it to be the same...just as surely as I knew it never would be.

SOMEONE BANGED LOUDLY ON THE DOOR.

"Yeah?" I called, rising from the boxes I was in the middle of packing and went to open it. "Frankie—"

I shouldn't have been surprised to find my sister on the other side, but I was because I'd hoped I'd get a little more time before having to do this. But clearly, the news had spread to the rest of my family about what had happened with Aurora. I knew I couldn't keep it from them forever. But I'd hoped for a few days where I could figure out what to say—*how I was going to fucking survive.*

"Do you have a brain injury?" Her harsh tone didn't match the soft worry that etched her face as she barreled inside, arms waving.

I jerked. "What?"

"All this time, all those injuries, and no one ever realized you had a brain injury. I'm shocked."

Damn, she was pissed. I shook my head. I didn't know what to say—didn't even have the fucking energy to growl at her that this was ridiculous. Gritting my teeth, I returned to the two open boxes I had left to fill.

I'd almost finished carefully wrapping and packing all of Aurora's dry specimens. I would've finished a lot earlier this morning if I hadn't stopped and decided to sketch them all. Not for me or for the gallery, but for her. I'd picked up the moon snail shell—the first *carcass* she'd left for me and recalled her wish to be even just a little artistic so she could include illustrations with her paper. I couldn't give her hardly anything she deserved, but I could give her that.

So, I'd drawn them all. Each of the thirty-two samples left in containers on the shelves. And that was why, after hours of being back at the lighthouse, I'd only packed about a third of them.

"Why did you let her leave?" My sister followed me.

Jesus.

"I didn't *let* her do anything because she's an adult who can make her own decisions about her own life," I said, stacking textbook after textbook into the box. "A life that she was going back to in the city at some point anyway."

I grabbed another container off the shelf.

"And how can she make the right decision without all the information?"

"What are you talking about?"

"Did you tell her you love her?"

Did I—love her—"What?" I choked and shook my head. "Enough, Frankie."

"Why didn't you tell her?"

I traced my finger along Aurora's handwriting on the label. So smooth and sure, so certain. Unlike me. I tucked it into a wad of bubble wrap and set it in the box. One after another. Stacked and ready to go back to the woman who understood them.

I wish I could pack myself in the box. I wish I could go back to the one person who understood me.

"It doesn't matter."

I heard Frankie roam around me, frustration oozing from every step. "Seriously, Kit? Why are you doing this?" Her anger broke in the sharp grip of sadness.

"Get a grip, Frankie," I swore and spun, everything inside me burning. "What was I supposed to do? Force her to stay? Kidnap her? Her dad is sick. Her semester is almost over. She had to go home—she was never meant to stay."

"But you could've—"

"No, I couldn't have gone back there," I said angrily, hating myself for every weak word—hating myself for not being healed. "I couldn't have gone with her to Boston, I'm sorry. I know you want me to be strong. I know you want to see me as some hero—someone who survived war and a gunshot wound to the head and the Boston Marathon bombing—"

Instantly, her anger dropped. "I don't *want* to see you as a hero, Kit. You *are* a hero. My hero."

"But I'm not." The words pushed out like a bullet from my chest, fired from the very deepest part of my pain. "All I did was survive, Frankie, and some would argue even that is questionable." I motioned around me to the lighthouse—*to my life*.

She strode up to me, angling her head and glaring at me.

"You're not my hero because you survived the impossible, Kit. You're my hero because no matter how bad things were, how bad the pain was, how hard the healing was, how much you wanted to give up, you kept fighting for everyone else around you."

"Frankie..."

"You know what I heard when you were in the hospital?" The fury in her eyes sharpened with pain. "Your doctor pulled Jamie out of the room to talk to him while the rest of us stayed by your bed. When they were done, Jamie insisted we should all get something to eat while they prepped you for surgery. Jamie said that was what the doctor wanted—to explain the surgery to him. What they were going to do. And Jamie didn't want us to hear."

My brow creased. Why hadn't I heard this before?

"I-I forgot my sweater in your room, so I went back,

grabbed my sweater, but stopped because I overheard your doctor and a nurse or PA talking right outside the door. They said you'd lost too much blood. That even with the transfusions, it was so risky, but because of the burns, they had to do it before things got worse."

Her head shook as she spoke, and I understood. Her body didn't want to go back to the memory because it was too painful.

"I remember the nurse asked *What did you tell him?*' She meant Jamie. The doctor said something, but I must've moved because he saw me through the window to the room. He looked at me. Looked at the nurse. And then told her to prep you." Frankie's voice turned hollow. "I saw through her fake smile when she came into the room. I saw the pain in her eyes. She said I needed to leave so they could do what they needed to do, and I told her I wasn't leaving until she told me what the doctor said."

"And?"

"The doctor told Jamie you had a less-than-ten percent chance of surviving."

My teeth ground together. I'd heard enough comments during my recovery—*miracles* and all that— to know the odds hadn't been good. But for someone to tell my sister that when she was only seventeen years old? Granted, seventeen-year-old Frankie was just as stubborn as twenty-seven-year-old Frankie.

"I ran to the bed—to your side—and I begged you, Kit," she cried. "I begged you to live. I told that we needed you—that I needed you, and I sobbed until the nurse had to have Jamie come back and carry me away."

"Frankie..."

"When they told us you made it through, that same

nurse approached me. She pulled me to the side and told me that it had to be because you'd heard me—that somehow you heard how much we needed you, knowing that was the only way someone in your condition would've survived."

My jaw locked, wishing there was something to say but there wasn't. Could I hear Frankie screaming for me? Begging for me to live? *Yeah, I could.* With perfect fucking clarity. But did I remember it, or was I just able to imagine it? I had no idea. I had no other memory of that time. Yet, I felt her story in the very marrow of my bones. As though there were parts of my body that could still remember even if my brain couldn't.

"You came back, and I know it was because I asked —because I begged you," she sobbed harder. "It's my fault. I know it would've been easier and less painful and more peaceful for you to just...let go—"

"Frankie—" My eyes burned with my own tears, watching her break down.

"But you fought for me because I told you I needed you. Because I begged you to live." Her entire body shook with the force of her cries.

"Jesus, Frankie." I hauled her against me. "Of course, I did. Of course, I fought for you. I'll always fight for you."

Her head swiveled against my chest, and she fought my hold, her small fist banging against my chest as she pushed back, tears streaming down her face. "That's the point," she charged tremulously, and I didn't understand her ripple of anger. "You will always fight for us. Fight the odds. Fight the pain. You'll sacrifice to give us whatever we need—whatever you think we need—and that's why you're our hero."

My throat felt thick—almost too thick to breathe.

"But for once, Kit...for just once, I wish you'd give the rest of us a chance to be yours. Your hero," she choked on the last. "I wish you'd give us the chance—the choice to fight for you."

Fight for me. The idea stopped me—stunned me. My mouth opened, but there was nothing to say—nothing to do except draw her back in for a tight hug and let her unload the rest of her tears into my chest.

"I'm sorry," I rasped when her shaking started to subside.

"She loves you," Frankie added, her voice softer now. "She would've fought for you."

The band around my chest clamped another degree tighter.

"She needed to go back to her dad—her life," I murmured softly and drew back to look Frankie in the eyes. "Just like I do."

I wiped her tears and tried not to think about when I'd done the same for Aurora.

"You were happy, Kit," she said so quietly that I wished I wouldn't have heard her. "You were finally happy."

"And I'll be happy again," I risked promising her—promising myself—with a smile that didn't quite reach my eyes. "Can you help me finish packing these?"

Her head gave a little nod, and I guided her over to the desk so she could pack up Aurora's remaining textbooks and notebooks.

"What are you going to do?" she asked when we'd finished.

"Take these to the post office." I lifted the first box—the heaviest—into my arms and nodded to the door.

"That's not..." She sighed and opened it. "What I meant."

I could've walked through without saying anything else—without answering because God knows, I didn't have much of an answer to give.

Instead, I paused in the doorway and said low, "I don't know, Frankie. I don't know what I'm going to do."

Maybe the answer wasn't anything, but from the look on her face, maybe it was everything. Maybe the shift from believing there was nothing I could do to being unsure what I was going to do was the biggest change there was.

And maybe that was why she helped me load the rest of the boxes into my truck without any more questions.

WHEN I RETURNED TO THE LIGHTHOUSE, FRANKIE'S car was gone, and I didn't know whether to be relieved or worried. Sure, there'd be no more questions, but that meant I was alone again and not with my own thoughts, but with hers.

Give us the chance to fight for you.

She would've fought for you.

She loves you.

"Fuck," I muttered, pushed open the door, and stopped just inside the threshold. "What the..."

My paints were strewn across the living room like someone had riffled through every bottle to get to the ones at the very bottom, and as I did a slow turn through the room, I realized why.

The bright colors were at the bottom. The bold colors. *The brave ones.* Reds and yellows and oranges and purples. The colors of the brightest dawn.

I took in the slashes of those brave colors painted over the brown and faded wallpaper inside the house, the words *Chasing Dawn* painted with my sister's commanding strokes over and over and over again.

Chasing Dawn.

Chasing the light.

Chasing Aurora.

Maybe I did know what to do after all.

CHAPTER 20
AURORA

"Dad?" I called when I heard something clatter to the ground.

When the muffled curse followed, I pushed out of my seat and rushed to the kitchen where I'd thought he'd gone for a glass of water. Instead, I found him in front of the pantry closet, climbing on a stepstool, a plastic spice jar rolling on the floor where it had fallen.

"What are you doing?" I exclaimed and grabbed his arm, forcefully guiding him back down.

"I needed a new jar of jam for my toast," he huffed, moving aside to let me get it for him. "I'm not an invalid, Aurora."

No, Richard Cross was a lot of things—stubborn, thoughtful, independent—but invalid was very last on the list.

He'd recovered phenomenally from his heart attack and subsequent surgery. I couldn't believe that he was ready to go home only three days after it happened, with only a handful of diet and exertion restrictions. It was probably why I'd overdone it, playing nursemaid to the point of annoyance, but I'd almost lost him. *And I was desperately trying to avoid thinking about the other man I did lose.*

"You just had a triple bypass last week, and your doctors told you to take it easy." I picked the jar from the top shelf, the weight of it—the feel of it achingly familiar in my hands.

I didn't have to look—probably shouldn't have—to see that it was Maine Blueberry jam from Stonebar Farms.

"Aurora?"

"When did you start buying this?" I asked thickly, like it mattered.

"Well, after you mentioned meeting the owners in Friendship, it caught my eye in the store, so I decided to try it. Pretty darn good stuff." He smiled at me, the white scruff of his beard coming in thicker since he hadn't shaved in a few days.

My throat tightened, and I nodded, too afraid to speak. Dad would know in an instant something was wrong. As it was, it was only because of my worry over him and his health that I was able to hide the pain of a broken heart.

I'd never...not been smart.

Reckless, sure. Obstinate, maybe. Bold, definitely. And whatever I'd gotten myself involved in with Kit was certainly all those things, but for the first time, that *experiment* had also made me an idiot. Maybe I was incredibly smart...unless I was in love. Then I was incredibly stupid.

The old adage was right, it seemed. *Only fools rush in.*

And I'd rushed in like a fool. I'd rushed to understand the man in the lighthouse. I'd rushed into his arms, desperate to know more of his touch. And I'd rushed my heart straight from my chest, too caught up in every moment to even consider what happened when the rushing stopped.

Well, it had. And in the moments between worrying about my dad's life and then his health and then his recovery, I desperately tried to forget how, in response to Kit calling us an experiment, I'd almost confessed to loving him—and insisted that he loved me in return.

It was the first time my lips blocked the words that were on my mind. Self-preservation superseding infectious honesty.

"Aurora." Dad touched my arm, and I flinched, the jar slipping from my tense fingers. I gasped, but he caught it in time, looking up at me curiously. "Are you all right?"

Not in the slightest, I thought, feeling the fresh crack in my heart from a silly jar of jam.

"Yeah," I assured him and stepped off the stool, folding it and moving by him to put it away. *This had to get better at some point. It had to.* I tried to head back to the living room, where I was holed up at the desk in the corner, finishing the final touches on my paper, but he didn't let me.

"You've been a little distracted since you've been home," he said calmly while spreading the jam on his English muffin.

"Dad." I folded my arms, giving him my best stern face. "You just had a massive heart attack, a huge surgery, and my final paper is due on Monday. Don't you think that's enough to keep me a little distracted?"

He paused and looked at me for a long second, then nodded.

I rolled my bottom lip through my teeth and then said softly, "I have to finish my paper. Please, just call for me before you climb anything."

I walked away—back to my paper. Back to my distractions. I'd just settled into my chair when I felt his hand on my shoulder.

"If you want to talk about it, you know I'm always here for you, sweetheart." His warm voice rumbled, always strong and soothing.

"Talk about what?" I asked, trying to keep my expression blank. "There's nothing to talk about. I'm just focused."

The sympathy in his eyes killed me. The pain. The knowing. "I wake up every morning and see the face of someone who lost the person they love. If you don't think I can recognize that look on anyone by now, then you don't give your old man enough credit."

My heart skipped and then stumbled, my eyes burning with the tears I tried to hold back. He knew. Of course, Dad knew. Months of phone conversations about the sea, and I hadn't held back mentions of the lighthouse and its keeper. I hadn't told him about *us*, but I had told him about Kit. And the Kinkades. And the art. And the candles. And the jam. I guess it hadn't taken very many words to paint a bigger picture for Dad of what was really happening.

"I didn't lose him, Dad. I just left." *And he hadn't stopped me.*

"Can you go back?"

No.

"It wouldn't matter. He doesn't love me back," I said, blinking quickly.

"Are you sure?"

I opened my mouth to say *"positive,"* but the image of Kit's face the day I left flashed in my mind. His drawn expression. The torture in his eyes. I'd seen them before—when he'd talked about moving to the lighthouse to spare his family the pain of seeing him broken.

I quickly shoved the image aside. An expression didn't mean anything—it didn't mean he felt the same when it came to me.

"I have to get back to work."

Thankfully, he didn't push the issue. He squeezed my shoulder, bent down to kiss my head, and then returned to his recliner in front of the wood-burning stove where his book was waiting for him.

Minutes ticked by while I worked and he read. I forced myself to scan through every word of my paper one more time, ignoring the significance of the sketches attached to the document that Kit had done and sent with the boxes of my things, and then attached it to the email to my professor and hit send. I didn't realize how hard the finality of the moment would hit me until it was too late.

I sat back in my chair with a loud exhale, feeling like I'd just been kicked in the chest.

That was it. *The end.*

Of my research. Of my paper. Of Friendship and the lighthouse and the experiment of us.

The tears I'd held back suddenly overflowed, spilling down my cheeks just as there was a loud knock on the front door.

"I'll get it," I said quickly, swiped my cheeks clean, and stood.

Dad was already asleep in front of the wood-burning stove, his open book toppled onto his chest. Even though he was on medical leave from the college for the rest of the semester and then on break until the fall, he still wouldn't take time to actually relax. But I couldn't blame him because I would be the same way.

My heart rose into my throat as I got closer to the door. It couldn't be Kit; he wouldn't be in Boston. Couldn't be. I willed my hopes back down into my chest and opened it.

"Frankie?" I gaped at the woman on my doorstep. It was Frankie, but it looked nothing like her. Fitted pants. A loose blouse underneath a sweater vest.

"Aurora!" Her eyes went wide, and then she smiled in relief. "Thank God." And then I was knocked back by the force of her hug.

"What are you doing here?" I asked, squeezing her back like she could magically transport me back to Maine. *Back to him.* "Does your brother know you're here?"

"God, no." She shook her head and the last of my hopes that Kit had sent her deflated. "He'd probably kill me."

I hummed and closed the door behind her. "What are you wearing?" I'd never seen her dressed so...professionally before.

"Oh, I borrowed this from Lou." *That made more sense.* "I just wasn't sure what to expect when I got here, so I figured I shouldn't look like a wax-stained slob on your doorstep." Then her eyes raked over me. "What are *you* wearing?"

I looked down at what I had on. Sweatpants. A T-shirt, and a zip-up. "What's wrong with what I'm wearing?"

"It's *gray*."

I blinked, and I realized I'd hardly worn any color since coming home. Grays and blacks and beige. I could claim I wasn't paying attention, but deep down, my brain knew I wasn't ready for color—knew I didn't feel very colorful right now.

But what did that matter? Wearing a color wouldn't change anything.

"What are you doing here, Frankie?" I asked again, suddenly feeling like every second in her presence was like peeling a scab over a wound that was trying to heal.

I tucked my arms over my chest, holding myself tight.

"I came to convince you," she declared. "You have to come back, Aurora. Kit is in love with you."

I reeled, my shoulder bumping into the wall in the hallway. She certainly didn't beat around the bush.

"No." My head swiveled, resisting the sting I felt behind my eyes. *In love with me?* No. She was wrong. "No, he's not. We were just a fling—"

"A fling?" She choked and shook her head. "Oh no. If you were a fling, then I'm going to go back to calling sea stars starfish because you and my brother were about as close to a fling as sea stars are actual fish."

My head ducked.

"You know my brother, Aurora. You have been around him more in the last four months than anyone has been in the last decade. He let *you* into his world—"

"He didn't have a choice—"

"Bullshit," she scoffed. "We thought he didn't have

a choice when he came home and lived at Mom's...next thing we knew, he'd moved into a lighthouse—*a freaking lighthouse*, Aurora." She jerked her head. "No, if Kit Kinkade doesn't want to be around people, he will find a way." Her expression softened. "But he wanted to be around you. He wanted to be with you. You helped him be better, and in the end, he pushed you away for the same reason he pushed the rest of us away—because he thought you deserved better."

"Did he?"

"How can you not think that? After seeing what he wrote? What he drew?"

Wrote? Drew? My brow pulled together. "What are you talking about?"

Now, she looked as confused as I was.

"The journal."

"What journal?"

Her confusion deepened. "Did you get my note?"

I exhaled loudly. "Note? No. What note? I never got a note."

Her eyes bulged.

"I was at the hospital for several days with my dad, but I checked all the mail—"

"It wasn't in the mail. It was in the box. Didn't you open all the boxes?"

My jaw slackened, heat flooding my cheeks. "No," I admitted softly and then led her to the back of our old brownstone townhouse to the office where I'd only partially unloaded all the things Kit had shipped back.

I told him to ship me all my specimens, not because I needed them to finish my paper—I was too close to the end for that—but because by leaving them, it felt like I was leaving a piece of me with a man who didn't want me. So, when the boxes were delivered, I'd only opened two of the three, the last still sitting taped up in the corner of the room.

"That's the one," Frankie said softly, folding her arms. "I left you a note in there to message me when you got it."

My throat bobbed as I tried to swallow. "Frankie..."

"You have to open it, Aurora," she insisted, her voice pleading. "Otherwise, you'll never know."

Know.

I stared at her. That was all I wanted. To know him. To know his secrets. His pain. His smiles. *His love.* And when he shut me out, I thought it was safest to not let my mind know any more—think any more about him.

"Please."

My head thudded quicker, and I paused for a second, letting my brain catch up to the reckless ruler in my chest that had already decided what I was going to do. And then I bent and slid the box to the center of the room, carefully picking at the end of the tape to peel it open. It zipped off the box with a tearing sound.

I folded the ends back, my brow creasing when the first thing I saw was some of my textbooks on top.

"I had to hide it so he wouldn't know I'd sent it with your things," she said as I lifted them out of the box and then stopped short when I saw the smaller, leather notebook tucked in their midst.

His journal.

"Frankie..." I sighed and shook my head, my fingers trembling as I lifted it. She shouldn't have taken this for me. It belonged to Kit. On top, I found the quick note she'd scribbled on one of my stickies. *Message me when you get this. We need a plan.*

My chest panged. *Frankie and her plans.*

"Just open it."

I couldn't resist, even if I wanted to. I was weak. I missed Kit with every breath, and if I could know some of his thoughts for just a few minutes, I'd take that relief like it was one more hit of a drug, willing to pay the price for my addiction later.

I peeled open the worn flap, the first page dating back two years ago, and on it were the notes of the light-house keeper: the state of the lighthouse, the weather and sea conditions, and notable activity near the shore. Using my thumb, I let the pages flip by, watching the scribbled dates in the corner tick closer to the present. And then I hit a page that was dogeared.

The day I arrived.

My eyes greedily scanned his notes. *Student at lighthouse. Says she's studying sea creatures. Aurora Cross.* But it wasn't the notes that held my attention; it was what was below them. A sketch. Of me in my waders standing on the rocks. There wasn't much detail, just a rough outline of the moment he first saw me.

I flipped to the next page, finding another mention, this time of the *nudibranch,* an outline of the shell *carcass* I'd left on the counter.

As the days went on, I watched the notes change. Grow. No longer were the pages only sparsely filled with brief meteorological and oceanographic notations, but they grew consumed with details—observations about me.

Sketches of my face when I found Stuart. My smile. The happiness in my eyes. Drawings of me biting my lip as I worked. From the concentrated furrow of my brow to the dimples in my cheeks, I watched each page reveal myself one detail at a time—weeks upon weeks when I'd been the object of his study just as much as he'd been of mine.

When I reached the final pages of the journal, embarrassment flamed my cheeks. The sketches turned more personal. More erotic. Images of me lying naked in his bed. Another one of me smiling at him from the shower. I sucked in a breath when I reached one of the final ones—my head tipped back with pleasure, my hands cupped over my breasts, his hands on my waist—the perspective of a man who was thoroughly enjoying himself from the vantage point between my thighs.

"You saw this?" I croaked, feeling the color in my cheeks deepen.

"Don't worry, no one else did," she murmured.

"Frankie...I don't..." I closed the journal, unsure what to say—what to think.

"He loves you," she blurted out, reaching for my hand. "He loves you, Aurora. He just needed to realize that he was wrong—that he's not a burden. That no one's better off without him."

Emotion welled so suddenly and strongly in my chest I struggled to breathe, my heart racing to keep up with every new piece I fit into this puzzle.

"If you don't love him or want to be—"

"I do," I said instantly. "I do love him." I flipped back through the pages of the journal, my mind already playing tricks on me that the drawings weren't real—that none of this was.

The first time I looked through the pages, I was struck knowing that he watched me—drew me. But by the time I reached the end, it wasn't the fact that he'd drawn me that stunned me...it was how he saw me that had my heart pounding in my chest.

Every image I recognized. I recognized the fullness in my cheeks, the frame of my glasses, every curve and roll of my skin...and while I loved myself, I never looked at myself the way he did. The woman in these drawings was mischievous and tempting. Beautiful and utterly seductive. *The woman in these drawings was someone he loved.* And it was as evident as every line and stroke of his pencil.

"So, you'll come back for the gallery show tomorrow?" Frankie asks, the gleam in her eyes shining with hope.

Yes. The word was right there on the tip of my tongue but I held it back, looking at her, thinking about what that show meant to Kit, and then gave my answer, "I have a better plan."

It definitely didn't feel like an hour had passed by the time I watched Frankie descend the steps out front to her car and close the door behind her. *Tomorrow.* There was so much to do. To pack. To think about.

To talk to Dad.

I couldn't leave him. Not so soon after what happened. But to ask him to move...or to commute back and forth...I didn't know what I was going to do.

"Aurora..."

I turned, too lost in thought to realize Dad had

woken up. As he came over to me, I saw the tears in his eyes. *Shoot.* I wished I could've come up with a plan before needing to have this conversation. I didn't want him to have any stress right now.

"How much did you hear?" I asked softly.

He smiled and pulled me in for a hug. "Enough to know that we're going on a trip."

"We?"

He drew back, incredulous. "You think you're going to leave me behind? Absolutely not." He chuckled. "They always say the sea air is good for your health. I think I could be easily convinced to live in a small seaside town in Maine for the next few months while I recuperate."

"Really?" A small cry slipped out.

"Well, they do have my favorite blueberry jam there," he mused warmly, and then with a twinkle in his eye, added, "And the man my daughter loves."

I let out a sob and wrapped my arms around his neck.

"I love you, Dad."

"Love you, too, sweetheart." He patted my back. "I do have one condition though..."

I tipped back and looked at him. "What?"

"I want to be part of this plan."

CHAPTER 21
KIT

"Hey, Kit." Mom's neighbor, Brian, patted me on the back, and when I felt the ripple of tension run through me, I didn't try to fight it.

I hadn't tried to fight it for the last two weeks. Every time I felt the hum of panic or the chill of fear, I let it in. When I went to the Maine Squeeze each morning for a cup of coffee. When I stopped at the grocery store, the art supply store, and even at Mom's, I didn't fight the darkness. I let it come...and then I let it fade against what burned inside me.

The light she'd lit. The need to be better. To understand. *To want more.*

And that was what I'd fought for since my argument with Frankie. I'd fought against my instincts to shelter and hide, accepting that they weren't instincts but plain old fear. Instead of sheltering from the threat of panic, I gave myself doses of it. Daily. Because if I could understand it, I wouldn't have to fear it.

I started slow. A coffee in the morning at first.

Lingering at the counter at the Maine Squeeze, distracting myself by talking to Lou. Then, I'd added in visits to Mom's. A stop by Jamie's shop. The grocery store. A walk down the street. I dosed myself with people and situations that could trigger me and worked through my body's reactions.

My first goal was the gallery show. To make it through the event okay. That was my litmus test, and if I could make it through that, then I would let myself consider going to her.

It wasn't about proving it to her—I'd never needed to prove myself to Aurora; she'd always believed in me. I needed to prove to myself that I could do this. That I could fight for more. *And that I was willing to let other people fight for me.*

And I had. I looked around the room, seeing every person in my family here, fighting for me.

Mom and Frankie and Gigi mingled with the crowd, talking to people about my work and only funneling through to me those who were truly interested in making a purchase. Jamie manned the desk at the back with Violet. She knew how crippling panic attacks could be; she suffered from them, too. So, she moved the desk forward a little and blocked off the larger space behind it as a designated area for Jamie to do packaging, but its dual purpose was a safe space. Away from the people. Away from the noise. If I felt the darkness closing in, I had a place to retreat to.

And Lou...Lou ran the ship. She chatted. She directed. She told stories about my paintings that I'd even forgotten I'd shared with her. She invoiced and took payments. She...she killed it. Then again, it was her future she was working for, too.

With them around, it was hard for the darkness to get close.

If I made it through this, I could reach out to her. Go to her. If I made it through this, it was proof that I could be better—that I could regenerate and grow back the part of me I'd lost.

"Hey, Brian." I reached out and shook his hand. "Thanks for coming. I really appreciate your support." I saw him come in almost...*forty-five* minutes ago...but hadn't had a chance to say hello yet.

"Of course." He smiled wide and then nodded over his shoulder to a man about his age who was chatting with Jamie. "That's my cousin, Steve Miller. The one I was telling you about. He just got here."

I nodded, recalling the last week when we'd run into each other at the hardware store, and he told me he had a cousin who was a buyer for some very avid and very wealthy art collectors in Boston. He mentioned sending his cousin a photo of some of my new ink drawings and how his cousin immediately made plans to come to the show to buy some pieces for his clients.

I was shocked. Grateful, but shocked. And it wasn't the first time.

The more time I spent in town, the more people approached me to tell me how excited they were about my show. Maybe it was me. Maybe it was pity. Or the mystery of the man who lived in the lighthouse that they wanted to see. But all that mattered was that they came because supporting me meant supporting Lou, and no matter how she busied herself organizing this event, I still caught the glimmer of worry in her gaze— worry that it wouldn't be enough to win the inn back.

"I'll be sure to say hello," I assured Brian with a smile.

"Oh, don't worry, he won't be leaving without talking to you—or with empty hands." He smiled warmly and made his way toward his cousin.

I started to follow, but Max and Nox stopped me to say hello, with Max introducing me to his two friends who'd invested in MaineStems. Then it was Judy, Carol, and Christine who manned the Stonebar Farms store in town. After that it was Lauren and Jenna from the Maine Squeeze and Jenna's dad, the mayor of Friendship. Everywhere I looked, people had turned out to support me, and for a second, I regretted all the time I spent hiding from the people who cared about me.

"Kit!" Lou rushed over, a pen tucked behind each ear and a stack of papers in her hand. "I need you over here." She tugged me to the other side of the room in front of my drawing of the whelk shell and beamed when she introduced me to an older woman waiting in front of it. "Mrs. Johnson, this is the artist and my brother, Kit Kinkade. He can tell you a little bit more about the drawing you're purchasing."

I tipped my head and winked at Lou.

She was incredible. She was running the show with the attention, ease, and grace of a conductor in front of an orchestra. She welcomed people. Introduced them. Guided them through the small exhibit she'd set up. She'd organized the purchasing process ahead of time so it could be done seamlessly from her phone anywhere in the gallery, the artwork then only moved to the back for Mom and Gigi to package up.

"It's a pleasure to meet you, Mrs. Johnson." I shook the older woman's hand gently.

"You're quite talented, young man." She eyed me and then the drawing.

"Thank you." I smiled. "This is a waved whelk. Some might say the smaller cousin to a conch shell."

She nodded for me to continue, her smile encouraging me that she was enjoying the scientific details as much as I was enjoying giving them. Every time I shared information about the animals in the drawings, it brought back memories of Aurora. Her amazement. Her excitement. And that funneled through me like an infectious beam of light.

"How fascinating." She pressed her hand to her chest, staring at the drawing once more. "I love shells. My condo is filled with all kinds that I've collected over the years. I'd love to add this to my living room wall. May I purchase it?"

"Of course." I smiled, and before I even had to look for her, Lou appeared next to me, easily injecting herself into the conversation to facilitate the purchase.

"Kit." I turned and found Frankie by my side, her hand on my arm. "This is Mr.—"

"Just Richard, please," the portly, older man insisted as he moved shoulder-to-shoulder with Frankie and adjusted his thick round glasses.

Air whooshed from my lungs, the slight movement hitting me like a bag of bricks to my sternum. For a split second, all I saw was Aurora. *Silly,* I thought with a shake of my head. Anyone who wore glasses would bump them just the same.

I cleared my throat. "Pleasure to meet you."

"Yes, quite." His eyes twinkled, looking at me more intently than he'd even glanced at the drawing.

"You were interested in this one?"

"Yes. The starfish." His smile quirked.

"Sea star," I corrected without thinking. Lou would argue that if he bought the drawing, he could call it whatever he liked, but I couldn't. I just couldn't.

His bushy brows lifted. "Oh?"

"Technically, they aren't fish, so the proper name for them is a sea star," I explained, shoving my hands into my pockets.

"Fascinating." He stroked his chin. "So, you're an artist and a zoologist?"

"Just an artist," I assured him. "The rest I learned... from a friend."

He looked from side to side, scanning the breadth of other paintings of mine hanging on the walls.

"Must be quite a friend."

"Excuse me?" I lowered my voice.

"Well, the rest of your paintings are landscapes. I presume that the person who gave you the facts was the one who also prompted you to switch subjects...and mediums." His head tipped. "A big change, I would think, so it must be someone special."

I tensed. I didn't want to share—didn't want to talk about her. Right now, all I had were her memories, and I didn't want to give them away to some stranger in my gallery. But then I looked back at the drawing of Stuart and his three legs and breathed through the tightness in my chest, remembering that this was why I was here— why they were here. *To know me. To know my art.* And if Aurora were here, she would've been halfway through the tale of her daring rescue of Stuart during the storm.

"She is," I rasped, feeling my lips tip upward even as the ache in my chest intensified. I stepped forward, closer to the drawing, and felt the crowd fade away. "His name is Stuart." I glanced back. "The sea star," I clarified. "She found him injured during a storm, so she brought him inside my li—my house, got him a little aquarium, and I've been watching him regenerate ever since."

The man—Richard—was silent for a moment. "Fascinating," he finally said low.

"Once his arms are regenerated, I'll put him back in the ocean."

"Not a pet then?"

I shook my head. "He belongs back in the ocean. The lighthouse was just a temporary stay to heal." As soon as the words left my mouth, they boomeranged right back against my chest.

The lighthouse was my temporary place to heal. It still was. But one day, I'd have that whole piece again.

"Well, we all need one of those once in a while," he murmured softly, and the conversation drifted to a heavy silence for a moment—a feat considering the crush inside the gallery. But then the older man turned to me with a warm smile and revealed, "I'll be honest, Mr. Kinkade, I'm an amateur art collector, so this is all new to me."

This was all pretty new to me, too, but I kept that thought to myself.

"What brought you into the art world?"

"There's only one world, Mr. Kinkade. Full of art and science. People and animals and...sea stars." He chuckled. "I was already in it, I just wasn't looking." Slowly, his head turned from the drawing to look at me. "Funny how you can live in a world for so long and miss out on so much of it, even beautiful things that bring you joy, things that you love."

My throat tightened, and before I could think of a better answer, an honest one slipped out. "Yeah."

I blinked, and I saw her smile. Heard her laugh. Smelled her sweetness. I saw my family and friends. The way they embraced me. Sheltered me. Respected me. *Fought* for me.

His hand on my shoulder brought me back to the present. "Good thing it's never too late to stop missing out on them," he said with a tone that made the conversation feel so much deeper than a discussion about art. But before I could think more on it, he added, "Sorry for my rambling, but on that note, I think I'd like to buy this one if it's still available."

"Of course. Let me grab my sister." I waved Lou over. "Richard would like to purchase the sea star, if it's still available."

"You're in luck, it's the only ink drawing that hasn't been sold." Lou's smile at me split her face.

My jaw dropped. *The only...holy shit.* I stared at her, silently passing along the question, *Everything else sold already?*

She tried to keep her nod discreet, but there were practically fireworks of excitement in her eyes.

"Oh, good. So, I'm not too late." Richard took the invoice she handed him.

"Not too late at all," she promised, cheerily chatting on about the packaging process and shipping options available if he would prefer. "Let me grab the piece, and then I'll take you to the back while it's wrapped."

He stepped back and let her remove the frame from the wall.

"Thank you," I said and shook his hand again just before he went to follow Lou.

Richard paused and placed his other hand on top of mine. "It's not too late for you, either," he said and then disappeared into the crowd after Lou.

What the...

"Mr. Kinkade." This time when I turned, it was Brian's cousin who'd finally made his way over to me.

"Mr. Miller. It's a pleasure to finally meet you."

"Steve, please." He shook my hand eagerly.

"Call me Kit," I returned.

"Really incredible work here. Phenomenal. I've managed to snag two of your drawings and the small seascape from the window for my clients. Do you do commissioned work? Because I have a few more people who would love to have something done like these."

"I—I'd be happy to take a look at the request and see if it's something I can do." Commissions weren't something I'd ever done, ever considered, but I could... consider them.

"Awesome." He shook both of his fists in excitement before tucking them to his chest. "I won't keep you. I know we're pushing the end of the show, but Lou said I had to ask you..." He trailed off and angled his body. I followed the rise of his arm, knowing in an instant where it was going to point. "Is that painting for sale?"

The painting of the lighthouse. The one that always stopped Aurora in her tracks.

My jaw went slack. The answer should've been "yes" because everything in here was for sale. Or was supposed to be. Or had been until this very moment when the thought of selling it—when the thought of anyone else having that painting except *her* changed my mind.

"While I'm very grateful for your support," I began hoarsely, "unfortunately, that painting is already spoken for."

"Damn." He smiled and shook his head. "She told me she didn't think it was available, but said it didn't hurt to ask."

He shook my hand, assured me that he'd be in touch, and then went to the back desk to collect his purchases. Meanwhile, my gaze searched for my sister, finding Lou watching me intently with a small smile on her face, hopeful that she was right.

Hopeful that I wouldn't sell the painting Aurora loved.

Within minutes, everyone worked their way out of the store, leaving only me and my family inside. My brother was the first to approach, pride oozing from his gaze.

"You did it." He rested his hand on my shoulder and squeezed.

"All of the drawings sold, Kit," Lou said, coming over. "And only two paintings are left, including the lighthouse."

"You're going to have to close the gallery for a few weeks to give you time to restock," Violet said.

"And to give Lou time to count all her money," Frankie chimed in, smiling even wider when Lou nudged her with her elbow. "What? It's a good thing.

Now, you'll be ready to place an offer as soon as the listing goes up."

As predicted, the inn hadn't been listed for sale as soon as Lou thought it would. The photographer had come out, along with the realtor, but as of yet, there was no new news.

"Christopher!" Gigi pushed through the rest of them and grasped my arm. "What are you waiting for?"

I stared at her for a long moment, something passing between us that was both silent and screaming. *Chasing Dawn.*

"One more thing," I murmured and then looked at Jamie. "Can you grab me the step stool from the back?"

While he went to grab it, I cleared a space in front of the wall.

He brought it over, and I climbed up to unhook the painting of the lighthouse, where I'd just replaced it earlier this morning.

"It's finally finished," Lou said quietly; she was probably the only one who knew that the painting on the wall this morning wasn't the same as it was left yesterday.

I held the frame, staring at one of my oldest paintings. The seascape shone with new life.

I'd stopped by the gallery late last night to check on a few last-minute things. Maybe it was nerves in anticipation of today. Maybe it was getting harder and harder to spend each night in my bed alone. I missed her. I missed her so damn much, I felt like a fish trying to live without water. But when I saw the painting on the wall —the one she always stared at—I found myself drawn to it, too. I used to be able to recognize myself in the dark clouds, the tumultuous storm, the hollow shell trying to stay in one piece...but last night, I didn't recognize anything, and I couldn't let it go.

I'd taken the painting back to the lighthouse and worked into the deepest hours of the night. Stars dotted the sky, and the moon was at its peak by the time I'd finished adding—altering the painting how I wanted. Only then did I finally sleep and return it this morning.

It felt right the way it looked now, but it felt wrong to put it back on the wall. And now, I realized why. It didn't belong on the wall, it belonged with her. Even if she didn't want me, I wanted her to have this. I wanted her to know how she'd changed me. For the better.

"Almost," I rasped and turned toward the door. "I have to go." Suddenly, my blood began to hum, an urgency erupting in it that wouldn't stay still. I'd played this moment over and over in my mind for the last week —what I would do if I made it through the show. Would I text her? Call her? Beg her to forgive me and come back to the lighthouse? But only now, the answer was clear. "I have to go to Boston."

Mom made a small noise, her hand quickly coming to cover her mouth.

"You know what?" Frankie stepped forward. "I have to go to Boston to get this new scent I want to use. It's super exclusive. Can I come with you?"

My gaze met hers, and I hardly nodded before Jamie spoke.

"I actually have a customer in Boston who I need to measure for a custom bed frame for, any chance I can tag along too?"

"Yeah—"

"Oh, you know, a supplier reached out to me about providing new glass jars for the farm," Mom added, joining the ranks. "They were going to send someone up here, but if you're going to Boston, I can just pop in and speak with them in the city."

I looked across all of them, their excuses were as transparent as the plea in their eyes. *Let us come. Let us be there for you. Let us be strong for you. Let us help you be strong.* They knew going back to Boston was a far cry from having an art show in a small town. They knew, like I did, what the risks were. And they wanted to make sure I had every support.

Sometimes the bravest thing you could do was to let someone else fight with you—for you. For love.

"And you?" I turned to Lou. "What's your excuse?"

"Me?" She gaped, and then smiled and took the painting from my hands. "I'm your gallery manager. It's my job to make sure every painting makes it to its final destination in perfect condition."

A smile flitted over my face, and I shook my head. "And you, Gigi?"

She chuckled and smiled so big, her eyes almost completely crinkled shut before she swatted my arm. "I'm ninety-seven years old, Christopher. I stopped needing an excuse to do what I want a long time ago."

"Fair enough," I rasped. "Meet me at the lighthouse, and we'll leave from there."

MY MIND WAS A SEA OF THOUGHTS BY THE TIME I parked in front of the house, the white, weathered structure seeming taller and brighter than it ever had before.

I wanted to grab a bag, just in case I didn't come back tonight. I didn't want to have expectations, but I also wanted to be prepared. I also wanted to give one of my sisters instructions on how to take care of Stuart in case I ended up away for a few days.

What if she couldn't come back here?

What if her father wasn't doing well and she had to stay in Boston?

Could I stay there?

The band in my chest tightened, and I slowly absorbed the fear. *There was no point in worrying about that now.* Right now, I just needed to talk to her. I needed to tell her this wasn't an experiment—that I loved her.

I was almost to the door when a noise stopped me.

A familiar, high-pitched squeal.

My head jerked, and then it hit me. The flash of dark curls just above the rocks. The scent of orange and vanilla clings to the sea breeze. *Was I imagining it?* I moved like lightning to the bluff, my heart galloping in my chest when I reached the edge.

No, I wasn't imagining it at all.

"Aurora? *Richard?*"

Maybe if there was one thing to be said about me, it was that I knew how to make a statement. And standing on the rocky bank of the lighthouse, wearing a bright flame-colored dress, and holding a waved whelk in my hands, I surely made quite a statement to the man standing at the edge of the rocks above, looking at me as though I were a ghost.

"Kit."

"What are you"—his head swiveled to Dad—"What are you doing here?" he demanded, extending his hand to make sure Dad made it off the rocks steadily.

Dad's smile broadened as he clasped Kit's hand and looked between him and me. "I had to meet the man my daughter fell in love with."

Heat bloomed in my cheeks, and I adjusted my glasses.

"Daughter..." He trailed off. His eyes widened ever so slightly as though he'd just put the pieces together.

"Had to make sure you deserved her."

I sucked in a breath, watching Kit's jaw flex. "And do I?"

Dad patted his hand reassuringly. "Any man who fills a gallery with only creatures my daughter loves—a man who risked the sale of every one of his drawings because he was too concerned with sharing the inspiration from the woman behind them, is more than deserving."

My breath caught, watching Dad embrace Kit, whose stormy eyes were only on me. And when they were done, Dad walked toward the drive where Ailene and Kit's siblings had just pulled in—all part of our plan.

"You're here," he croaked, reaching for my hand and then for me, lifting me almost completely over the last boulder and onto flat ground. "You came back." He cupped my face like he still couldn't believe it was me.

I licked my lips. "I couldn't stay away."

"Why not?" The hope in his voice made my heart swell.

I reached up and placed my hands over his. "I love you, Kit Kinkade. And I will always, *always* fight for you," I promised him. "But don't you ever push me away again—don't you ever think I would be better off without you."

He let out a low groan, dropping his forehead to mine. "I couldn't. I tried, but I couldn't." He let out a deep exhale. "Come with me."

Before I could ask where and why, he led me to the house. I opened my mouth to warn him that his family was right outside, in case his plan was...*experimentation*...but the words died in my throat when I walked inside.

"Oh my...Kit." I pressed my hand to my mouth, a choked sob wrenching from my chest as I looked around the room.

Gone was the old, tearing gray wallpaper and the dreary interior, and in its place were vibrant, bold colors. Not just colors. *Specimens.* Kit had painted massive, colorful seascapes like murals on the walls. Sea stars. Whelks and periwinkles. Crabs and lobsters. They filled every inch of the walls in reds and oranges, blues, and purples, bringing a new kind of life to the space that had felt almost...forgotten before.

"What did you..." He led me into the bedroom where there was even more. *Including the moon snail and bushy-backed nudibranch.*

"It didn't feel right here without them," he said quietly, taking me in his arms. "And it didn't feel like home anymore without you."

Tears flowed down my cheeks. "Kit..."

He gently kissed away the escaping droplets. "I love you, Aurora. I love you so much—"

My lip quivered as I pressed my mouth to his, needing to kiss him. Hold him. *Needing him.* "I love you," I murmured as he held me tighter and deepened the embrace.

There was a knock on the door, and Kit groaned. "Go away."

I giggled and ducked my head to his chest.

"You forgot something," Frankie called from the other side.

With a huff, he stalked to the door and yanked it open, the annoyance quickly deflating from his posture when he reached out and took whatever it was she'd brought.

The door closed, and I realized it was a painting. *No.* My heart stopped. *Not just any painting.*

"Is that..."

"I fixed it...finished it." Kit cleared his throat, handing me the frame. "I was going to drive to Boston to bring it to you."

I tried to say his name and choked on my effort. I couldn't believe what I was looking at—couldn't believe this was the same ominous, stormy painting of the lighthouse I'd stared at for weeks.

Gone were the storm clouds that darkened the horizon, instead a vibrant red dawn welcomed the sunrise. The sea that had appeared tumultuous and angry before now crashed eagerly on the shore, as though beckoning whoever was near to explore its depths. And the lighthouse...

Tears sped down my cheeks, and I didn't bother to stop them as I reached out and let my finger trace over the windows of the house that now glowed with a warm light and then slid them up the height of the tower, the brightest light beaming out to the very edges of the canvas from its peak.

He hadn't just changed the tone of the scene; he'd given the lighthouse back its light.

"All this time, it was missing its light," he rumbled low. "Just like I was missing you."

My shoulders started to shake.

"I wasn't the lighthouse, Aurora, you were. You were the one that continued to shine no matter what storms I threw against you. You were the one who reached out in the depths of my darkness and guided me safely to shore. You didn't save me, but I couldn't have saved myself without you."

"Kit." My lip wobbled traitorously.

"I love you," he murmured, dropping his head close to mine, his lips teasing mine with the warmth of his breath. "Will you stay with me? Be with me?"

I let out a sob and wrapped my arms around his neck, nodding.

"Is that a yes, sea star?" he rumbled low. "Tell me that's a yes."

"That's more than a yes." I threaded my hands through his hair and pulled his mouth to mine. "That's a 'I don't belong anywhere else.'"

"Good," he growled, pressing a kiss to my lips. "Because I'm never letting you go."

"Promise?" I shivered, desire warming my blood.

Another kiss to my cheek. "Better than a promise." And to the soft skin just below my ear.

"Kit..."

"An experiment," he whispered, dragging his mouth back to mine. "An experiment in forever."

And then he kissed me. Deeply. Madly. *Consumingly.*

Distantly, I heard cheers erupt from outside the house.

"The plan worked!" Frankie's shout echoed through the house's walls, announcing to the rest of his—*our*—family how this ended.

Kit growled and broke the kiss. "Hold that thought." He strode to the door and pulled it open again. "Show's over, Frankie. Take everyone home."

"Aurora's staying?" I heard her ask.

"Only if you're going," he warned.

"We're going," she squeaked, and I heard her retreat across the gravel as she yelled, "See you soon, Aurora!"

I bit my lip, doing a poor job of holding back my laugh as he shut the door. "What plan?"

My mouth opened and shut, and I pulled my lower lip between my teeth. "Frankie...came to see me in Boston."

He arched a brow, his eyes tracking me as I went to my bag that I'd set on the counter earlier, pulling out the worn leather journal tucked inside.

His gaze went wide. "I wondered where the hell..." He shook his head and came over to me.

"She wanted me to see your notes. Your drawings." The pages fluttered as he thumbed through them.

"All this time...I tracked all the things that stayed the same. Then you came into my life, and suddenly my notes included you. Your knowledge. Your smiles. They evolved—revolved around you. Little by little. Day by day. Until it was impossible to deny how things had changed—how I had changed because of you," he said low, his gaze capturing mine. "I wanted more—had more because of you."

I cupped his cheek and pulled him close. "You made me want more, too. More than science and specimens."

"More than sex?" he teased, his nose brushing mine as he set the journal on the counter.

"You made me want everything." I looped my arms around his neck and pressed my mouth to his.

The next thing I knew, I was upside down and over his shoulder as he carried me into the bedroom. "Kit!"

He flipped me upright, and my back hit the door. "You know what two weeks without you does to a man?" he growled and flushed himself to me, his hands roaming a path of hot possession over my hips and sides.

I shuddered, welcoming back the feel of his massive, hot body imposing on mine, especially the hard ridge of him digging into my stomach.

"No," I murmured throatily, rocking myself against him. "Tell me."

He grinned. "I think I'd rather show you."

And then I was lost, sinking willingly—blissfully—into the possession of his kiss.

ONE MONTH LATER...

"Kit!"

He broke the kiss with a groan, pulling away from me and sliding me off the desk in the back of the gallery.

"Oh." Lou stopped quickly and then looked around awkwardly while I straightened my shirt. "Sorry," she murmured, her cheeks red.

"What's up, Lou?"

Her smile spread like lightning. "My realtor just called and said that the buyer just withdrew their offer."

"Seriously?" Kit's jaw dropped, and I was equally as shocked.

Sure enough, a few days after I'd returned to Friendship, the Lamplight Inn had been put up for sale. *Again*. And, as expected, there were several offers placed almost immediately, including Lou's. According to her realtor, the offer she'd sent was very attractive, but the owner wanted to weigh his options. Days ticked by in uncertainty until Lou got the call that they were going to accept another offer. She was devastated. Her realtor cautioned that there was still time for something to happen—for someone to change their mind—but she didn't believe it would happen. We could all see it; the entirety of her demeanor changed, and no one seemed more affected by it than Frankie.

And then, a week later, another call came in that the buyer had withdrawn their offer. It wasn't uncommon. These things happened after inspections and those kinds of things. But what was uncommon were the rumors that started up—rumors of a ghost inside the old inn. As quickly as they swelled, the rumors died off as another offer was accepted. *Again, not Lou's.* And she was equally, if not more, devastated the second time around.

"Did she say why?"

Lou opened her mouth and then shut it again.

"Lou..."

"Apparently, they also claimed that the inn was haunted," she said, folding her arms.

Kit swore and shook his head. "That's ridiculous. It's not haunted."

"Well, whatever it is, it's closer to being mine," Lou declared and smiled again. "I have to go tell Frankie." And then she was gone as quick as she came.

"Do you really think it's haunted?" I asked after she left.

"No." He shook his head. "Unless the ghost has a particular grudge against being under new ownership."

I chuckled and reached for the letter on the desk— the one that prompted a celebratory kiss that quickly devolved into something far less appropriate to be doing in public.

"Congratulations." Kit pressed a kiss to my nose. "I'm so proud of you."

I reread the letter stating that I'd passed my final research class and earned my master's degree, pride swelling in my chest.

"I love you, sea star," he murmured, trailing kisses over my cheek and onto my neck.

"I love you, too." I sighed, perfectly willing to admit that the best thing to come out of my education wasn't this degree but him. "I have to tell my dad," I said as soon as the thought hit me.

"Let's tell him and my family together," he suggested.

I smiled. "That's a great idea."

"You know what's really great about it?" He slid his arms around my waist, his hands drifting lower to grip my ass.

I hummed, letting him pull me hard to him as he kissed up my neck. "What?"

"That dinner time isn't for another three hours, so we have plenty of time to celebrate *privately* before I have to share."

We celebrated there—in his studio. Then again in the truck. And finally, once more, back at the lighthouse, surrounded by light and color and laughter and love.

EPILOGUE

ONE YEAR LATER

"We can always stay," I murmured, coming up behind my wife and clasping her shoulders. I pressed a kiss to the top of her head as she stared out the windows of the lantern room, the sunset like a toppled paint can of burnt reds and oranges.

For a decade, I'd been in...hibernation, or so I liked to think of it. Sleeping through life in the dark. In solitude. Until Aurora's sunshine woke me up. And I'd lived the last year making up for the time I was gone.

There was still darkness and panic and fear—*but there always would be*. That was the point. There was no hiding or escaping or sheltering from darkness. The only way to eradicate it was through understanding. *Through light*. So, I brought as much light into my world as I could.

I proposed to Aurora a month after Lou caught us in the gallery that day, and we were married three weeks later at the lighthouse in front of our family and friends. I wore my uniform, and Aurora had seashells in her hair, and I swore to love her until the day the sun stopped rising.

And tonight...tonight was our last night in the lighthouse. Tomorrow, we moved into our new home—an old farmhouse attached to a barn that was both close to town and close to Mom's yet far enough away for us to enjoy our quiet moments like we did here.

"I think about it sometimes," she murmured as she turned, her stomach protruding between us. "Staying here."

My hands slid down the swell. "We can't raise a baby at a lighthouse."

Her full lips quirked. "It could be an experiment."

I laughed low. *This woman. My woman.* "I think we have plenty of those going right now," I murmured and pressed a kiss to her lips.

In four months, we would be parents. Between now and then, we'd move into a new home, and the lighthouse would be turned into an environmental education center with Aurora and her father at its helm.

"We do." She sighed and angled her head for another kiss, which I happily obliged. "I love you."

My chest swelled. "I love you too, my light." And then I kissed her again. Deeper this time. Unable to stop myself from wanting her—wanting to lose myself in her again.

Sometimes, I still pulled out that label and stared at Gigi's handwriting. I'd thought the day Aurora came back to Friendship for me was the day I'd finally caught her. But every day since, I realized I was wrong.

Chasing Dawn.

I was always chasing her. Chasing her smiles. Chasing her laughter. Chasing her thoughts. Chasing her light. Love wasn't about finding what you were looking for, it was about fighting for it. So every day, I fought for her. For my family. For us.

I would forever be the chaser of her light.

"Where are you going?" she asked when I tried to lead her to the stairwell.

"Downstairs," I said, even as I caught the way her eyes darkened as she stepped closer and lowered her other hand to the front of my pants. I groaned. "You're playing with fire, sea star." I cupped her face and lowered my head. "Let me take you to bed and worship you where you'll be comfy."

Her response was only to stroke my dick more firmly. "I don't want comfy, Kit. I want your cock."

Fuck, I loved her—and her pregnancy hormones.

I took her mouth in a rough kiss, my tongue angling long strokes against hers. Her fingers fumbled for the waist of my pants, her soft moans mingling with pants of frustration.

"Let me take care of you," I cooed, lowering my mouth down the side of her neck as I turned her toward the glass, forcing her to release me.

Her head tipped back onto my chest, letting my lips have their way with the soft skin above her pulse while my hands went to the hem of her shirt. *My shirt.* They were all she wore around the house, and I couldn't get enough, especially the way her growing body filled them out.

One hand laid a possessive claim over where our baby grew inside her, and the other went to her breasts. They were even bigger now. More lush. They overflowed from my grasp in a way that drove me wild.

I continued to kiss the side of her neck as my hand on her stomach moved to her underwear, tugging them down over her hips. She tipped forward, holding on to the rail as I got the fabric just far enough to where my fingers could slide between the backs of her legs to find her wet center.

And if she was responsive before the pregnancy—

"Kit!" She buckled at the first brush of my fingers. I pinched the sensitive bud and then worked my thumb over it in firm strokes until she was coming apart on my hand.

"I've got you." I kissed the side of her neck and pushed two fingers inside her, soaking them with her desire and then drawing them back to the heavy length of my cock.

She whimpered, bending forward a little more as I moved my own clothes out of the way and notched myself at the entrance to her body. I had to be careful from this angle. From behind, I could go deep—uncomfortably deep for her right now—but there was no way in hell I was going to lay her on the dirty floor right now.

"Fuck, you feel incredible," I groaned, pushing the tip of my dick inside her and then forcing myself to stop. "Move back on me, sea star. Take my cock slow until it's comfortable."

Using the rail as a lever, she pushed herself back slowly on my length. Meanwhile, I gritted my teeth and rubbed my hands on the outside of her hips, forcing my body to remain perfectly still while she impaled herself on me.

"Kit..." she moaned low when the head of my cock rubbed her G-spot. "Right there."

I gripped her tight and rocked into her body. Thrust after thrust. Deeper and deeper. Within seconds, she was coming apart on me, her cries filling the small room as her body milked my own release free.

"You're incredible," I muttered several moments later, acutely aware that she couldn't be comfortable like this. With a groan, I slid from her, put us both back together, and then drew her to me. "You okay?" I rasped. "I didn't hurt you, did I?"

"No." She smiled and locked her arms around my neck. "Never."

"Good," I rumbled. "Let's go down."

Her arms tightened. "Will you miss it?"

"The lighthouse?"

"Yeah."

I lifted my gaze to the horizon, staring at the panorama I'd been surrounded by for the last decade, and then looked back at the woman in my arms. *Yeah, there was nothing that compared to her. Nothing that ever would.*

"No," I answered her with a smile. "You're my haven. My shelter. You're my lighthouse, now."

"Does that make you my keeper?" she murmured huskily.

My smile widened, and I lowered my mouth to hers as I said, "No, it makes you mine. The keeper of my light."

A LOOK AT BOOK THREE:
THE CANDLEMAKER

Francesca 'Frankie' Kinkade has a penchant for trouble.

By day, she runs her candle shop. By night, she plays matchmaker for everyone but herself. When a grumpy out-of-towner shows up to sell the inn her sister's dreamed of buying, Frankie's ready to scare off the competition—literally.

Chandler Collins doesn't do feelings. Or small towns. Inheriting the inn was never part of his plan, and selling it should've been simple. But one by one, buyers keep backing out...until he realizes someone's behind it.

Frankie wouldn't say her plan was a great one, but who wants to buy an inn that's haunted? No one. When her master class in ghosting leaves her sister as the only buyer left, Frankie is sure the city slicker will take the offer and head back to his skyscrapers. But when Chandler calls her bluff and decides to stay at the inn himself, she matches him step for step.

One week. One inn. One dare neither of them meant to lose.

But under flickering candlelight, sparks fly, and Frankie's about to learn what happens when you mix business, pleasure... and one *very* unexpected surprise.

AVAILABLE OCTOBER 2025

Rebecca Sharp is a contemporary romance author of over thirty published novels and dentist living in Pennsylvania with her amazing husband, affectionately referred to as Mr. GQ.

She writes a wide variety of contemporary romance. From new adult to extreme sports and forbidden romance to romantic comedies, her books will always give you strong heroines, hot alphas, unique love stories, and guaranteed happily ever after. When she's not writing or seeing patients, she loves to travel with her husband, snowboard, and cook.

www.drrebeccasharp.com
Rebecca Sharp's Sexy Little Sharpies